COMBAT CAMERA

T0131374

COMBAT CAMERA

A NOVEL

A.J. Somerset

BIBLIOASIS

FIRST EDITION

Library and Archives Canada Cataloguing in Publication

Somerset, A. J., 1969-
    Combat camera / A. J. Somerset.

ISBN 978-1-897231-92-0

    I. Title.

PS8637.O449C66 2010   C813'.6   C2010-904591-2

Canada Council **Conseil des Arts**
for the Arts **du Canada**

Canadian Patrimoine
Heritage canadien

ONTARIO ARTS COUNCIL
CONSEIL DES ARTS DE L'ONTARIO

Recycled
Supporting responsible use
of forest resources
www.fsc.org Cert no. SGS-COC-003153
© 1996 Forest Stewardship Council

Biblioasis acknowledges the ongoing financial support of the Government
of Canada through The Canada Council for the Arts, Canadian Heritage,
the Book Publishing Industry Development Program (BPIDP); and the
Government of Ontario through the Ontario Arts Council.

PRINTED AND BOUND IN CANADA

for Vicky

Part One

Chapter One

The most alarming development now confronting Zane was his suddenly frangible reality. Even his routine moments had become fraught with risk. Suppose, for example, a glint of sunlight was to catch the crack traversing his grime-smeared windshield; a disturbance as trivial as this could inexplicably fracture the entire tableau, could set fragments of his past tilting and sliding through his mind like pieces of coloured glass in a broken kaleidoscope. Things finally come to rest in a jagged landscape of unwelcome memories, and then where in hell are you?

On checking his rear-view mirror, Zane might find his back seat now occupied by Liberian child soldiers, their eyes glassy with drugs, their small hands grasping hand-me-down Russian assault rifles approximately four sizes too large. A West African horizon might replace outer Mississauga's industrial wasteland, under the same dissipated sun. A dead man, installing himself uninvited in the passenger seat, might speak. Panic rushes in, sweat popping from cold pores, the sour taste of bile and adrenalin, pain in the gut.

It was getting so he couldn't even drive to work.

Above all, it was essential to remain grounded. This demanded continuous attention to detail. Pavement humming under the tires, afternoon sun flaring in the film of grime covering his windshield, and the breathy clatter of valves from the cylinder heads, heralds of an impending catastrophic engine failure: these things belonged indisputably to the here and now. These things provided fixed reference points from which Zane could triangulate his position. Mississauga vice Freetown, in this particular case: he was on his way to a shoot. For now, Zane remained safe in the present.

The main thing was to deal in facts. Valve clatter was a fact. The rest did not bear considering. The mind, allowed to wander, can easily stray into a bad neighbourhood. Then you're calling missing persons, handing out recent photos, sitting up late, fearing the worst. You wonder where you went wrong when all the while, in your heart, you already know.

Zane kept his eyes on the road. It didn't pay to look back. Neither did it pay to aim high in steering.

* * *

In the studio, bare fluorescent tubes hung suspended amidst loops and garlands of wiring, illuminating two thirds of a motel room: three walls painted a nondescript beige, a door that opened to nowhere, a window blocked by threadbare curtains. The curtains opened not onto glass but to a plain white sheet, the face of an improvised lightbox that, when illuminated, created the illusion of sunlight falling through the non-existent glass to set the curtains aglow. A faded yellow carpet, a double bed without blankets, and an old floor lamp completed the set.

Richard Barker sat at a desk in the corner of the studio, considering the display of flesh on his computer monitor. He possessed the confident air of a one-time all-star high-school quarterback, twenty years after the fact, who had moved from the gridiron to the sales floor without ever failing to make himself the centre of attention. Barker was the kind of man who crushed your hand to shake it, gripping your arm with his free hand while his gold watch and class ring glittered hard and cold, his eyes pinning you to the mat all the while. He had clearly never felt uncomfortable in his own skin.

He looked up from the monitor as Zane walked in, and pushed back his chair and leaned back and knit his hands behind his head.

"You look like death warmed over."

"I don't feel much better."

"Seriously, you look sick."

"I just didn't sleep well last night."

Zane felt no pressing need to elaborate. What's to say? Your ghosts get bored haunting your dreams, they start dropping by uninvited in prime time. We interrupt your regular programming to bring you this brief and disconcerting hallucination: Christine, freshly exhumed, with pale crumbs of clay in her hair. Christine was quite dead, and had been for over twenty years, but she had recently started to visit, and Zane had come to resent her disrespect for propriety. It isn't decent, to ignore the conscious divide. He'd had enough of her long, freighted silences, her reproachful stare. Christine was getting on his nerves.

He told her to get lost.

She offered no reply. He closed his eyes and waited, and when he reopened them, she had left. Nevertheless, sleep had remained a difficult prospect.

This sort of thing, Zane thought, would be difficult to explain to a man like Richard Barker.

* * *

Explaining Christine would require that he first explain certain background matters, matters that he had glossed over rapidly during his perfunctory job interview. On that occasion, to Zane's relief, Barker had done most of the talking; Zane had yet to discover that this was entirely in character.

Zane had gone to such lengths as donning a tie and dusting off his portfolio for the occasion, not that it revealed much in the way of applicable experience, but Barker did not even glance at it. He simply asked Zane what experience he had as a photographer.

Zane said, I did some journalism.

Some journalism: twenty-two years in El Salvador, in Nicaragua, in Honduras and Guatemala and Panama, in Beirut and Lebanon, in the West Bank and the Gaza Strip, in Northern Ireland and in South Africa, in Angola, in Ethiopia and Eritrea and Somalia and Sudan, in Romania, in the fractured remains of Yugoslavia, in Afghanistan and Chechnya, in Sierra Leone and in Liberia. One hell of a list, yes sir, and I'm sure I've left several out. Eventually, all places merge into one. Who can keep it all straight? Iraq, I skipped. I was on vacation.

None of this did Richard Barker need to know. Details such as these can lead only to still more details, and ultimately into conversational territory best avoided. If pressed, Zane would say he had no more interest in discussing his twenty years on the job than would a man who spent his life in the manufacture of light switches. He had no interest in war stories.

So he said, I did some journalism.

Barker looked at Zane askance, said, you're not doing some exposé, are you?

I'm not doing some exposé, he said. I'm through with all that bullshit. And he was.

* * *

Barker returned to the task at hand, a review of the pictures from their last shoot. It had not gone well.

The girl looked young and her face seemed oddly ill-proportioned, her cheekbones too wide, her mouth too small, her eyes too close together; a hint, perhaps, of fetal alcohol syndrome. She showed little enthusiasm or interest in proceedings. Half-way through the scene, she declined to participate further.

Show business is not without its challenges: Bill, cast in the role of the leading lady's love interest, complained that these interruptions made it difficult to stay in character.

I'm losing my hard-on, he said. What am I, a fucking machine? You're a pro, said Barker. And Bill did, indeed, move with mechanical precision, a steam engine reduced to its simplest elements, piston and wheel.

That's right: I'm a pro, said Bill. And I can't work under these conditions.

They took ten, while Barker discussed with her the elements of contract, standards of professional conduct, and the problem of getting paid. The girl returned to work with renewed commitment, but soon began to cry. The shoot continued, heedless. The show must go on. Afterwards, Bill got badly drunk.

And Bill, who had just arrived for work, didn't want to see the pictures now. Worthless, he said. Why're you lookin' at that shit? Waste of time. Bitch looks like a deer in the fucking headlights.

"You're wrong," said Barker. "This is good stuff. What we got here is a work of genius."

The photograph in question is flesh and eyes, the blur of a shark tattoo, all ink and teeth, and masculine fingers indenting flesh. The girl's name now escapes recollection but the whites of her eyes pull bad memories out of the depths of Zane's mind, a hospital in Beirut, blood on the floor. And the eyes, the way that all the pleading faded out of them, the way they faded into exhaustion and hopelessness, like lights going out.

Zane looked down at his camera bag, pushed the images from his mind. Barker's voice went on, an immortal drone, while he mechanically checked his camera's myriad switches.

"Only you could do it, Zane. Only you could give me this. You are a certifiable genius."

Zane busied himself with his camera gear, with his ritual of cleaning and inventory. Something in Barker's manner had always reminded him of his high-school Phys-Ed teacher, the football coach, the basketball coach, the coach of all things organized;

perhaps his forced bonhomie, his optimism, and the volume of his voice were responsible, or the breadth of his shoulders, his physical presence. The cause was immaterial. Zane hated team sports and harboured a long-term aversion toward their coaches.

"Bitch is about to start crying," said Bill.

"Your problem is, you don't think about this business in terms of audience. Diamond Blue Productions is consistently profitable because we bring diverse product offerings to the marketplace. In other words, to translate, not everyone wants to jack off to some boob-job porn star who can suck a golf ball through a garden hose."

"We better hope not."

"You can't buy acting like this."

Bill announced that he had to take a leak, and, having adequately articulated his point of view on the matter, left.

"This is why you're a genius," said Barker, indicating the computer screen like a museum tour guide introducing his group to the centrepiece of an exhibit.

Voila: the girl in close-up, choking, Bill's hand gripping her skull and pulling her face to his crotch. Veins and tendons stood out from the back of his hand, muscle and sinew, her one visible eye turned to the camera, pleading, wide, panicked; the iris stands out in a striking, pale blue, tiny red blood vessels snaking across the white. Good lighting.

The fear in her eyes dredged his subconscious, muck-flowers blooming in dark waters, something shapeless stirring below. Zane looked away.

"That," said Barker, "is genius."

Light falls from the sun, or from artificial lights ultimately powered thereby, and, directly or indirectly, illuminates the subject. Part is absorbed, but certain wavelengths reflect, bend within the extra-low dispersion glass of the camera lens, within fourteen glass elements in eleven groups; thus channelled, the light bounces upwards off the reflex mirror and passes through the focusing screen into the pentaprism, where it ricochets around wildly until it rights itself again. The resulting image flies out through the eye-piece, through the cornea, the aqueous humour, the lens of the eye itself, through the vitreous humour, and then falls against the retina like a wad of wet toilet paper hitting the locker room wall: splat. The impact trembles along the optic nerve, vibrates within the thalamus, through synapse and neuron, resonates within the visual cortex. The mind is a camera; you might as well blame the sun. What I'm saying is, don't look at me. I didn't do it.

Zane removed the battery pack from his camera, snapped in a new set of rechargeables and slid the battery pack into place, and then turned the camera on and checked the status display. He had already done this, but it bore repeating.

"Why d'you think I wanted to hire a real photographer?"

"I never really thought about it."

"I mean, it's not like I went to film school."

The job interview: what we're doing here, you got to understand, this is not Los Angeles. What we are is a niche producer. We serve a niche market. We aren't doing, you know, high production values. We don't do, you know, stories. We got no plots and storylines. We don't set up all kinds of lights and, you know, camera angles. We just get the girl in a room and then Bill fucks her. You got to get your pictures when you can.

"You know what the genius of this is?" Barker waved his hand at the screen and leaned forward to tap his index finger repeatedly on the girl's left eyeball. "Just like they say, the eyes are the window to the soul."

Zane did not believe in souls, or in that particular photographic cliché. The eyes, in his view, were the window to diddly-squat.

"I'm serious, here. Our man, he's after a certain thrill. You know what he wants?" Barker's index finger continually sought new targets: the computer screen, Barker's temple, the heavens; now it stabbed at Zane.

"I never really thought about it."

"Let's not be modest. You know the look, man."

Zane didn't.

"Our man wants to feel confidence. These boob-job porn stars, they scare him. He knows he's not getting any of that. He knows that's out of his league. Our man, he doesn't do well with women."

Zane sat fixed and staring in the jacklight of Barker's eyes.

"He wants the girl next door who isn't getting any. He wants her desperate. He wants to be in control."

Barker pointed at the monitor again. Zane did his best to ignore the eyes imploring him from the photograph.

"What I'm saying is it's the eyes. It's not the skin that gets our man going, it's the eyes. That's where he gets off, man." Barker stabbed his finger at him again. "The genius here is the humanity. It's the humanity."

"You missed your calling."

"How so?"

"You should have been a shrink."

"It's all upstairs in this biz." The index finger tapped his temple. "You got to know what makes people tick. Take you."

A disconcerting vision: Zane lies back on the couch while Barker, with goatee, sucks a pipe. Barker frowns profoundly and writes in his notebook, repressed this, suppressed that, the redirected rage is channelled etcetera. And why do you think this deceased woman, this Christine, visits you? You say she is "reproachful." Why do you feel she is disappointed in you? Yes, very interesting. I see. Yes, very interesting, indeed.

"You're all about the money," said Barker.

This will not look good on a headstone. But on balance, it's probably fair. And there's at least some risk that it's true.

* * *

Jade Barker stood with her arms crossed, weight on one leg, one high-heeled toe tapping the linoleum, her clothes and manner pulled directly from the cover of one of the trashier women's magazines, those that advertise more and better sex to the super-market checkout line. All that she missed to complete the effect were tag lines, floating in the glaring, fluorescent air: Look Sexy! (Ten Tips That Actually Work), Twenty New Sex Tricks To Drive Him Wild, Guys Confess: What Men Really Want. But what men really want, Jade already knew.

"She's late again," she said.

Bill stared off into space. Zane fiddled with his camera.

"A couple of minutes," said Barker.

"Fifteen minutes, to be precise."

Barker said nothing.

"It's the second time in a row."

"I know."

"What I'm saying is, you better talk to her."

"We need Melissa," said Barker. "That girl is money in the bank."

"She's just another girl."

"No, she's not. This girl can act."

Jade rolled her eyes back, and her head followed.

"I mean it," said Barker.

"She's got you fooled, anyway."

"Melissa, I can build a site around. This girl is a product line all on her own."

"This girl," said Jade, "is a mishap in the offing."

"I'll deal with Melissa. I got a plan."

"You better. We're all on the clock here."

Zane fussed at an imaginary spot on his lens. It was like finding yourself trapped in a room with a married couple, trying not to pay attention to their marital spat. And that was probably because that's exactly what it was.

* * *

At first glance, Melissa didn't much look like money in the bank, or a product line all her own. She looked, in most respects, fairly ordinary: young, modestly pretty, and too short to be a model. Dark hair, eyebrows a touch heavy, one of them continually cocked, and something in her smile that suggested she was sizing you up and had discovered some flaw that amused her.

To Barker, she gushed an apology; she had missed the bus. Public transit and its frustrations threatened to overwhelm her. Her performance appeared to nullify Barker's index finger from the outset, and his manner quickly softened.

"This is a family business," he said. "We treat each other like family."

Melissa nodded; if she understood what he was driving at, she was alone.

"Don't worry about the bus. Zane'll drive you. He lives in your part of town."

Melissa cocked her eyebrow and subjected Zane to a careful appraisal, as if calculating the probability that he was some kind of pervert.

Another childhood lesson, lately discarded: the clothes make the man, Lucas. Although, in all likelihood, not one tailor today living could compensate for your cadaverous appearance. Zane essayed a sunny smile, in effect somewhat closer to a death rictus. It was a problem he'd been having.

"Shit, Zane, you sick or something? You look like the night of the living dead."

"I think I'm coming down with something."

Zane felt vile, but above all, he simply felt tired.

"I hope you're taking something for that," said Jade. Jade carried antiseptic wipes in her purse, inspected restaurant cutlery with care, kept a small bottle of hand sanitizer on hand at all times. The studio reeked of it, the chemical smell recalling a doctor's office, tongue depressors, the clinical penetration of a cold otoscope into the ear canal.

Zane said nothing. What he was coming down with, specifically, was the sudden onset of bad memories. And Zane was indeed taking something for that: he drank.

This choice of medication had done little to improve the quality of his sleep. He had begun to suspect, furthermore, that it might be responsible for his blotchy appearance, which had recently begun to attract comment.

Zane fussed with his cameras and looked up to see Melissa studying him carefully. He felt that he had become completely transparent.

* * *

Melissa departed for the change room, an incongruous token of modesty, and returned as Alyssa, who wore a tartan skirt, knee-high socks, a white shirt and a surprisingly elastic cardigan that was a clear example of one size failing to fit any. To compound the effect, she had fixed her hair neatly into pigtails and tied them with coloured ribbons, which she fussed with as she sat down on the bed.

Barker had provided the script, such as it was. Alyssa had spent her tuition money and was without money for rent; her Dad was so gonna kill her. But then she'd seen this ad in the paper. And so on, ad lib.

Zane had always preferred to work in close. If your pictures aren't good enough, you aren't close enough; so Robert Capa had said. Then Capa stepped on a land mine. Melissa looked directly into Zane's lens and tilted her eyebrow, then dropped it again. Grey irises, flecked with brown, eyes the colour of a rusting blade. He tripped the shutter: snap.

"Hi, Alyssa," said Bill.

She giggled, threw a shrug. Snap. A sidelong look, biting her lip. Snap.

"So I went down to the campus, and look what I found," said Bill. "And you're not just your average, garden-variety slut, are you?"

Shakes her head, giggles. Snap.

"Alyssa here needs a little money for tuition, so's she doesn't get kicked out of school. Isn't that right?"

"I like, spent all my money. My dad's so going to kill me."

Light falls from suspended fixtures, reflects from this woman with the cocked eyebrow, bends through fourteen elements in eleven groups, bounces off the reflex mirror and casts an image on the focusing screen. The retina scans that image and feeds it through the optic nerve and thalamus to the primary and secondary visual cortices, who discuss among themselves matters of form, contrast and colour. The important thing is to stay grounded; as for the rest, it's really not up to you.

"Well, we don't want that to happen to a hot girl like you. And we've got a way for you to earn that money, don't we?"

Melissa giggled and averted her eyes, then looked up again and parted her lips and touched her lower lip with the tip of her tongue.

Zane concentrated on the hum of the computer's cooling fan, the clack of his camera's reflex mirror, the whine of the capacitor charging in his flash. This girl has a fake name and a fake outfit and she sits on a fake bed in a fake motel room; triangulation becomes somewhat tricky.

"And I'll bet you want to earn that money, don't you? Look at that, you're blushing. Tell us how you're going to earn that money."

Melissa giggled and fanned her face with her hand. This woman can blush on demand: money in the bank.

Zane heard the fluorescent tubes humming overhead, one concrete fact for his mind to latch onto. You reach out for anything you can. A drowning man grabs at a lifeline; the lifeline smiles, steps back, plays hard to get.

CHAPTER TWO

It had begun to rain. Traffic crept along the rain-black pavement in the usual rainy-day Toronto fashion, which is to say slowly, ten thousand drivers eyeing the wet roadway with distrust. Better keep your eyes on the road; factions among the puddles plot mayhem, lie in wait to prey on the inattentive. Anything could happen. Consequently, a million people arrive late home for supper. Zane watched brake lights glow and fade through the smear of his windshield wipers with irritation swelling in his chest.

In Nicaragua, when a good rain hit, the streets would be knee-deep, lost under brown, roiling water laden with silt and garbage. Under all that, you could never be sure that the road was still there. And probably, sizeable chunks of it weren't. So then, then it made sense to slow down. But a little rain like this, a little rain is nothing. Long pedal on the right, full speed ahead. The puddles are not going to jump out and hurt you. You people, you people in your Beemers and your mall-assault land tanks, sport futility vehicles, you people don't know how good you have it.

Drizzle flecks the windshield, fracturing the light, brake lights swelling in glowing red splatter. The passenger-side wiper blade has split and the loose end trails across the glass, leaving a refracted smear in its wake. About time you fixed that wiper. That's not the sort of thing you ought to let go. Road safety is no laughing matter, etcetera.

Melissa emanated from his passenger seat.

Zane was a creature of routine, and recently, solitude had become the central element of that routine. Melissa's presence was a serious disturbance in the quiet field of his existence, a standing wave creating sympathetic vibrations of ever-increasing amplitude, the kind of thing that took down the Tacoma Narrows bridge. Zane was no engineer; his solution to such problems was to ignore them until they dissipated. He papered her over with layers of silence and concentrated on the road.

It was not that Zane was ignorant of social convention and its demand for small talk. He simply felt that his present situation highlighted a serious omission from even the finest etiquette books: how one is to make small talk with a stranger, having just watched her act out the fantasies of a compulsive masturbator. It was difficult to identify an appropriate conversational gambit. Above all, one had to avoid any suggestion of ulterior motives. It would not be appropriate, for example, to compliment her mastery of the finer technical points of her trade, nor even her grasp on certain fundamentals.

The safest course, therefore, seemed to be to deliver Melissa to her home at best possible speed, and thus to remove the disturbance from the quiet field of his existence. But Zane was fighting the inevitable. All lines of pressure now bent in her direction; the conversational barometer was falling like a brick down a well. Sooner or later, something was going to get said.

"Nice weather we're having," said Melissa.

Zane peered at the gloom above, the glow of illuminated signs through the steady drizzle: an Indian restaurant, a donut shop, an adult video store with its windows painted over.

"For a duck, I mean. Nice weather for a duck."

He considered it essential to pay close attention to traffic.

"So I guess you're the strong and silent type." She leaned against the passenger door, elbow propped on the window frame. The cocked eyebrow, the smile of amusement. He felt that she should be wearing her seat belt.

"I was just watching the puddles. For ducks."

An arrested laugh: her head fell back, her mouth opened, but nothing issued.

"A sense of humour. This date might just work out after all."
Zane glanced across at her, saw young love, laughter flashing in darkened streets, tearful breakups, rent troubles. Twenty-five years before, at an age when he fell in love approximately once a week, Melissa would have rendered him doe-eyed and helpless. As things stood, he wanted only to get her out into the rain.

"I bet all the girls think you're creepy."

Time to get that wiper fixed; it grows irritating. Zane reached for the radio knob, turned it on with the volume down low. Some inane DJ chatter, an advertisement for payday loans, followed by another for a bankruptcy trustee. Now this, this is a business plan that Richard Barker himself would admire. You get the suckers coming and going.

"Yeah, you got serial killer written all over you. Next thing, you're gonna start talkin' to yourself or something."

"There's room for you in the trunk."

"Another funny."

"You think I'm joking."

"I think you're just shy."

Offering her a long walk in the rain seemed an appropriate rejoinder, but that would be to concede defeat. The lesson came long in the learning: they can't get your goat if they don't know where it's tied. His father's words. Don't show them where it's tied.

Melissa was now discovering the location of every farm animal that Zane had ever owned.

"I don't feel well. I didn't sleep last night. I'm really not in the mood."

"Maybe I can get you in the mood."

"Maybe you can walk home."

Melissa lapsed into silence. Zane celebrated victory over the length of an entire city block, then pulled up at a red light. At this rate, you'll never be rid of her. The rain was coming down hard now, pounding on the roof.

"How'd you get into this, anyway?"

"Get into what?" Barker got me into this. He said, drive her home. So I'm driving you home.

"I mean, the business. How'd you get into the business."

"How did you?"

She shook her head. "I asked you first."

"I answered an ad."

"You just don't seem to belong, you know?"

Zane knew, but pretended otherwise.

"You're not the type."

He drove for a moment, absorbed this.

"Bill's the type. Rich is the type. You're not the type."

He dodged a car waiting to turn left. So you're not the type. What type? And why does anybody do anything, anyway?

"I'm in it for the money," she said. "The money's great. I'm gonna make a bundle and then get out, so I don't have to work some shit job."

He wanted to ask just what constituted a shit job, in her mind, but thought better of it.

"It just happens to be my shit job."

"You're in it for the free peep show. Admit it."

Is it impolite to inform her that her finest work does nothing for you?

"Yeah, I bet you go home and jack off to all your pictures."

"Barker keeps all the pictures."

"I bet you keep your favourites."

"Barker takes the card. He's afraid I'd just turn around and sell them to someone else."

"Would you?"

"Probably."

"That's all you really think about? Selling them?"

"After a while, skin is just skin."

On the radio, the DJ attempted a joke, with uncertain results, and then took refuge in the next song. Melissa became a blank face staring out into the rain. Ahead, a traffic light turned orange and Zane stamped on the gas, blew through on the red.

"You always drive this fast?"

Zane checked his speedometer and eased back. "I just want to get home and get some sleep."

"Mind if I join you?"

The same smile of amusement, the same cocked eyebrow. The question filled him with a discomfiting sense of his advancing age, not to mention unwelcome memories of Bill in action. In my day, young lady, sweaty entanglements of the sort you so disingenuously propose were preceded by an appropriate period of mooning about and holding hands. Now, you get the AIDS test, you do your interview segment with Bill, you tell us just how you want to earn that money.

Helicopters rain Agent Orange on the Garden of Eden; the tree of life grows cancer apples as Adam frolics in the grass. The serpent drapes himself over Eve's naked shoulders, says, hey babe, you can do a lot better than this. We could take this snake act on the road, make us some good money. We won't have to work no shit jobs.

"Not tonight."

"You gay?"

"No." Furthermore, don't flatter yourself. You are not, in fact, all that.

Some things, you prefer not to explain. Ladies, this is the captain speaking: we are experiencing difficulties with the engines, and have been for some time.

"Shit, Zane, you're wound tight as they come."

"How 'bout we talk about your problems?"

"You're a walking hangup, man."

The bleat of a car horn, briefly dopplering, a falling note of futility.

"Thanks for the insight."

Zane made a left turn and accelerated. The valve clatter was growing worrisome. A mechanic would first recoil in horror, then consider his bank account, like a dentist peering into the mouth of a child raised entirely on candy. The motherlode. Best to let the engine die a natural death.

"Maybe you'd like me as a cheerleader," she said.

"That kind of crap's for assholes who never grew out of high school."

"Or I can be your daughter. I bet you'd like that."

"Give it up."

"Lots of guys like that."

"I said give it a rest."

"And what if I don't? You want to give me a good spanking?"

"You can get out and walk."

She laughed, head back against the passenger window. He pictured the door falling open behind her, the look on her face as she fell backwards to land in a puddle.

"Why can't you just chat about the fucking weather?"

"Shit, Zane, I already tried that."

This, Zane could not refute. He foundered on a lack of gambits. Beyond meteorology lies hockey, the universal Canadian topic. Zane hated hockey. Work was not a topic he wished to explore. Still, it was essential to maintain the initiative.

"Where do you go from here?"

"Left at the next lights."

"I meant in a broader sense."

"I don't think that far ahead."

"I meant tonight."

"You mean your place is out?"

"Seriously."

"I'm going to get solidly baked."

"That's how you deal with it, is it?"

The car was filled with a regrettable hit of the 1970s, the clink and squeak of a windshield wiper reaching the limits of its arc, and the sound of the rain. It occurred to Zane that he had slipped from small talk to much larger talk. Served her right. He thought he would just leave it at that.

"I'm not some kind of *victim*, Zane."

She shifted her body to sit back in her seat, and at last he had quiet.

* * *

You get to see a lot of victims.

Christine was his first. When Zane first saw her, she was dead.

He found Christine in El Salvador, on the road to a small town near the Honduran border, a place called Guarjila. Guarjila was in the middle of what would eventually be called the *Zona_Roja*, the red zone. Romero was dead and in San Salvador the police were firing on demonstrators, and Zane had come to El Salvador to cover that story. He had three Nikon camera bodies, six lenses, a case filled with black-and-white developing gear and chemicals, and the contact information of a dozen photo editors to whom he expected to sell his pictures. He was out to comfort the afflicted and afflict the comfortable. He was out to stop the killing. He was out to win the Pulitzer. Lucas Zane was almost twenty-two years old, and El Salvador was his first war.

In San Salvador, he met Terry Lapierre, whom he had long idolized. Lapierre had shot every war from Vietnam forward, won the Pulitzer, and had three times been awarded the Robert Capa Gold Medal for his work. Zane spotted Lapierre outside the Hilton San Salvador and introduced himself. He said he was in-country shooting freelance and Lapierre said, for who.

Just freelance, he said. I came here after Romero.

And you know no one, you have no contacts, said Lapierre.

Zane did not reply.

You better stick with me, then, said Lapierre.

In a war, you don't work without contacts, he said. You have to be with one side, or be with the other. If you do not have friends, you will be killed. So you always make sure to have friends. And you must have contacts so that you can know the next story before it begins. These demonstrations, they are the last story.

Lapierre said that the next story was up in the mountains, in Chalatenango. So Lapierre headed to Chalatenango, to Guarjila, and Zane followed, and found Christine.

The first sign of trouble was a green-and-white van pulled over at the edge of an open field, its doors hanging open. The wheels were almost in the ditch and the van leaned towards the hills as if drunk. Luggage and papers and bundles of clothing were strewn in the grass and along the road, and as they drew closer Zane saw that some of the bundles of clothing were not bundles of clothing but bodies, collapsed in the curious shapelessness of death. Outside of the sterile confines of the funeral home where he had seen his father, dull and deflated in his casket, these were the the first dead bodies Zane had ever seen.

The dead were four women. One had blonde hair that clearly marked her as a foreigner. She lay on her back. Her vacant blue eyes, on which flies now lighted, implored an indifferent sky. All four had been raped.

A small voice in the back of his head, a voice out of a textbook, demanded that he shoot the scene in a way that preserved the dignity of the victims, and his mind reeled at the suggestion. It could not be done. Nothing he framed worked, nothing explained the scene. He continued shooting to the end of the roll, rejecting each frame as useless even as he shot it, and then mechanically loaded a new roll. As he threaded the film leader onto the sprockets he absently noted the shaking of his fingers. His head swam in the heat and his ears were full of the droning buzz of cicadas.

The youngest of the victims was a dark-haired woman of about twenty, lying face-up in the grass. They had shot her in the chest, twice, and bayoneted her through the ribs. Her purse, brown vinyl cracked at the corners, lay spilled in the grass beside her. He knelt and began picking up her things, putting them back into the purse. It just seemed like the right thing to do.

A few sheets of notepaper, a pen, a flat tin of Aspirin, two tampons. A letter, written in a girlish hand, with big, open loops and careful circles dotting the i's. Zane searched and found the envelope, addressed to someone named Christine. A return address in North Dakota.

A photograph. An Instamatic shot, the dead girl with two others, at a picnic table. All of them smiling at the camera. He noted that they were all a little bit blurred by the combination of poor camera technique and a poor quality lens. Nothing written on the back. Kodak paper.

Zane laid the photo in the grass beside her outstretched hand and changed lenses, switched to the fifty-five macro. He leaned in close and took a shot of her hand, dark with dried blood, with the photo lying beside it in the grass. Long slashes, no doubt from the bayonet, crossed her palm. He picked up the photo and the letter and tucked them carefully inside the envelope, and put the envelope in the front pouch of his camera bag. It was the only identification he could find.

Lucas Zane didn't yet know it, but he had just won the Pulitzer Prize.

* * *

Zane inhabited a one-bedroom apartment on the second floor of a three-storey walk-up, far enough off Queen Street West to escape any trend toward urban renewal, rising rent or creeping fashionability. The place had a small and dingy bathroom that successfully resisted all attempts at cleaning; no amount of scrubbing ever quite effaced the granular feel of the bathtub enamel. Sitting room and kitchen were a single space, divided by a counter and by the cupboards suspended above. The furniture, provided, consisted of a battered couch, a coffee table, and an old television, and Zane had cable on the sly, as long as at least one of his neighbours paid the bill. His kitchen window overlooked the street, and when the television proved too demanding, Zane often stood at the window, watching.

On the windowsill behind the television, a spider plant in a coffee can slowly died of neglect. The plant was the gift of Zane's neighbour, a large black woman with a thick Caribbean accent, a woman he carefully avoided, suspecting that she was insane. She seemed to him entirely too friendly and talkative to be completely stable.

Zane had few other possessions: a few dishes, a camera bag containing the tools of his trade, a toothbrush, a razor, the other essentials. In the corner of the sitting room was a small stack of cardboard boxes that he had never unpacked, bearing dust dating from the day he moved in. He had never needed the things inside. He had forgotten what the boxes contained.

His job with Barker paid the rent and the grocery bill. The work, which consisted of shooting the photos and then taking care of the photo editing, left him plenty of free time, and Zane could easily have found more work and made himself comfortable, but he felt no ambition toward comfort. Zane felt no detectable ambition at all.

In the mornings he got out of bed, shaved, showered, and cleaned up after the night before. Then, if he had no work to do and if no domestic chores presented themselves, he went out into the street and found ways to pass the day.

He shopped for groceries, for cleaning supplies, for abrasives with which to attack the granular surface of the bathtub. He browsed bookstores but never bought a book, thumbed through magazines, but avoided newspapers. Sometimes, he sat and drank coffee and watched the life of the street pass him by. He drifted into pawn shops, considered musical instruments in hock and cheap cameras abandoned. Not once did Zane take a photograph in the street. He never felt that urge.

In the early part of that summer Zane passed time in the park, where he amused himself by feeding the squirrels and the pigeons; this ceased after he saw a decrepit old woman mumbling to herself while doing the same. Her eyes possessed a rheumy vacancy that disturbed him far more than a glance in his bathroom mirror. He found new hobbies.

Sometimes, he rode the subway, pointlessly travelling east or north, lost in the anonymity of public transit. He observed men deep in their newspapers, women bathing in novels, kids staring vacantly at their reflected selves with wires hanging from their ears. He thought about Walker Evans but felt no desire to emulate him. Between subway maps and ads for career training services he read poems posted as a project in public art, and wondered just what distinguishes a poem from a run-on sentence interrupted by superfluous carriage·returns. He got off at random stops and walked. He looked into shop windows. He invented purpose where he could find it.

Recently, he had started on museums. He went to art galleries, considered sculpture, looked at photographs. He tried reading *National Geographic* again, for the photography, but all of the mighty had fallen; Abell and Harvey and Allard had retired and what remained seemed empty. Most of the junk in the galleries he explored was the work of pygmies who imagined themselves somehow better than those mere journalists. Their greatest achievements lay in their artist statements, towers of finely crafted babble in which they explained the subjects their crap *investigated* and *explored*. Zane mentally composed an artist statement of his own, one he wished had accompanied his own exhibits in New York: just shut up and look at the pictures.

Once, he went to the zoo, where he passed an entire afternoon in watching a troop of monkeys. None of the monkeys had ever composed an artist statement, but each still seethed with unrealized ambition. He learned their personalities, gave them names, had a brief but earnest conversation on the subject of their internal politics with a six-year-old girl. He felt quite confident that he had this thing about nailed. Then the girl's mother dragged her away by the hand. The look she gave Zane blistered his paint.

Throughout each day, he kept himself in motion. In the evenings, as the city slowed, stalled, and settled into quiet, he sat at home and locked the doors. It was only then that he started acting crazy.

* * *

Among Zane's less terrifying symptoms was a recent tendency to talk to himself. Not that he carried on full-blown conversations, which would indeed be worrisome; he simply punctuated his long stretches of domestic silence with occasional remarks, like the elliptical conversations of a long-married couple that has long since run out of new topics for discussion.

Disjointed phrases presented themselves, and he uttered them: "I think I've just about got this thing nailed," for example, or "the important thing now is to keep things plumb." Just what it was that he intended to nail, or why it was essential to keep things plumb, Zane had no idea. Perhaps, in some past life, he had been a carpenter, and some karmic offence – a hammer dropped on a stink bug, perhaps, or a careless glue spill that had pinned and drowned a spider – had consigned him to this unhappy plane. Or perhaps he was just going nuts.

To his credit, this last possibility did give him a sense of creeping unease. Zane felt a growing suspicion that he was not entirely in control of himself, a feeling that he was up to something behind his own back. Up to no good.

But on good nights, the words themselves, and more importantly, the confidence in his voice as he said them, were soothing. He heard the voice of a man in control of himself, a man who had it together. All was well, or perhaps soon would be. If indeed he was up to something behind his back, at least he seemed confident about it.

It was only on the bad nights that Zane really drank. He only started to run when he heard himself catching up.

* * *

Evening sunlight slanting through the resting air gilded the three-storey walk-up opposite, rendering brick and mortar, baked clay and powdered limestone, into gold. Alchemists toiled for centuries and never considered photography. Clay into gold, light into silver. The philosopher's stone, it transpires, is multi-coated, low-dispersion glass.

Now is the magic hour. It is impossible to take a bad picture now, but it is easy to make a cliché. The problem is never the light but what you choose to do with it.

Below Zane's apartment window, the street has fallen into shadow. A man crosses with a woman, shortening his stride to keep pace with her small, quick steps. She wears a light cotton dress, a flowered print. Reflections flee the windows of his passenger door as he opens it for her in a sudden, uncomfortable moment of formality. Her teeth flash in a smile, eyes catching reflected light, her bare leg retracting into the darkness of the passenger seat. Zane watched until the car pulled out into traffic. He had never lost the habit of staring.

Now you shoot chromes, high-speed chromes in defiance of the conventional wisdom, let the grain take over, let the lights along the street burn through the film. Chromes give the colours of the cars and the buildings weight and depth, render shadows a deeper black, conceal the eyes of people drinking in their shirt sleeves on the patio of the restaurant next door. Drag the shutter: the couple on the street blend into a blur of togetherness, all detail lost to shadow and motion, unknowable. The picture is as compelling as a dream.

But the picture says nothing. The picture is just a circus trick that lets you work with the impossible light. Shooting available darkness, you do what you can and alchemy takes care of the rest, silver halides and dye couplers distilling life and motion into a silent dream in which nothing is specific. Gone are the quickness in his step, his rush to beat her to the door, the shyness of her movements, his momentary awkwardness. The couple is silenced, stilled, suspended in a net of gelatin and grain and flash trickery. What remains is an eloquent lie. In the silence of the photograph, you will never see that this is their first date. And you will never see the breakup.

Die knowing something, Walker Evans said; you are not here long. So stare, listen, pry, eavesdrop. But you know nothing now, and every day, you know less.

Zane drained his beer and put the bottle on the counter by the sink and opened the fridge to find another. An unsteady step explained his uncharacteristic explorations beyond mere facts; a few beers and you abandon all your commitments, let the mind run free. Time to return to the facts. Among said facts, half this case remains. We'll need to buy another, but that's tomorrow's project. Let us now focus on today's. Zane twisted open another bottle and threw the cap in the sink.

Time for a change. You've seen enough imploring eyes, provided enough chauffeur service for Richard Barker, been appraised as a potential pervert on one too many occasions. Time to get moving. This exile has gone on long enough. It's time to find a new gig. And the only way out is back through the same door you came in.

Zane found the telephone and dialed the New York number of his agent. The office was closed. He let it ring through to voice mail, then hung up and called Jack at home.

"Zane, let's not go through this same old shit again."

This was not the greeting he had hoped for.

Jack, fussing with his tie, inspecting his fingernails, immaculate. His hair would be neatly combed. An aging dandy in an Italian suit, silk tie and pocket square. As if to compensate for his effeminacy, Jack swore non-stop.

"I want a story," said Zane.

"You're drunk."

"Not particularly."

Zane enunciated with care, but the word contained too many syllables.

"You know the answer. We've been through the motions more times than a twenty-dollar hooker."

"I need work."

Zane left his bottle on the counter and wandered to the toilet. The beer was making its presence felt.

"You don't want a story, Zane. You want to believe in a story."

"I can't keep doing this, Jack."

"What exactly are you doing?"

"I'm taking a piss."

In the long pause that followed, Zane completed the task at hand. For a moment, he thought that Jack had hung up on him.

"I mean, what exactly can't you keep doing."

Zane considered this carefully: I am photographing less-than-perfectly attractive young ladies engaged in various acts of a sexual nature, in an explicit manner, for the interest and enjoyment of the members of a predominantly, perhaps exclusively, male audience. I am not working in Los Angeles; my work therefore falls outside the mainstream of this genre. Although remunerative, it is decidedly low-rent.

"I'm *en vacances*."

"Zane, are you okay?"

Zane tucked the phone under his ear and washed his hands and regarded his reflection. A long, diagonal crack transected the mirror and split his face into two halves that didn't quite align. The more he looked at the faces, the less familiar they became. The man in the mirror was tired and unkempt. His hair rioted in disarray. He looked blotchy, had bags under his eyes like bruises. The man in the mirror was obviously not well.

"I think I'm coming down with something."

"What I mean is, how are you doing these days."

"I know what you mean. I'm fine."

"I don't think you are."

Zane stared absently at his reflection and listened to the silence of the telephone line.

"It's still the same deal," said Jack. "Get yourself straightened out, come up with a story, pitch it to me, we'll see."

"I am straightened out."

"I'd like to believe that."

"Believe it."

"Can't talk myself into that one."

"I can do this, Jack."

"Stop getting drunk and calling me at home. I'm going to change my number. Goodbye, Zane."

Zane leaned in closer to the mirror for a better look. The glass was streaked and dirty and somehow never seemed to come clean. His eyes were hollow pits. He looked as if someone had punched him out some days ago, and his face was just now returning to normal.

Had someone punched him out? If someone punched you out, you'd remember. Besides, who would make the effort? Anything's possible, but.

These questions are too difficult to consider.

Food is simpler, if uninteresting. He made a turkey sandwich on white with a skim of low-fat mayo, accompanied it with a cup of skim-milk yogurt, approximately as appealing as a can of white paint and a poor match for beer. At a field hospital in northern Pakistan, the American surgeon asked casually what he had eaten for breakfast. Morphine allowed Zane to take this for small talk, and he joked of eating things that would be unobtainable in Afghanistan: bacon, eggs, hash browns.

Above his surgical mask the doctor's eyes betrayed no hint of a smile. We need to identify the foreign matter in the abdominal cavity, he said. Then he cut out almost one third of the small intestine. Over time, the remaining intestine was supposed to adapt, to learn to deal with real food again. And Zane hadn't tasted bacon, eggs, or hash browns since.

It starts to get you down. After a while, you start to wonder if this is living.

So you take certain precautions. The apartment contained no fixtures sufficiently solid to aid Zane in hanging himself, and the windows were insufficiently high for him to accomplish anything by jumping, beyond breaking his legs and thus making a fool of himself. His stove was electric, rather than gas. He did not own any old-fashioned razor blades, and his medicine cabinet contained no drugs powerful enough to overdose even a domestic cat. To shoot yourself, you need a gun; Zane had carefully ensured that he did not own one. This left slashing his wrists with a kitchen knife, something he was fairly certain he was too cowardly and squeamish to do.

The television spouted its usual comforting inanities. Lift the plot of one sitcom and drop it in another; nothing changes but the faces. Zane flopped onto the couch and opened his camera bag. He turned on his camera and the LCD display flashed at him. He zoomed the lens to about twenty millimetres, comfortably wide. He set the white balance to auto, threw the aperture wide open and set aperture priority. He didn't need to think.

With the camera at eye level he tested the autofocus on the kitchen faucet and then on the cupboards and the television. He found the remote and switched to the weather channel where an enthusiastic young woman expounded on the likelihood of rain on the prairies, a low-pressure system sweeping in from the west; all this was a matter of pressing national interest today. Zane framed the desolate room with the television nattering away at its edge and released the shutter. On the LCD screen, the shot looked like nothing more than distilled loneliness.

What the hell are you doing here? Is this some kind of purgatory? There is nothing here to shoot. The camera is useless.

Zane slipped the camera strap from around his neck, widened the zoom to about seventeen millimetres, and held the camera at arm's length, the lens aimed directly at his face. The glass stared back at him, black and implacable, splashes of colour catching the light, fragments of his apartment in cyan and magenta, his face reflected in the glass. He stared straight into the lens and then he released the shutter.

Light passes through the lens and forms an image on the sensor, confirming at least that you exist and are reflecting light in the normal way. On the LCD screen, Zane's face still looked blotchy and unshaven, and his hair remained a chaotic mess. Crow's feet around the eyes and deepening signs of age. A complete absence of expression. It looked like an ID card photo.

It will look good over your obituary: Lucas Zane, erstwhile combat photographer of some repute, was found dead in his apartment today at the age of forty-six. An image left on his camera's flash card confirmed that Mr. Zane had committed suicide by shooting himself once in the head with a wide-angle lens. In his suicide note, hastily scrawled on the wall of his squalid domicile in unused pixels, Mr. Zane complained that even his own small intestine had abandoned him. Mr. Zane is survived by his photographs, which have taken on the life that he intended, but that he now regrets.

Zane stared at the image for a few moments, and then deleted it.

CHAPTER THREE

At about the age of ten, Zane decided that what he could not remember must never have happened.

He arrived at this theory lying awake in his bed at night, on nights when the sounds of the furnace coming on and of the wind in the birch tree outside his window failed to coalesce into the certainty that something was watching him from behind. On those nights, he allowed the events of the day to pass through his mind in instant replay. What he remembered, had happened. What he did not remember might well not have happened at all. The only way to be certain of anything would be to memorize it.

His speculations deepened. Perhaps all experience was nothing more than the playback of memories. It seemed conceivable that he had already reached the end of his life and was now only witnessing the playback. If one were to die at the age of ten, say, of something sneaking up in the dark, for example, and if one had failed to be properly attentive up to that time, then the entire playback of one's memories might take only a year or two. It was a sobering possibility. And each day's film seemed disappointingly short.

So: it was essential to be attentive. Lying in bed, Zane concentrated: okay, I know that this moment is real, that this is happening to me, because I am thinking that I can remember it, and therefore I must actually be remembering it, from some future vantage point. And if I think I remember it, then I must be able to remember that I am thinking that. Otherwise, I would not know I was thinking it.

At some point in his philosophical struggles, young Zane invariably fell asleep. The onset of unconsciousness he naturally failed to remember, since sleep necessarily follows from a failure of attention. On the following evening, this fact became grist for further ruminations. If he could not remember falling asleep, had he slept at all? If not, how had he awakened?

It seemed to Zane that a lot of life was lost in the playback. It did not occur to him then that this is a tragic thought to have rattling around the inside of your head at the age of ten. And it was not until much later that he realized that the memories he most wanted to retain inevitably collapsed into footnotes, while the experience that remained consisted chiefly of things he would rather forget.

* * *

Someone had knocked a carton of eggs off the supermarket shelf. It was the fractured shape of an eggshell, lying on the tiles, that set him off.

At first, Zane's mind refused to make sense of the scene. A man lay on his side in the road. He looked almost as if he was resting, but for the blood and dirt on his face. He had not been dead long, had not yet started to smell with that terrible smell that soap can never remove. The executioner's bullet had carried away the back of his head, and the sun shone into his empty skull, glared bright across the white edge of shattered bone.

Zane got to work. He went down on his knees with the fifty-five macro, focused in close. The exit wound gaped, a cave entrance, darkness behind a threshold of white bone. He leaned in to get a better shot. Too dark. The camera shook. He cranked up the shutter speed to fight the shakes, shot with the lens wide open. A trickle of sweat stung his dominant eye and he could feel his pulse in his chest.

You're going to have to push this roll to get anything.

You are in the supermarket. You are in Toronto. You are shopping for groceries.

Oppressive humidity and the smell of garbage and tropical flowers, sickly sweet. Sweat stinging your eye, tickling between your shoulder blades.

Lapierre's hand on your shoulder. Zane came to his senses, crouching beside the body, the front element of his lens only inches from the exit wound. Taking close-ups of the inside of a human skull. Too dark to show anything, even if he wanted to. He stopped, looked up. Sunlight pierced his eyes.

"Who is going to buy that picture, Lucas?"

Now he could hear again: the thrum of the truck engine and the buzzing of cicadas in the trees. Heat and humidity enclosed him. He stood, brushed the red dust of the road off his knees.

"I don't know what I was thinking."

"Don't worry about it." Lapierre lit two cigarettes and handed one to Zane. One of his vile French Gauloises. Zane took the smoke but did not take a drag. He wasn't sure his stomach could take it.

"Sometimes all you can think is to make a picture," said Lapierre. The picture doesn't have to make sense. Sometimes, you can't make a picture that makes sense. Sometimes, having a camera in front of your eyes lets you avoid seeing. Lapierre said all these things, at one time or another.

Zane kept seeing the edges of the skull.

He tried not to look at the eggshells, concentrated on slowing his breathing and calming his heart. You are in Toronto, in the supermarket, standing in the rush of cool air coming off a refrigerated cabinet filled with egg cartons. You can smell stale milk, spilled from a leaking carton. You came here to buy groceries.

"Are you all right?"

He had seen this woman before, working the cash. He had noticed her face as she rang up his groceries. Pretty, in a delicate way, her pale skin white over the bridge of her nose. She was thin, looked impossibly fragile.

He could still smell the smoke from Lapierre's Gauloise.

"Dizzy spell," he said. Sweat on his forehead, the pace of his breathing, the thrum of his heart.

"Do you need to sit down? I can call someone."

You are beautiful in every sense. Normal people keep their distance. Normal people call the cops on weirdos who break out sweating and start freaking out in public places. That's how you get tasered. Every cop loves a weirdo.

"I'll be fine."

"Are you sure? Can I get you a glass of water?"

"No, I'm okay. Thanks."

What you need is a bolt-hole, someplace dark and quiet where you can hole up away from all these people. What you need is space and distance. Not this public freak show.

"You don't look so good."

"I'm okay."

"Let me get you a chair."

"Just please leave me the fuck alone, will you?"

You want to pull cans and cartons down from the shelves, throw jars, break glass, trash the place. As long as we're making a scene, let's make a scene. You want a freak show I'll give you a fucking freak show, people.

In the parking lot, the sudden weight of humid air and the sun stabbing your eyes. My kingdom for someone to hit. Just give me a reason, any reason at all, knuckles splitting against smiling teeth, blood spilt on hot asphalt. You light up like a flood of gasoline and it feels good. It feels clean. As he reached the sidewalk he started to run, and people turned to stare. Crazy man in blue jeans, running down the street.

He was just going to have to do without groceries.

* * *

Zane was perturbed.

The ultimate cause of Zane's agitation was one Richard Barker, who had telephoned earlier and asked him to drive Melissa to work.

To refuse Barker would be like refusing the wind. The wind blows on, heedless, carries in storms, kicks up dust, demolishes carefully ordered hairstyles and the occasional trailer park. The wind is everywhere, a law unto itself. The wind is a fact. You don't refuse it.

So Zane telephoned Melissa, who then insisted on walking down to his place and meeting him there. He was not to go out of his way to pick her up. But the last thing Zane wanted was an intruder in his sanctuary, particularly one who could render him transparent with her eyes. A brief standoff ensued.

"It's really not very far out of my way," he said.

"It's okay. I'll just walk on over."

"You shouldn't be walking round out there alone."

"Shit, Zane, don't be such an old maid. It really isn't that far."

So, logically, it should be no trouble for me to pick you up. But now is the time to recognize defeat, to accept your lot with maturity and grace. One can sustain such a rally only so long before superficial politeness is revealed for what it is. Beyond that point, further resistance can only lead once more to the question you so hope to avoid, to wit, what's wrong with you. She had him cornered.

And: *an old maid?*

Zane told her to come for half-past one. He made sure to do the dishes.

And now the immediate cause of Zane's agitation was knocking at his door. He needed to pee but went to the door instead.

Melissa, her head balloon-swollen in the fisheye lens of his peephole, twitched like a ferret at the entrance to a rabbit warren. And like a rabbit, Zane froze. In this way, the rabbit hopes to remain unseen, and thus to avoid being torn into bite-sized pieces. As a survival strategy, remaining perfectly still in the face of onrushing death is not a consistent success; the species compensates by profligate breeding. That option was not open to Zane. He opened the door.

"You're early."

"It was much closer than I thought."

"That's why I offered to pick you up. Remember?"

"So do I get to come in, or should I wait in the hall?"

Zane stepped out of the way. She brushed past him. A faint scent of lemon, of flowers, and the mind reels. A good thing you took a shower and found a clean shirt.

"Nice place. You live like a king."

He made for the kitchen.

It is essential that we keep things plumb. Also, to control ourselves; should you suddenly insist, apropos of nothing, on this imperative to keep things plumb, she will probably form the opinion that you are distinctly odd. Especially if you then admit that you haven't the faintest idea what you actually mean by that.

"You sure have done a lot with this place. I mean, look at this couch. You get this from the dump?"

The couch was among his landlord's excuses for calling the place furnished. Likewise the television, of late 1980s vintage.

"I gotta take a leak," he said.

"Thanks for sharing."

Zane closed himself into the bathroom, his inner sanctum, the one place where he alone still ruled. Relief, on more than one count.

But above the splash and rush from the toilet bowl, he heard another sound. Melissa moving around, and something else, just below the mutter of the television. It occurred to him that Melissa's interest in his apartment might be based solely on the value of its contents, specifically his cameras, at the nearest pawn shop. He knew nothing about her, save that she was not the kind of girl one takes home to meet mother.

His mother's likely reaction to that introduction beggared the imagination. Yes, mother, this is Melissa, who as it happens, works as an actress in pornographic films.

A porno girl! How *interesting*! We simply *must* compare notes sometime. Chattering thus, the womenfolk proceed to the kitchen of the Zane homestead, presumably to exchange recipes therein.

This sound could be the sound of twenty-five thousand dollars departing in his old-fashioned canvas camera bag. Meanwhile, Zane was otherwise engaged. He finished as quickly as he could.

When he emerged, Melissa and his cameras were right where he had left them. She sat on the couch with her feet on his battered coffee table, holding a large book with a black cover, Lapierre's posthumous career retrospective. Foreword by Lucas Zane.

"*Lucas* Zane? Lucas?"

"Where'd you find that?"

She pointed at the pile of boxes in the corner.

"You always snoop through other people's stuff?"

She dismissed his question with a wave of her hand; no harm, no foul, objection overruled.

"I always figured Zane was your first name."

"Only my friends call me Lucas."

"I never heard anybody call you that."

He went to the cupboard and found a glass and filled it with water from the tap.

"Maybe I'll start calling you Luke."

"Nobody calls me Luke."

"Luke Skywalker. Cool Hand Luke."

"I just go by Zane."

"Lucky Luke. Luke the Kook." Again the smile of amusement, the mocking smirk. She turned back to the book, flipped quickly through the pages and closed it to look at the cover.

"So this guy was, like, famous."

"Define famous."

"You been holding out on me, man. Just who the hell are you?"

This is a question that interests us all.

"They got this picture of you in Nicaragua or someplace." She opened the book to the page in question, his foreword, held it up to show him.

"The guy who took those pictures was a good friend of mine."

"I can't picture you in places like that."

43

Zane didn't want to picture places like that.

You should have put the boxes in the closet. You shouldn't have left them out. You should have thrown all that stuff out, long ago. But you didn't, and now the ferrets are on the loose, appraising the furniture, checking out the family heirlooms.

"Zane, what the fuck are you doing?"

"What am I doing what?"

She put the book on the coffee table and stood up.

"I mean, what are you doing working for Rich?"

"It buys the groceries."

"Oh, bullshit." She picked the book up and waved it at him. The ferrets go on a rampage, smashing the china, setting the couch on fire. "Why are you doing this cheap-shit porno when you could be in Iraq?"

"What do you know about Iraq?"

"Shit, Zane, you think I'm just some dumb porno chick? I watch the news."

"Why would I want to go to Iraq?"

"You could be doing something that matters, man."

This is what you get for dealing with ferrets. The species is not known for its manners. They're nosy; they pry. Also, they like the taste of blood. He heard his mother's voice: well, she seems very *nice*, dear, but not particularly *well brought up*. You have no *idea* what she told me in the kitchen. Where exactly did you say you met?

"I don't want to talk about it."

She shook her head. "I don't get you at all."

"Why don't we talk about your personal life?"

"We're talking about you, buster."

"No, we're not." And: *buster?* Zane picked up his camera bag and slung the strap over his shoulder and dug out his car keys. You should have burned that book, years ago. "You're talking about me, and I'm getting ready for work."

"I just think it's a waste."

"How old are you?"

"Twenty-one."

"Go look in the mirror and tell me about a waste." He took the book from her, carried it back into the kitchen and threw it in the garbage with unnecessary force. "We're going to be late."

So Melissa finds all your farm animals, again. You never do learn, after all. The outcome, however, provided some small satisfaction that overrode the urge to apologize: Melissa remained silent thereafter.

* * *

In his first months in El Salvador, after any particularly difficult day, Zane would chance the vagaries of the Salvadoran telephone system and the resulting bill, and call home to Trish, the woman to whom he was then engaged.

Zane first met Trish at a restaurant in Toronto, where she worked as a waitress. He found her features striking enough that he returned often, more often than he could afford. Eventually, with the abandon of one too many glasses of wine and the desperation of a man at the limits of his already limited credit, he informed her that he found her nose remarkable. This, she might have written off entirely had he not followed up with a stream of nonsense to the effect that, as a photographer, he collected unusual faces. Her eyes narrowed, calculating risk. After a stream of qualifications and clarifications – not unusual bad, I mean, just unusual striking, interesting – he lapsed into silence.

The truth of the matter was much simpler: he thought her lips looked edible, and furthermore had on several occasions gained a fine view of her cleavage as she leaned over to clear tables. This, he wished to investigate. Her remarkable nose was merely the fine print.

She said her name was Trish, agreed to meet him for coffee. Just for coffee, she said. Something in her voice said we've been down this road before. You pick up the waitress; what a cliché. He expected her to stand him up.

She didn't. Zane remained on his best behaviour, didn't mention photography again. He didn't say anything about photography until she said, aren't you going to ask to take my picture?

"I don't really do portraits."

Again her eyes narrowed. "What exactly do you do?"

"I'm more in the vein of candid street photography. I'm interested in showing things as they are."

"Portraits don't show people as they are?"

"Portraits show people striking poses." He unzipped his jacket pocket and pulled out a small album of four-by-six black-and-white prints. "This is the kind of stuff I do."

Zane's portfolio at that time was a collection of clichés, student work, all ironic juxtapositions and alienated tension, in imitation of the masters. But Trish had no background in photography. She said they looked witty and intelligent.

"I thought you might like this one." He had kept the shot in an envelope up to now, Trish in profile at the bus stop a block down from the restaurant, where he had met her in the street and briefly chatted to her the week before. He thought of the picture as his Girl in Fulton Street, after Walker Evans.

"I took that Tuesday. After talking to you at the bus stop."

She frowned at it, lips tightening.

"Is that what you do? Follow girls around and take their pictures?"

He deflated like a bad tire.

"I'm sorry. Forget it."

"I was going to ask you out. I took that to have a picture to give you. Even if you said no. You can keep it."

"I'm sorry."

"I thought it was a nice shot. I don't usually do stuff like that. I thought it was a good one."

"It is a good one. Thank you." She reached across the table to touch his hand. And by the time he got to El Salvador, they were engaged.

* * *

On the evening after they found the bodies, an evening on which Zane felt particularly helpless, the alchemical rituals of his improvised darkroom did nothing to relieve his mood. He hung his film to dry and didn't bother with contact prints. He had nothing. Only the unprintable record of the deaths of five people, a series of images that no one in middle America would want to see over a bowl of Rice Krispies, sunlight breaking through daffodils in a North Dakota kitchen. Defeat.

Zane left his film hanging from the shower rod and turned out the bathroom light and closed the bathroom door to keep out the dust. The final remains of his ice supply swam in the ice bucket. He fished the cubes out and splashed rum over them and then got the dead woman's letter from his camera bag and sat down on the bed. He still could not bring himself to read it. Instead he took her picture out of the envelope and stared at it for a long while.

Had Lapierre been in the room he would certainly have advised Zane not to obsess over dead people he had never met, and in particular not to construct sentimental fantasies of their quiet lives in North Dakota farm towns. Furthermore, Lapierre would have warned Zane to lay off the rum. Lapierre did not drink, having formed the opinion in Vietnam that self-medication was the path to ruin. This was the only one of Lapierre's working principles that Zane routinely ignored, purely on the grounds that it was no fun. And besides, Lapierre was not in the room.

Zane tucked the picture back into the envelope and then looked at the telephone for a long moment before he picked it up and dialed. Trish picked up on the fifth ring, her voice tinny through the long-distance static.

"Trish," he said.

"Lucas, it's really late. And you sound like you've been drinking."

How can she get that from a single word? "Had a rough day."

"We can't afford this. It's too expensive."

He started slowly, then spilled the whole story, the abandoned van and the bodies in the grass and the flies and the victims' vacant, desiccated eyes, his inability to make visual sense of it, and the fact that Christine looked just like her, a fact that was utterly untrue but which had become true in his mind as he developed his film. The words rushed out fast until he exhausted his supply.

"You're my lifeline, Trish," he said.

"I want you to come home. I don't want you to stay there anymore."

"I can't come home. I have to finish this."

After a long pause, he realized that there was nothing left to say. He said his goodbyes and hung up. Afterwards, he stared up at the ceiling for a long time. He remained in Central America until he was wounded, and then returned to Toronto. By the time he got back to El Salvador, he was no longer engaged. And these memories, try as he might to retrieve them, had long since collapsed into footnotes. He couldn't remember the name of the restaurant, or where they went for coffee, or the smell of her hairspray. He couldn't remember a thing.

* * *

Zane waited for an oncoming furniture truck to pass and then took the corner, drove slowly past the corner grocery and the flower shop and a run-down Ethiopian restaurant. He was just a few blocks short of normal; that is to say, he had only to drop Melissa off, and then could return home and lapse back into the comfortable pattern of his life: couch, beer, television, solitude.

"So what now?"

The question caught him off balance.

"What do you do now? Drink 'til you pass out on that wonderful couch?"

"Why would you think that?"

"You got more beer in your fridge than food."

"I haven't been shopping."

"Seriously. What do you do now?"

"Seriously? I go back home, have a couple beers, and get on with my life."

"Sounds lonely."

Somewhere in the English language there exists some combination of words that will get this woman to shut up and leave you alone.

"You want to share those couple beers, Zane?"

Zane hesitated. The scent of a ferret wafts on the breeze, a scent that, deeply ingrained in racial memory, scares the shit out of rabbits.

"You're half my age."

"What the fuck does that mean?"

That's the risk you take, moving beyond concrete facts. Sometimes a couple of beers is just a couple of beers; Freud said that. I'll let you cry in my beer, if I can cry in yours.

"It's not complicated," she said. "I just want company."

"All right, then." He attempted to concentrate on traffic, realized he had omitted the word etiquette demanded, and tacked it on as an afterthought. "Sorry."

Melissa said nothing.

So much for peace and quiet. One moment of weakness and you've got her in your apartment again, drinking your beer, socks on your coffee table, controlling the TV remote, digging through your stuff when you leave the room to take a leak.

Remarking on your spider plant, for example: "Shit, Zane, you ever water that thing?"

She hadn't sat down yet, he hadn't put his keys away. Just through the door and already there's something.

"I mean, if you're going to keep a plant."

"It's not really mine."

"What, it just lives here?"

"No."

"It comes and goes as it pleases? It has its own key?"

"My neighbour gave it to me."

"So you kill it. Nice."

"She gives everyone spider plants."

"So you might as well kill yours?"

"She'll only give me another. She hands them out to everyone. She'd give you one, too."

"How sweet," said Melissa, with not one hint of irony.

"She's not all there."

Melissa looked at him for some time, then said two devastating words: okay, then. She turned away and dropped her bag on the coffee table.

No, I'm telling you: this woman is not all there. But it's futile; she's not going to listen. Let her meet the neighbour one of these days, find out for herself. This woman talks your ear off with an accent you can barely comprehend and then presses another spider plant into your hands. Before you know it, you're choked with all this jungle foliage. Zane had killed three to date.

Zane left Melissa in the living room and took his camera bag through to the bedroom and left it there.

Melissa called after him: "Look, you mind if I take a shower?"

Seems reasonable, with what you've been up to. The bathroom was civilized when last seen although the tub still feels like sandpaper. Chances of finding a clean towel are at least fifty-fifty. He told her to go nuts, said he'd find her a towel.

She went into the bathroom and closed the door. The sound of water splashing in the tub. Zane found himself a beer and opened it and then headed for the bedroom closet.

Something here is badly askew, several degrees out of plumb. A serious disturbance in the magnetic field, and it centres on the bathroom. Some boundaries, one does not cross, a matter of good manners. Even the ghosts retain a certain decorum. Christine never visits while you're on the toilet. But Melissa has now penetrated the final refuge.

The foolish man invites the vampire into his home. Thereafter, he is powerless to resist. So says the legend. This being the case, you're in serious trouble. You've got no holy water, no crosses, no Bible, only the remnants of a bottle of garlic powder. And you can't just ambush people with garlic powder; it's not done. Garlic powder in her hair and stuck to her eyelashes. She'll feel compelled to inquire as to exactly what's wrong with you. And here we go again.

He left the folded towel on the end of the kitchen counter. Melissa's voice carried through the sound of the water, singing, clear and on key. A tune that Zane recognized but could not name. Zane went into the living room and sat down and listened until she stopped, and then he turned on the television.

A photogenic anchor spoke in grave tones, but having come in halfway through the story Zane couldn't make sense of it. Murder and mayhem, police lifting yellow crime scene tape that blocked the driveway of a large suburban home. A woman's head, crying. A man's head, angry. A wavering shot of broken glass and blood on the front step. Memory returns like a drain backing up: a house in Kosovo, glass and crockery broken on the kitchen floor, the decomposed bodies of a woman and her child, skulls with hair blackened by decay. He changed the channel.

"You got that towel?"

The splashing had stopped. Zane returned to the kitchen, picked the towel off the counter and knocked on the bathroom door. The door opened and he looked away to hand the towel to her, and she laughed at him.

"Shit, Zane, you seen a lot more than that."

"That was different."

She left the door open, so he retreated from the kitchen and sat down again on the couch. Presently she emerged, wrapped in the towel, and Zane heard the fridge open and the caps popping off two beer bottles.

She stood by the counter wearing the towel, her hair tousled and backlit, her smile mocking him. Zane considered her for a minute, mentally calculating the exposure that would make a halo of her hair while leaving detail in her face.

"I know what you're thinking. I'm going to put my clothes on, before you lose control of yourself."

She brought him the beer and then disappeared back into the bathroom. Zane returned his attention to the television. After a few minutes Melissa reappeared in jeans and T-shirt. She went into the kitchen and rummaged around under the sink and came out to the living room carrying Lapierre's book. The dust jacket was missing.

"The cover's all wrecked," she said.

"I threw that out because I wanted it out."

"You threw it out because you were pissed off at me."

"Put it back in the trash."

She stood for a moment backlit in the kitchen light and then simply walked to the boxes in the corner and put the book away and closed the box.

He pretended to be interested in the television.

Melissa went back out to the kitchen and washed her hands and then took a place at the other end of the couch. The sitcom came to its end and the credits rolled. Zane got up and went into the kitchen and made himself a sandwich. Then he remembered his manners and made her one, too, identically bland. He brought the plates out to the living room and handed one to her without saying anything and then sat down. They ate in silence.

"Was it a nice wedding?"

The laugh track bubbled on, but Zane had missed the joke.

"I was wondering when we got married. You know, sitting here watching TV, nothing to say."

"What's to say?"

"Shit, Zane, you amaze me. You really do."

"I really don't have much to say." Hard to find acceptable topics: Zane was working hard to lose track of his own history, and had no interest in hers.

"Oh, I'm sure you'll think of something."

Zane studied her face.

"What was that you were singing?"

"What?"

"In the shower. What was that song?"

"Had your eye pressed to the keyhole, did you?"

"And you wonder why I don't make conversation."

"It was just some song off the radio."

"You're a good singer. I had no idea."

"You have no idea about a lot of things, buster."

"What do you actually do? Other than the obvious, I mean."

"I strip."

"You're a stripper."

"How else would I end up doing porn? What else you gonna do with dance lessons?"

She took a pull from her beer and stared blankly at the television for a moment, ran her fingers through her hair. The blue light of the television played over her face and Zane thought about how it would look on film. Then she looked down at her beer bottle and ran her finger around the rim, and then tossed her head back as if shaking off a chill.

"Yeah, you know, I learned to act and dance and sing but you can't get a job with that. You get some shit job ringing in groceries. So, you do what you can. You learned to dance, might as well dance. I make good money. If I make a pile of money, I won't have to do this shit anymore."

"Then what?"

She paused for a long while, staring at the television.

"Then I go home."

"Where's home?"

"Vancouver."

"That's a long way."

"I moved out here because this is the place if you want to act, but there isn't anything here. Now I just want to go back. Go back to school, I don't know. I just want to make enough money to start over."

"Here's to fresh starts." He raised his bottle. All of us trying to outrun ourselves. Nobody ever gets a fresh start. But that's a lesson we all have to learn on our own. And this kid still believes she can reinvent herself.

Zane felt he had to make a gesture. When she left, he gave her the spider plant. It was about the only thing he had to give.

CHAPTER FOUR

Two outs, bottom of the ninth, bases loaded: Zane hefts the bat and wiggles it experimentally, as if feeling nuances unknown to mortal men, then steps to the plate and kicks his toes firmly into the dirt. A hush falls over the crowd and the dugout falls silent. The din of hope and expectation settles out of the air and comes to rest firmly on his shoulders, but its weight does not bow him. He raises his eyes, sets his jaw and spits, then squints at the pitcher. He is ready.

Except that Zane is seven years old, the pitcher is a machine, and the din of expectation has seeped through the skin of his shoulders and alighted in the pit of his stomach, where it has settled into a jumpy backbeat over which a saxophone blows wild and crazy bebop. The sun is in his eyes and he prays that the shaking of the bat will not betray his terror. He hears his father's shout.

"Go get 'em, Luke!"

The elder Zane is firmly in favour of team sports, in general, and specifically of baseball. He is a staunch adherent of the view, commonly held among his peers of the police force, that team sports are essential to a healthy childhood. *Mens sana in corpore sano.* Carrying the burden of a team's hopes Builds Character. All for one and one for all.

For his part, Zane finds that carrying the burden of a team's hopes builds only his urge to puke. He hates baseball, but he continues to play, in part to satisfy his father and in part because he hopes that one day he will stare squint-eyed into the sun, dig in his toes, and live up to the expectations placed on him by knocking the ball clean over the fence. He wants to hear his father say, "That's my boy."

He adjusts the batting helmet. A size too big for him, it rides his hair like a loaf of bread balancing on a lemon. His coach, standing by the pitching machine, catches his eye and nods, drops the ball into the whirling maw of the machine.

Zane tenses. The machine burps and ejects the ball, which arcs quickly towards him. He closes his eyes, swings, and whiffs.

He hears giggles from behind, quickly hushed, feels the hot surge of a shameful flush wash over his face and neck. His father's voice reaches out again.

"Come on, Luke. Let's go."

The ball sails past him again, fearless of his wild swing. He can hear kids on the other team giggling and behind him the voice of a teammate: man, why'd we have to get windmill-boy?

Zane knows he should feel defiance, but instead he feels sick and wobbly and ashamed. When the last ball comes he swats ineffectually at it and then drops the bat and walks back to the bleachers without looking up.

"Nice going, doofus."

His teammate's remark somewhat undermines the popular notion that baseball teaches Team Spirit. Zane's coach lays a hand on his shoulder and tells him not to worry about it. On the ride home, his father says nothing. Presumably, he does not want to interfere in the character-building process.

* * *

Everything had changed. The motel room had disappeared. The bed and the cheap carpet were gone. In their place were a plain wooden desk and a utilitarian office chair, on a tile floor. A blackboard now covered the false window. On it was written "Anatomy 101," and in the corner "Professor Payne." On top of the desk sat a globe.

Why does an anatomy classroom require a globe? The head bone's connected to the Kashmir; the Kashmir's connected to the clavicle. The mind interprets these signals from the optic nerve and tells the retinas to get lost. Go away, the two of you, get together and get your story straight. And don't come back until you're prepared to be sensible.

Bill pulled out the desk chair and sat down with the confident enthusiasm of a man who never tires of his work. In résumé-speak, he had found his passion. He always clocked in five minutes early, never called in sick. He wore chinos, a dress shirt, and reading glasses, but the disguise was incomplete, as the shark tattoo still grinned from beneath his collar. Not a professor in the country looked like Bill.

Jade brought the girl in, a bleached-blonde kid with a thin face and a long nose, wearing an ill-fitting tartan skirt, white knee socks, glasses, pigtails, and a plain white blouse open to the third button. Wardrobe remained a problem. Also, the ring through her nose somewhat undermined the intended effect. She uncrossed her arms, bones wrapped in tissue paper, to fuss with her ponytails, revealing track marks and bruises. Not a virgin in the country looked like this girl.

"When do I get the money?"

"When we're finished," said Barker.

"Don't worry," said Jade. "This is easy. You've done it all before."

Zane wondered what experience Jade had, precisely, that allowed her to assure the girl that this was going to be easy. Lacking applicable experience, he suspected it would be anything but. Bill got out of the chair and Jade led the girl over to it and motioned for her to sit.

"What name we using, again?" said Bill.

She shrugged.

"What the fuck is this?" Bill lifted his arms in a gesture of help-lessness. His creative powers were overtaxed as things stood.

"Ashley," said Barker. "We don't have an Ashley."

Bill pointed to her with his open hand, as if explaining gravity to an obtuse child; you drop things, they fall. She looked at him as if he were a precipice over which she had no choice but to jump.

Bill essayed his best impression of a professor by rubbing his chin and frowning thoughtfully. Thoughtfulness, apparently, was foreign to him, and the effect was correspondingly insincere. He pursed his lips to add to the effect, and now more closely resembled a chimpanzee pondering its choice of bananas.

"So what seems to be the problem, Ashley?"

"Oh, Professor Payne." At once wooden and overly theatric. "It's this F you gave me on my term paper. My daddy's going to just kill me when he finds out."

"It just wasn't a very good paper, Ashley."

She looked at him with something resembling entreaty.

"Isn't there anything I can do?"

"You're just going to have to learn your anatomy, Ashley. You don't know a cock from a coccyx." A self-satisfied smirk.

Zane concentrated on the picture space, abstracting its contents into light and shadow, reading the status display across the bottom of the viewfinder. Light passes through the lens and bounces off the reflex mirror, through the pentaprism and thence onto the retina. The mind, still upset about the whole incident of the globe, tells the optic nerves to pound salt. Zane and the camera were one, but the dialogue was playing hell with his exposure meter.

"Why don't we start by taking a look at your anatomy, Ashley?"

The girl stood and lifted her skirt to reveal plain, white cotton panties, a part of the costume. Legs like two sticks, pasty white, hipbones like ridgepoles under the cotton. She had the body of an underfed child.

"Is this good?"

"It's a start," said Bill. "But I'm going to work you a lot harder than that. And I will not accept shoddy work."

Things went rapidly downhill from there.

Bill had moved on to deep throat, and Ashley was failing the lesson. He held on and thrust as she gagged and struggled to breathe, panic shining from the whites of her eyes. Tears smeared her mascara into charcoal runnels down her cheeks. She broke free and pulled back, spit drooling from her mouth like wet string.

"Come on, Ashley," said Bill. "Work for that B minus."

It all took only an instant. Ashley struggled, twisted her head, pulled back, her face and neck convulsing as she gagged. Bill tried again and she kept her mouth closed. He went for the nostrils but she jerked her head away, and he hit her.

Zane heard the dull wet smack as his open hand connected, the sound of the blow merging with the clack of the reflex mirror, and he mentally congratulated himself on his excellent shutter timing. Blood and spit and tears and the remains of her makeup smeared over Ashley's face. Bill hit her again, this time with his fist.

The first thing you noticed, the one thing that overrode all others, was the smell of the bodies inside the ruined house. It was a smell you never forgot. It was a smell that never left you. It stayed in your clothes and in your hair, clung to you, conceded only grudgingly to lather, rinse, and infinite repeat. And even then you still smelled it when no-one else could.

Rubble lay in the street and the girl lay backed against a wall pock-marked with bullet-holes, fresh blood blackening the front of her blouse. From the bubbles at the corners of her lips Zane knew she was bleeding into her lungs, drowning in her own blood. You can handle this: you tape a piece of plastic over the entrance wound and hope to seal it, to ease the breathing until you can get her to a surgeon. But fear paralyzed him. To move would be suicide. The sniper would be waiting.

And then he was back. Bill was half dressed. Ashley sat on the linoleum and her small body heaved as she breathed through her sobs. Zane discovered himself backed against Barker's desk. His hands shook. He could not keep the frame steady.

Jade shoved Bill towards the door.

"Get the fuck out of here."

"Bitch tried to bite me."

"Give it up. Zane! Enough with the pictures. What the fuck is wrong with you?"

What the fuck was wrong with him had recently become a matter of great interest to Zane himself, but the question remained unanswered. He hadn't even been aware that he was still taking pictures. The hands carry on, autonomous response. He turned off his camera and checked the lens for blood spatter.

Jade drew a blanket around the girl's shoulders and crouched down to rub her back. The girl's mouth dripped blood over her chest. She looked like a shot deer, all heaving ribs and sightless eyes. Jade put an arm around her and pulled her to her feet.

Barker waited for the door to close behind them and then took two quick steps and kicked the nearest chair, which skidded into the false wall at the back of the set where one of its legs punched a hole through the drywall. Zane remained shaky and the hole reminded him unpleasantly of a bullet-hole.

"That asshole is all dick and no brain."

Zane was too rattled to deal with this anatomically puzzling image.

"He doesn't think. He just doesn't think. You just can't fuck around in this business."

Zane started packing. His hands still shook and he tried to keep them out of sight, but Barker wasn't watching.

"So now she goes to the cops. Where am I? Bill goes to jail, we're shut down. Cops sniffing around. I'm paying lawyers. You know what I spend on lawyers? We lost a night's production, we can't use this stuff. And all the time I'm bleeding money to the office of Shylock, Billable and Upchuck."

You aren't out of here until Barker finds a new audience. What we have here is one simple fact, a mess of blood in the middle of the floor. The longer he talks the higher he'll build on that fact. Soon we'll have a conspiracy of lawyers, police, do-gooders, feminazis, politicians and Bill's dick, all dedicated to the crucifixion of one Richard Barker. Any response will only encourage further litanies. Here it comes, the tower of babble. Zane stopped packing and sat.

"You want Bill's job?"

"I lack Bill's natural talents."

"Well, that's refreshingly honest." Barker pulled out Professor Payne's desk chair and sat. "I tell you, a nine-inch dick is a hard thing to find. And then when you find one, it's attached to a moron."

Zane returned to his cameras, concentrated on the removal of flash guns and the checking of batteries and the flipping of switches, and on various cleaning tasks that had suddenly become essential. He struggled to replace his lens caps, which refused to align with the filter threads.

"I got all these leeches hanging off me. I pay lawyers, I pay rent, I pay for this girl's dental surgery, I pay for drugs and I pay to keep the goddamn cops off my back. I pay to create all this shit and I pay for server space to put it up where people steal it and put it up on their own sites and pretend it's theirs. So then I pay more lawyers to chase those fuckers around. I pay to put my shit up for free where people can steal it. And then I pay half my fucking income to the goddamn government just so some welfare asshole can sit home and jack off looking at pictures somebody stole from me in the first place."

Barker jumped up again, knocking the chair onto its back, and then turned and kicked it. Zane considered that he was not being paid enough to put up with this shit, but felt also that this was perhaps not the most opportune time to broach the issue. Certainly not in those particular terms.

"I pay all this shit to keep Jade in buttons and bows and boob jobs. I got an ex-wife moved down to Tucson, I pay her alimony so she can shack up with some hippie-dippy craft artist and smoke dope. I'm paying for the whole goddamn world here. What if I just stopped, eh? What if I just up and stopped? What then?"

Merciful silence, in all likelihood. Zane felt it was high time that Barker just upped and stopped. He was running out of switches to fiddle with.

"You ever stop and think how many people are sucking the tit of a single creative entrepreneur such as myself? I generate the content, I generate the wealth that pays for the whole fuckin' system of links and servers and free preview sites. It's people like me driving the Internet, Zane. The Internet! The most important technological innovation in the history of mankind. I am the fucking fountainhead!"

Barker let his arms drop to his sides and crossed to his desk where he righted his chair and then flopped into it, deflated. Zane detected a lull. Escape was at hand. He put his camera in his bag and closed the clasps, stood, felt he should say something but couldn't think what.

The door opened six inches. Jade looked through, caught Barker's eye. She held the door while the girl entered, dressed now in her street clothes. Her face was a mess, her mouth bruised and puffy where Bill had punched her.

"I think we're going to have a little problem," said Jade.

"I'm going to go," said Zane.

Barker ignored him. He took a bottle of whisky and three glasses out of the desk drawer and poured a generous measure into the first glass.

"I think we all need a drink."

Zane paused, his hand on the door handle, and looked back. Barker pressed the glass into the girl's hand, and then poured two smaller drinks, talking nonstop.

"When girls come to work for us, we treat them like family. What I mean is, we're going to take care of you. We're going to fix you up."

"We do detest these mishaps," said Jade.

Barker reached into the desk drawer and retrieved a small bag containing a pale, brownish powder. Zane had seen enough. He let the door close behind him.

* * *

Zane slipped the camera bag from his shoulder and locked his apartment door and put on the chain. Here, at least, we have some guarantees. For example, here, nobody's going to beat the shit out of a gawky and possibly underage drug addict. No risk of finding yourself entangled in the lives of people whose given names keep changing without warning. With all the changing names and fake rooms it's impossible to keep things straight. If this keeps up you'll end up a shut-in, go back to feeding pigeons in the park.

Zane had taken to avoiding hard liquor as a means of demonstrating to himself that he was not an alcoholic. Nevertheless, something stronger than beer was now in order. He took a bottle of rum from the cupboard, the emergency reserve. All the glasses were in the sink, covered with god knows what. He considered them, rejected them, found a single coffee mug on the counter. The stain therein suggested it had held only coffee. He quickly rinsed it, and then half-filled it with rum.

Rattling around Zane's head was the question Jade had so eloquently articulated: what the fuck is wrong with you? The easy answer is nothing, but that one's beginning to lose credibility. Still, one hesitates to consider the alternatives. Some doors are best left unopened; there's the problem of just who you might find inside. Better to avoid situations in which this question comes out into the open. Problem solved, save the possible outcome that finds you returning to the pigeons.

Zane felt that something had come loose inside, something now spinning free, a pulley without its belt. You've come to a stop but you should be in motion.

He needed a shower. In the bathroom he put his drink down on the edge of the sink and took off his jeans and threw them in the corner. Now the scar collection: exhibit A, the left thigh. An antipersonnel mine, in Bosnia, in 1993. Put it down to bad luck. The mine killed the Bosniak militiaman who set it off. Stepping off the road was stupid, but the soldier did it anyway. Concrete and asphalt you could trust; earth, you could not. But after a while you look at the grass and think this could be an easy out. You step off the road and you know what's coming but you just don't care anymore.

Back from Croatia, in '92, Zane avoided stepping off the sidewalk, found himself nervous and agitated when he had to cross a lawn. Suburban children running through a sprinkler sent him into a sudden panic attack. After the wound it was worse. You get panic attacks in the street and then you get angry at yourself over the panic attacks. Everyone knows there are no minefields in Toronto or New York.

You get to thinking about luck. Staying alive is the ultimate good luck. You have your talismans; you change some tiny thing, someone gets hurt, you change back. It's stupid and you don't tell anyone but why take the risk. Then one day you wake up and realize that your whole career is nothing but luck. Like all the others you try to predict events, to minimize your risks and read the currents and anticipate the story, but in the end it's f/8 and be there and being there is simply a matter of luck.

Lapierre said you made your luck. It didn't matter being in the right place at the right time if you couldn't make a good picture. But in the end Lapierre ended up with bad luck.

Zane didn't want these memories. He peeled off his shirt. Exhibit B, the abdomen: this is the entrance wound caused by a 7.62 x 54 mm bullet, probably fired from a PKM general purpose machine gun, Russian-made, a testimony to the genius of Mikhail Kalashnikov who also gave the world the AK-47. Good old Mikhail, the failed poet, will have a lot to answer for when the Great Historian writes his final account, if indeed that ever comes to pass. If only he'd written better poetry. Exhibit C, the exit wound, does not bear considering. Put it down to bad luck; this wound accounted for Zane's dietary restrictions and for certain other problems.

It doesn't bear considering but it doesn't go away. The first thing you remember is the cold. Lying out in the desert with the sun beating down on, and yet feeling so cold.

He was getting good pictures. In an abandoned village, following a group of Afghan fighters, more guts than tactical sense, and their Special Forces advisors. No pictures of the latter, thank you. And there was a photographer working for one of the big news agencies, Dan Webster. The Taliban opened up from the hillsides with machine guns and RPGs and there they were, trapped in this village.

So you keep still and you keep your head down. You stay out of sight. Zane hunched down behind a stone wall. The Special Forces team leader called in an airstrike, calling in the orders in a calm, measured voice. They were in a bad spot, behind the wall. Loose stone walls and parked cars only give cover in the movies, but it was the only cover to hand. Still, nobody was shooting at them. Everyone was calm except Webster, and he was trying not to show it. It was Webster's first war.

Dust explodes from the top of the wall, the sharp crack of bullets passing overhead. One moment you're talking about restaurants and the next, your luck runs out. You don't feel pain, just the impact, a solid blow to the gut. Then the distant thumping of the machine gun firing catches up, shouts, rifle fire, the sound of bullets in the air like someone tearing strips off a huge sheet of aluminum foil.

You know it's bad. It has to be bad. An abdominal wound is always bad. Zane looked over at Webster, lying still, blood splashed dark on the ground beside him. His camera lying there with blood spattered on the lens.

Danny, I think we're in deep shit here.

Right arm folded under your body. Immobilized. Legs don't seem to work. You want to check for the exit wound, but your free hand is filthy. You keep a field dressing taped to the strap of your camera bag, but it's out of reach. And about now you wonder, in a detached and almost clinical way, if the bullet hit your spine. Bleeding to death seems academic. You're fucked in any case. This war looks to be your last.

Danny, it might be time to retire.

The sky a distant, faded blue.

Getting wounded, it's no big deal. Didn't you read the brochure? It's part of the job, down there in the fine print. It's like getting the runs when you go to Mexico. Just relax, there, Danny.

The important thing now is to remain calm. The important thing is to remain still. The more you struggle, the more blood you pump. The more blood you pump, the more blood you lose. It's an entirely sound line of reasoning, even if this advice to remain calm isn't entirely practical. The same reasoning applies to poisonous snakebite; the more blood you pump, the faster the toxin spreads. Just how you're supposed to remain calm and control your heart rate when you've got this cobra hanging off the end of your nose is never adequately explained. Theory and practice. That's book-learning for you.

Are you listening, Danny?

Bullets cracking overhead, the tearing sound they make in the air, the distant thump of the muzzle blast.

Some more book-learning for you: that sharp crack is the sound of the bullet passing overhead, faster than sound, and the dull thump is the muzzle blast catching up. Sound travels three hundred metres per second in dry air, which we most assuredly have here in Afghanistan, although altitude and barometric pressure also factor into it. Consequently, you can judge how far away the guns are, that is, if you can separate the sound of one gun from another when you've got all this firing going on and all these little metal death-hornets flying through the air and this big frigging cobra hanging off your nose.

Pay attention, Danny. This here book-learning's important.

Zane laid his face down in the dust to ease the pain in his neck, incipient muscle cramp, and a stone bit into his cheek. This is an indignity.

Starting to feel cold. When you start to feel cold, that's shock. Shock kills. And now the pain, a mass of pain building as the body begins to comprehend the scale of the damage. Pain is physiological indignation. The stone digging into your cheek rapidly loses relevance when you realize that you're going to die here, behind a stone wall at the edge of some ruined village in one of the poorest countries in the world.

Zane had no religion. You get to see a lot of victims. You get to see a lot of people die and it's always miserable, and there is no grace or redemption. No choirs of angels. Probably your awareness just fades away as the circuits of your brain shut down. The mind struggles to make sense of the failure of the brain's circuitry. All the circuits yammering in indignation come through as white noise, white light. The chill of shock is the chill of death. To lie there, knowing your life is ending, unable to tie up loose ends and say goodbye: this is unfair.

What the fuck, Danny. Just like Dad always said. Life isn't fair.

What a terribly mundane thing to feel at the transcendent moment. How utterly banal.

Sooner or later, it comes to us all: Capa, Larry Burrows, Henri Huet, Terry Lapierre. Werner Bischof, who never got his due. At least I got my due, Danny, whatever that's worth. Not much, anyway. I think it really is time for me to retire.

You want to keep it light. You've got to keep your mind off that cobra, even as he pumps more venom into you.

I'm going home, start shooting celebrities. You can take this particular job and shove it. And I'll make a lot more money, because that's all the news is these days. Mass-produced pop stars in skimpy tops and tight jeans are the future of journalism. Running around in the desert, a bunch of bearded guys with guns, what the hell is that?

Cold. He had no feeling in his arm, but his body swelled with pain. A pain balloon. And he was so cold now. High overhead, he heard the sound of a jet.

Someone dragging him, the sun and the ground gyrating wildly. A room with stone walls, a hole in the ceiling. Through which my spirit can ascend. Someone pressing down on his belly, and then they rolled him and he felt pressure on his back.

Shit, what a fucking mess.

Don't give him morphine. Not with that abdominal wound.

Makes no difference anyway, this one's not going to make it. What a fucking mess.

I'm in the room, dammit. If you don't mind. And bring on the fucking morphine.

A face floated into Zane's view, one of the Special Forces soldiers. Hang on, he said, we got a chopper coming.

Get Danny. You've got to get Danny out.

That other guy? Shit, half his head's gone. He was dead before he hit the ground.

On a stretcher, moving, swaying. And then the rotor downwash battered his face as they loaded him into the helicopter, and the helicopter whirled up into the air, and Zane whirled with it.

Zane traced the puckered scar with his finger and looked at himself in the mirror, haggard and blotchy. He picked up his drink from beside the sink and finished it and then started the shower. The chill was still on him so he ran it hot. When the water turned hot he stripped off his shorts and stepped into it, felt the heat playing over his skin.

He needed to get warm. He needed to get clean.

CHAPTER FIVE

Zane's first camera was an Olympus Quickmatic 600, a simple rangefinder with an automatic exposure system and a thirty-six millimetre lens that used zone focusing. The camera was a Christmas present from his maternal grandfather, a keen amateur photographer who developed his own film and gave Zane his first lessons in photography. The Quickmatic used Kodak Instamatic film, which yielded small, square prints, and Zane received three cartridges of film that same Christmas morning.

By the time his father carved the first slice of Christmas turkey, Zane had used up all three, producing 60 fuzzy pictures of the Christmas tree, the family cat, his parents, his younger sister Connie, the snow-covered front lawn, and other such essential subjects. He continued to frame potential pictures after all the film was gone. By mid-afternoon, after throwing a tantrum, Connie was sent to her room; Zane had received a better present than anything she got, as usual, and it wasn't fair.

Well, life isn't fair, said Zane's father. And: that girl is turning into a spoiled brat.

Connie had decided at an early age that she had been cheated on the family deal. Whether it was who got the last cookie or who had to stay in to practice the piano, it was unfair. Zane's mother clucked sympathetically, and always caved in. Zane's father, on the other hand, invariably replied simply that life is not fair, and this fact lodged firmly in Connie's mind where it swelled over time, like a subcutaneous infection, obscuring the fact that life's unfairness extended to people other than Connie. By fourteen, Connie had decided that the playing field was permanently tilted in Zane's favour.

It's easy for you, she said: you're a boy. You're just what Dad wanted.

But being just what Dad wanted introduced burdens of its own. Among these, thanks to Zane's incurable lack of athletic prowess, was a generalized difficulty with playing fields, tilted, level, or otherwise. Furthermore, as Zane discovered in later years, arriving home shit-faced and underage in the small hours of the morning was not seen as desirable in the son of a police officer who spent his Friday and Saturday evenings handing out tickets, fifty-three dollars and seventy-five cents each, to the shit-faced and underage.

The discovery that Zane was a bookish shit-disturber with artistic pretensions was to the elder Zane a sore trial; he could have found it in himself to forgive the disturbance of a certain amount of shit if only, for example, the kid could play football. Low-grade shit disturbance in a football player constitutes mere hijinks, a blowing off of steam. But football was not among Zane's talents. Instead, he liked to take pictures of things, pictures that to his father made no sense. It is, for example, a goddamn fire hydrant. Why do you need a picture of a fire hydrant? Looks like artsy-fartsy bullshit to me. And low-grade shit-disturbance coupled with artistic pretensions is immediately suspect: this kid is probably smoking dope.

None of this occurred to Connie. In retaliation for life's refusal to be fair she became her mother's daughter, and the family stool pigeon. It was no coincidence that Constable Zane happened to find himself at the head of the stairs each time Zane stumbled, shit-faced and underage, into the family home. Someone kept tipping off the cops.

This was all that remained to Zane when a drunk driver, distracted by the flashing lights of Constable Zane's police cruiser, weaved too far to the right and killed him as he checked a speeder's licence. Zane never had the opportunity to make a truce or to reach the kind of reconciliation that arrives when the barriers to things unsaid simply rust away.

Zane moved out, went off to school, got engaged, went to El Salvador, and returned with a hole in his head. With no one left to get all the breaks, Connie got over it, went off to school, started teaching, and met a plastic surgeon. Zane was in Tel Aviv when she got engaged, and sent a card. But the inexorable collapse of his mother's mind put the kibosh on their nascent reconciliation. Connie might have forgiven Zane the events of their childhood, or even his being overseas as Alzheimer's disease munched holes in her mother's hippocampus, but she could never forgive the simple fact that, in rare lucid moments, it was always Zane that the patient asked after.

Where's Lucas? He always took such nice pictures, she said.

* * *

Melissa stands at the kitchen window, in the soft wash of pale and indirect light that floods in through the dirty glass, flows over the walls and counters and cupboards, embraces and folds over surfaces. The light picks out her hair and separates her face sharply from the dingy wall behind. It picks out the cracks where the yellow paint is starting to peel, illuminates the point of her chin, the line of her jaw, her slightly upturned nose and the cryptic smile formed by her eyebrows and lips. You remain after all these years a collector of faces, prefer pretty to beautiful. It entails fewer complications.

This shot is easy. The light makes it easy. You can let the shadows fall to black. The rest is in the framing. You either get in close with a short tele and go for the profile, or you shoot wide, put the pretty girl in the context of the squalid apartment. You define what's in the story and what remains untold. She looks into the frame or she looks out. Looking out is better, but this shot is an obvious cliché: the girl looks into the light, suggesting youth, or hope, or a bright future. Another eloquent lie.

Melissa knocked back the remains of a bottle of beer, which completely ruined the effect but offered a more truthful perspective on her situation.

"What're you lookin' at?"

"I was thinking of taking your picture."

"Like you don't do that enough?"

"Garry Winogrand said he took pictures to see what things looked like photographed."

"You know what I look like."

She didn't bother asking who Winogrand was. He pressed on regardless.

"After a while you know what things are going to look like photographed. So you look at things in terms of what they'll look like photographed."

"Are you going anywhere with this, or are you just drunken rambling?"

Zane found this question difficult to address. You start off going somewhere but then she changes the subject. The conclusion flees and escapes, catches the next Greyhound back to its hometown. He took the empty bottle from her and fished two new ones out of the fridge. He had lost track of how many he had drunk, but he was reasonably sure that he was ahead. Zane had the drunk's habit of keeping tabs on what was left for him.

"I was going somewhere, but I forgot where it was."

Melissa found this tremendously funny, but Zane didn't see the joke. When she stopped laughing and looked at his face, she laughed still harder.

"Anyway, I was just thinking that the light was good."

"'The light's good.' Oh, you don't fool me with your artsy photo-talk, mister."

"That diffuse window light is always good."

"Zane with the artsy photo-talk. I'm losing the light here, people! Fuck harder!"

Zane didn't think it was quite that funny. He didn't find it funny at all.

"It's not – "

"Bill, what's your *motivation*? What's your *inner conflict*? Oh, yeah. Rich would just love that one."

"You might be surprised. He has some theories."

"Rich has all kinds of theories. The more he talks, the more theories he comes up with."

"Rich says I'm a genius."

A mouthful of beer sprays from Melissa's lips, a mist of fine droplets followed by a series of choking noises. Shit, beer up my nose, she says, coughing; that hurts. Serves her right. This notion of genius shouldn't be laughable, precisely.

Melissa retreated to the couch with an unsteady step. He heard the television come on, in the form of an advertisement for a telephone dating service that offered the chance to connect with local girls now. This he considered an unlikely prospect, given the paucity of ads offering local girls the reciprocal opportunity. Where do they find them all?

Zane stopped at the end of the kitchen counter and watched the light from the television play over Melissa as she sat on the couch. She took a small glass pipe out of the pocket of her jeans and loaded it, then lit it, a heavy smell filling the apartment, burnt grass clippings on a summer day.

"You thinking of taking my picture again, or are you working up to getting all artistic with me?"

"If you could be anywhere in the world right now, where would you be?"

"Other than your wonderful couch?"

"Play along."

"On a stage." She smirked, waved one dramatic hand. "Romeo and Juliet. I would be Juliet. As I stick myself with the knife, everyone weeps."

"And everyone throws flowers. Everyone falls in love with you."

"And then the curtain falls. I get up, run backstage, change into my street clothes and leave with someone far smarter than that dumb shit Romeo."

"Then where do you go?"

"A long, long way from anyplace I ever been."

Zane thought: fair enough.

* * *

Barker sat at his desk and worked the mouse with methodical efficiency.

"This girl," he said. "This girl has got potential."

Zane did not respond. He checked his lenses as he packed his gear, blew some dust off the camera eyepiece. As far as Zane was concerned, Barker was talking to himself. An easy mistake to make, although at the best of times, it was difficult to tell.

"Boundless potential. And once again, Zane, I must say that you are a genius. This deserves a drink."

Barker slid open his desk drawer and pulled out two tumblers and a bottle of Scotch. He poured Zane a generous one without waiting for him to accept the offer, and then slid the tumbler across the desk and raised his own glass.

The opportunity for a gracious exit thus evaporates. Things have slid well out of plumb: the onslaught of Melissa on your carefully ordered detachment, the question of what the fuck is wrong with you, a beating, a certain problem involving groceries. You get asked to use another supermarket. Faced with all this it becomes difficult to smile and nod on cue. Still, one must rise to the occasion. Also, there is the prospect of free booze to moderate the experience.

Zane sat. He picked up the glass, raised it in return. Whisky, do your work and make it quick. Barker, on the runway, acknowledged takeoff clearance for another flight of rhetoric. Roger; go with throttle up.

"Here's to genius, Zane."

Drinking to his own genius did nothing for Zane's balance. The great Lucas Zane had often been accused of genius, and Zane found the subject acutely uncomfortable. He hoped the Scotch would help.

"Do you know why you're a genius?"

"I never really thought about it."

"Because you *see*, Zane. You are a genius because you *see*."

Barker lifted his glass to sip at his drink. His index finger broke free to point at Zane as he sighted him over the glass with his dominant eye, as if aiming a pistol loaded with cheap Scotch.

"Now, this is a rare thing, Zane. I had this guy before, he couldn't take a good picture if it was hanging on the wall. The moment was wrong, faces were in shadow, you couldn't see shit. He'd catch the girl rolling her eyes or looking bored. Who the hell is gonna pay good money to jerk off to that? This guy would miss the goddamn money shot and get a picture of her wiping it off.

"I said to the guy, you gotta capture the *decisive moment*, man. He looks at me, he says, what the fuck, this isn't fuckin' *art*, man. If you can see her boobs then what the fuck, right? But you know what?"

Zane paid attention to his drink.

"He was wrong!" Barker leaned back with a look of triumph and smacked his glass down on the desk. Half of its contents sloshed over the rim. He seemed not to notice. "You know why he was wrong?"

Zane elected not to reply.

Barker put down his glass and raised his hand to make the point, counting on his fingers: "Kaitlyn, Amber, Melody, Sugar, Natalie. Not a Mary or Anne or Jane in the bunch. It's the same old game: 'Who do you want me to be?' Our customers, they all want to believe. The truth is too mundane. So we give the girls biographies. Melody here, she's nineteen and her favourite position is doggy style and she likes to swallow and her secret fantasy is to be gang-banged. In fact, we can't get her to do more than solo. But they believe this shit. And you know why?"

Zane asked no questions. You avoid getting engaged. You get into a bout of full-contact philosophy, you wake up three days later surrounded by empty Scotch bottles, your head pounding, thrumming with strange belief systems implanted by Barker using brute force and a number four Phillips screwdriver. The safe course is to play along. And at all times, stay between Barker and the door.

"They believe this shit because they want to." Barker sat back with an air of triumph, having arrived at a profound revelation. "They make a *willing suspension of disbelief*. Coleridge said that. They *know* it's fake, but they *want* to believe it.

"And that's what this asshole didn't get. They *want* to believe some kind of story here. This isn't just a bunch of chicks getting drilled. This is fucking art, Zane: art!"

Round and round and round he goes, stream of nonsenseness, like dropping acid and watching *Eraserhead*, an error of Zane's youth. Strange distorted images, sinister sounds. Somehow a baby is involved. None of this makes sense but you can't get away. The soundtrack is overwhelming, mechanical, grips you by the base of your skull and shakes hard. All you can do is hang on and hope it ends soon.

"I'm feeling the need for another drink."

Barker retrieved the bottle and casually poured another two fingers.

"Now, a lot of people would laugh at that. We're making art here: that's a good one! But those people are dickheads. Fact is, art is that which moves you. And sex, sex is not about your dick. Sex is all up here."

The index finger tapped Barker's temple three times and then took aim, right between Zane's eyes. Barker nodded earnestly; Zane tried to blink in a way that would suggest comprehension. He suspected that he had failed.

"What I'm saying is we got to get that willing suspension of disbelief. We got to get that *story* in there. You don't get that when the girl looks like she's compiling her grocery list. But we – and I mean, you and me, Zane – we are *making* that story. We are moving minds all across the *world*, and I got the credit card receipts to prove it. Tell me *that's* not fucking art!"

When Zane was still in high school, he once carried on a loud and passionate argument on a city bus, on the question of whether the back of a chair could be art. At the time, nothing seemed more important than the question of what art was and whether the chair back was it. But that was thirty years before, and Zane had grown out of it. More importantly, arguing the point would only encourage Barker.

Meanwhile, if you're going to suffer this, you might as well get compensation. Zane drained his glass and held it out for a refill.

Barker topped up Zane's glass and then turned to the computer monitor. He looked at it carefully for a long while, rolling the Scotch around the bottom of his glass. An opportunity for a quick exit, but there is this free Scotch to deal with. Zane drank quickly. This proved to be a serious lapse of judgment.

"Yes, this girl's got potential. This is a girl with potential. All we need to do now is to convince her to do more than solo. And we will.

"They all come around. A girl like this is sitting at home, thinking how she's gonna stretch the lousy few hundred bucks she gets paid at fucking Walmart. Then she sees in the want ads where she can make two grand a night. Two grand a night! Flexible hours. And stripping doesn't seem so bad, when you think about it. You done that before, right? But that time, you called it love. And it's only for a little while, so's she can get a leg up.

"But you know that doesn't work out. Instead of saving the money, she buys some things. Some clothes and shit, some nice stuff for her kid. She quits Walmart, cause the pay is shit. Maybe she starts using, just to take the edge off. You know, it's hard, you need to take the edge off. So now she *needs* the money.

"And then she starts to feel some power. Coke'll do that to you. She thinks, look at all them fools staring and drooling. So what the hell, they're only pictures, right? Anybody jacking off to their computer screen's got no place looking down on *me*. The coke makes her feel pretty good about things. Most of the time, she feels all right. And it's just once or twice, so's she can get a leg up."

Barker refilled their glasses. Zane's tongue had gone numb and he was beginning to lose track. He noticed that Barker put the cap back on the bottle one-handed, without looking. But Barker was doing all the talking. Zane was doing all the drinking, and clinging to any object that appeared to be stable. The closest object to hand was his glass.

"So she needs *more* money. It's my body, she thinks, I'll use it. It's just sex, you done that before, right? You're already doing lap dances." Barker motioned to the screen. "Give this girl five, six years, she's on crack and turning tricks to earn her next fix. And it's only so's she can get a leg up. Only 'til things start working out for her.

"Now, you're probably wondering where I'm going with all this."

Zane was wondering not only where Barker was going, but where he was at present. He felt strongly that he should rewind the tape, and get back to territory he more clearly understood.

"Let's get back to the part about me being a genius."

"We covered that. Stay with me. This is the thing. Without me, all this girl's got to look forward to is some dead-end job and a boyfriend beats the shit out of her. Anyone else in this business, they chew her up and spit her out and she's on the street. But me, I'm going to keep her out of those troubles. I'm going to keep her working for as long as she can work. I'll give her jobs. There's always something."

Barker put his glass down and then rubbed his eyes as if he was getting a headache. Zane felt that perhaps he was supposed to interject, but couldn't think what to add. The first thing that came to mind was "you want to clamp those glue joints firmly," and that had nothing to do with Barker's rambling or, indeed, with anything at all. Barker took his hand from his eyes and snapped his fingers at Zane and continued where he had left off.

"And you'll hear people saying, it's that Richard Barker. He's the guy that fucked up that kid. All the do-gooders and feminazis all saying, we need to shut him down. Like suddenly *I'm* the one who started it all. Shit, it's probably her daddy fucked her up. Me, I'm a legitimate businessman.

"Did I make this system? I just work here. Some people are gonna make a lot of money and get rich, and some people are gonna keep fucking up and stay poor. All those do-gooders might want to ask why those people keep fucking up. Me, at least I'm offering a leg up. *I'm* not pushing dope on them. And I'm not importing crackheads from Thailand and Russia. I'm working with local talent. Fuck, Zane. I'm giving back to the fucking *community* here!"

Barker paused and took a sip of his Scotch, his eyes appraising Zane over the rim of his glass. Zane struggled to make sense of the logic that led from his genius through Coleridge and the nature of art to the workings of the sex trade and ultimately to Richard Barker's role as a pillar of the community. Things were getting wobbly. It might have been the whisky.

"I really think we need to get back to the part about me being a genius."

"So you can demand more money. Abusing my hospitality. Gimme your glass."

Zane handed it over. Getting home was going to be problematical.

"I'm serious. This shit is going to happen. I don't put girls on crack. I don't hand out needles. I'm not forcing anybody. You got to remember what I always say: this is a *family*. I'm not like the others. I take care of my own. Without me, shit, they get a couple years, they're washed up.

"You see where I'm going with this, Zane?"

Zane's tongue felt thick and numb.

"I don't think I'll be driving home."

Barker shook his head as if Zane was a dog that simply could not be trained to sit.

"This girl, she's going to come around, and she's going to do more than solo. She's going to do it because she's going to need to do it. And we're gonna be there for her, because she's a part of the family. Right? We always got jobs for our girls. Jade keeps an eye on them, and we make sure they get what they need. Our girls don't have to leave the family."

He nodded at a point over Zane's right shoulder and Zane twisted his head to see Jade standing behind him in the doorway.

"All done your little chat?"

"I think we're done. And don't you worry about driving home, Zane. Jade's gonna drive you. You're part of the family."

Zane knocked back the rest of his Scotch and put the glass on the desk.

"Speaking of the family, how're you getting along with Melissa?"

"Just swimmingly," said Zane, and regretted it. The sibilants proved insurmountable. A simpler response would have sufficed, something straightforward, such as "okay," or perhaps "good." You live, you learn.

"That's good. I want that girl to stick around. She's got a lot of potential. A lot of potential."

Zane stood, stooped to pick up his camera bag, and lost his balance. Jade caught him by the arm. He was surprised by the strength of her grip.

"I think you see where we're going with this," she said.

* * *

Jade drove a black BMW with leather seats and an engine that Zane could barely hear. The interior still smelled new. She remarked on the quantity of Scotch he had downed during Barker's dissertation by way of cautioning him not to make a mess of the leather. He had difficulty holding his head erect, felt he was sinking, the seat swallowing him. The leather, an undead cow, takes revenge for a lifetime of hamburger.

"It's nice you're getting on so well with Melissa."

Barker called a spade a long-handled digging implement for manual excavation but it remained unmistakably a spade. No need to keep hammering this nail. Zane said nothing.

"Famously, is what I hear."

Obviously you haven't been keeping up with the news.

"We get along."

"You get along." Jade smiled, tapped a manicured fingernail on the leather cover of her steering wheel. "Tell me something: have you ever had a friendly conversation, or do you always behave as if you're under police interrogation?"

"My client declines to answer."

"Zane, you do make me laugh." Jade failed to laugh. She drove with precise care, barely over the speed limit, her every movement deliberate and controlled. "You'll probably say that it's none of my business. But Rich is pleased."

How perceptive: it is, in fact, none of your business.

"I wasn't aware Rich took such a close interest in my personal life."

"Rich takes an unusual approach to things."

A masterpiece of understatement. Pardon me if I find all this interest in my private life disturbing. It is, in Melissa's idiom, creepy as all fuck.

"We don't get along nearly as well as you seem to think."

"Oh, I hear things."

A source close to the incident has spoken under condition of anonymity. Zane let that go by. Jade looked over at him briefly as if to gauge the effect of her words.

"I know all about you two. I make it my business to know what's happening with our girls. It prevents what I call 'mishaps.'" She uttered this last word with a delicate distaste. Mishaps do occur, have occurred, but are not to be spoken of in polite company. "What I want to know is, do you actually see what Rich is getting at?"

His head felt decidedly wobbly, a delayed reaction as his final glass of Scotch worked its way into his bloodstream.

"Why don't you just tell me what everyone's getting at?"

"I thought as much." Jade smoothly shifted down through the gears, approaching a red light. "Rich has one very great fault. He sees himself as an ideas man. He hatches grandiose schemes. He talks endlessly without getting to the point."

The light turned green.

"So get to the point."

"Rich trusts that you will see where he's going, because he thinks you are uncannily perceptive. For my part, I think you're a dunce."

How refreshingly direct, if not precisely tactful. The supper table, *chez* Barker, vibrates with lively conversation. Barker pontificates; Jade tells him to shut up and eat his mashed potatoes, before they get cold.

"So you're going to get right to the point."

"Exactly. Do you know why our girls are here?"

"The details are fuzzy. I gather it has something to do with Walmart."

"The short answer is that they are losers. They are girls with problems, who can't take control of their own lives. Who can't take responsibility. So there's a kind of unpredictability to their relationships."

This was not getting to the point. Jade had spent too much time around Barker.

"And you expect a mishap."

"Exactly. I expect a mishap."

She turned to him and beamed. A dull pupil finally grasps the principles of long division; gold stars all round.

"I don't think we'll see any mishaps."

Zane calculated the risk of a mishap at approximately zero. He and Melissa had no relationship to go awry.

Jade returned to tapping her finger on the steering wheel. She steered fastidiously, with her fingertips.

"Rich sometimes gets funny ideas," she said. "Rich values your talents, as he does Melissa's. And on that point, at least, I have to agree with him. He has some notion of keeping the both of you happy."

"And otherwise?"

"I think what will keep you happy is a steady paycheque. Melissa is another problem." She pulled up short in the street below his apartment and he cracked the door open to get out, but she carried on speaking. "I am not looking forward to cleaning up after things go bad."

Zane got out and then leaned down to talk through the open door. "I don't think you need to worry."

"I certainly hope not." Zane closed the door, and she drove smoothly away.

* * *

Melissa was off the wall.

A couple of beers turns into a couple more beers and at some point you lose track. Some of us handle it better than others, which is largely a matter of practice; cocaine is another matter entirely. Melissa giggled, made jokes, splashed water at him in the kitchen. She spoke quickly and her eyes were unnaturally bright, radiating heat and light. She kept excusing herself to go to the bathroom. Zane wondered why she felt the need to hide what she was up to, but he decided not to ask. You don't want to push your luck. The brakes are long burned out and all you can do is hang on, Casey Jones, and hope this thing stays on the tracks.

At some point after her steps got wobbly, Melissa recounted the misadventures of her roommate, who went by the name of Clarissa. Clarissa's adventures were invariably sexual. She was a young woman of considerable athletic grace and prowess. Clarissa's most recent adventure involved a boyfriend who liked to take pictures. This young man wished to expand his horizons and Clarissa, being an obliging girl, had invited Melissa to participate in the general fun and games.

"So I said, what the hell." Melissa elaborated no further. "So now she owes me one, you know? If I ever wanted her to, you know, return the favour, with anyone."

Zane realized this story had no punchline. He found Clarissa's rhyming name an improbable coincidence.

"Clarissa sounds like a very friendly girl."

"You want to meet her?"

"Sure, sometime." He waved his hand vaguely, realizing only too late the implications of his response. He addressed himself to his beer bottle, a less complex interaction. There's no graceful way out of this one.

Up until now Zane had been able to stick to concrete facts. You have this girl, Melissa; she drinks; she gets drunk. She takes other things. Now we must face the question of what these facts signify and where they lead, what these facts expect and what they intend. These tales of brave Clarissa. Additional facts complicate the picture: Barker, Jade, a certain difficulty swimming with millstones. Mishaps loom.

The lingering effects of Zane's abdominal wound, or of the confusion that followed it, left Melissa's questionable virtue in no danger. The equipment was not serviceable. Which was not to imply that the man in the mirror, the same Zane who kept the apartment free of razor blades and other weapons of self-destruction, was incapable of using her as a lab rat, to see if anything had changed. There was no way to know.

"Shit, Zane, you're a real wet blanket. It's impossible to have fun with you."

"You've discovered the truth at last."

Yet Melissa's bounce did not diminish. She finished her beer and went to the bathroom. He didn't hear the toilet or the tap. On her way back she picked up two more beers and stopped in front of him and planted her feet and thrust her hips forward.

"Truth or dare."

"What?"

"Truth or dare."

"Get real."

"I want to find out what makes the great Lucas Zane tick."

"And you think I know?"

"Dare."

"What?" The facts were spinning out of control.

"Dare me."

"What's next, spin the bottle?"

"You got a bottle?"

We have no shortage in this department.

"This shit is for kids."

She affected a pout and flopped onto the couch next to him. He moved to the left to make room and she giggled and followed. Things were getting out of hand in the rabbit warren. Zane ran out of room to retreat, and stood up.

"Just stop. It's not funny."

"Party pooper." She stuck her tongue out at him and got up and made for the bathroom again, walking with the studied care of one whose balance is mildly askew.

This kid is a disaster in the offing, a walking mishap. You don't want to get mixed up in her terminal wipeout. Might as well leave the Boy Scout guide to knots lying around the apartment, opened to the chapter on nooses, a straight razor for a bookmark. Getting entangled in Melissa's problems will be a little more complex than razor blades but every bit as final.

A crash and a shout from the bathroom, a spate of swearing. Zane knocked at the door and called out to ask if she was okay, received only more swearing in reply. When he opened the door, the first thing he saw was the blood. Melissa stood at the counter gripping her right fist, bleeding copiously onto white porcelain. Pieces of mirror and splashes of blood decorated the counter and the floor. Her face was white.

Broken glass on the floor. It is essential to stay in control. To stay in the here and now. Zane took her by the elbow, steered her to the kitchen, away from the blood and the glass. In the kitchen he found a clean dishtowel and pressed it against her hand.

"Seven more years of bad fucking luck," she said.

"I don't think this was a question of luck."

He lifted the towel off her hand. The cuts were superficial, where the glass had slashed her knuckles.

"What did you do, punch it?"

He started the tap and held her hand under it. As the water hit the cuts she swore and yanked her hand back but he gripped her wrist and held it under the water.

"Don't be a such a baby."

"It fuckin' hurts."

"No shit." He took her hand out from under the water and inspected the cuts closely, looking for slivers of glass. "Why'd you go and do that?"

"I didn't like what I saw."

"How d'you like it now?" He pressed the dishtowel on her hand again. "Press down on that."

Zane made for the bathroom. An apartment bedroom in Sarajevo, the broken glass of the window scattered over the floor. The body of the sniper lay on the floor with dark blood pooled around his head and Zane stopped to take the picture that was there, of the man's body lying in the blood and the shards. He didn't stop to consider that he was standing in the light from the window until the bullet came, so close that it lifted his hair. He hit the floor, on top of the body and the glass, cut his palms going down, thinking, idiot. Pain wracking his guts, his insides tightening, still alive. You've been here too long. You've been here too long when you start to act like you're bulletproof. When your unconscious self decides it's time to make a separate peace. When you can't trust yourself to keep yourself alive.

His guts twisted at the memory. The chill of sudden sweat. You are in your apartment, in Toronto, and the stripper in your kitchen requires first aid. Just another tranquil domestic scene in the Zane household. The Band-Aids are where you left them, dear, next to the cocaine. He found a box of gauze, one formerly sterile dressing (package torn), and a near-empty bottle of antiseptic in the medicine cabinet. Time was, you had a fully stocked first aid kit. Povidone-iodine solution, pressure dressings, wound closure strips, tincture of benzoin. Then it ceased to be necessary. You get to be casual about these things, living in Toronto.

In the kitchen, Melissa had taken the towel off her hand to inspect the cuts. Fascinated, as if the hand in question was not hers. Blood dripped onto the floor.

"I told you to keep pressure on that."

"I didn't mean to break your mirror."

"It was cracked anyway."

He took her hand and pressed the towel to the cuts again, then inspected the damage. She had one nasty cut, over the middle knuckle. That one was going to leave a scar.

"Keep pressure on that. And don't go looking at it. It's not that interesting."

In the cupboard under the sink he found a hand broom and dustpan, which he used to sweep up the glass from the bathroom floor. The broom smeared blood over the floor and the counter, and he mopped it up with a wet towel and then ran water in the sink to wash away the blood. That sight nearly sent him spinning again. It was amazing, how much blood.

Why is my life so full of blood?

He filled the sink with water and put the towel in to soak, and returned to the kitchen. Melissa obediently clutched her injured hand to her chest. She had blood on her shirt but her colour had returned. He dabbed disinfectant on the cuts, again admonishing her not to be a baby. Then he took the dressing and pressed it to her knuckles and wrapped gauze around her hand to hold it in place. As he worked she leaned her face into him and he felt the heat of her breath on his neck, tracing the line of his jaw, her mouth looking for his. She darted her tongue against his lips, the smell of stale beer.

"You're pretty drunk," he said. "I think I better put you to bed."

"Yes. You better put me to bed."

She has that endless talent for innuendo. Zane took her by the elbow and steered her to the bedroom and sat her on the bed and took off her shoes. She giggled at his order to take her jeans off, and wriggled out of them and then stood in front of him. He reached past her and folded back the blanket and sat her down, discouraged her sudden and enthusiastic efforts to unfasten his belt.

"Go to sleep, kiddo, and don't punch any more mirrors tonight."

"What's your problem?"

"For starters, you're half my age."

"That never stopped anyone before."

"It's complicated."

On the other hand perhaps it's embarrassingly simple. But why go into details? He reached down and took her good hand and patted it in what he hoped was a sympathetic way. She gripped his hand.

"Nobody I like ever likes me."

How do I extract myself from this? Zane essayed a reassuring smile while attempting to twist his hand free.

"Melissa, if I was your age, I'd whisk you off to Vancouver tomorrow."

"All the way to Vancouver."

"Sure. But for now, just remember you're young enough to be my daughter."

She still refused to relinquish her grip.

"Do you have any kids?"

"No. I have no family at all."

"I could be your daughter."

If you think that's going to solve anything then you're drunker than I thought.

"Okay, kiddo." Zane extricated his hand. He left the door open while he retrieved a spare blanket from the closet, and then closed the door on her.

Zane threw the blanket on the couch and then went to the kitchen, where he mopped up the blood from the counter and floor with paper towels. He couldn't remember if her shout had followed the sound of breaking glass or preceded it. Anyway, it didn't much matter.

What a fucked-up kid.

When he was finished cleaning up he turned out the light and went into the bathroom, where he looked into the empty frame of the mirror. He was momentarily disturbed to discover that he had no reflection at all.

CHAPTER SIX

Sunlight spills over the building opposite, breaks over the windowsill where yet another backlit spider plant still clings to life in its coffee can, splashes against the walls and washes over Zane, inert and face down on the couch. The pattern of the couch fabric stamped into his face. Awake, awake and greet the day. A mouthful of paste and a head full of grog.

A persistent pain had settled in just behind his eyes. At first he thought he'd passed out there, on the couch, but then the events of the night before returned. He got up, went into the bathroom, checked for broken glass. Either you were less inebriated than you thought, or you're better with a broom than you ever knew. Don't drink and sweep. Don't think and weep. The evidence suggests that you're still drunk.

The worst symptom of hangover is the non-specific conviction that one is an incorrigible fuck-up. This time, there's no shortage of evidence to support that hypothesis. It's time to deal with the rest of the mess.

Bloody water and towels in the bathroom sink: these will forever after be formerly white. You are only a virgin once. He picked the towels out of the sink one by one, dripping pink water on the floor, pulled the plug and let the blood-tinged water drain. The blood was hard to handle and on a hangover it was worse. He had on one occasion dropped a glass of booze and when he saw it on the floor the liquid splattered among the shards was blood. He blinked hard and reality snapped back into place. It was about that time that he realized something was badly wrong. And the sight of blood remained disturbing in ways unfathomable to the merely squeamish. He wrung the towels out and rinsed them and and hung them over the shower rail and went to check on Melissa.

At the bedroom door he paused. What is the proper form for dealing with a wounded, hung-over, messed-up porno chick in one's bedroom? We wish to establish, at least, that she is still alive, but still, we must respect her privacy. Miss Manners, that bitch, never addresses such real-world problems. A compromise: he tapped lightly on the door before opening it. He needn't have bothered. She was still out and showed no sign of stirring.

Zane stood in the doorway for a moment and watched her sleep. Melissa lay face down, her head turned to the side, her breath slow and steady. A little bit of blood had seeped through the dressing in the night and showed as a small brown stain on the gauze. Her face was stilled by the slack-jawed stupidity of sleep, all its animation gone. The shape-shifter at rest.

Zane closed the door on her and went back into the kitchen. He started a pot of coffee. It was almost eleven but there was no need to wake her yet.

"This thing is just about ready to go," he said to himself. He liked the sound of the words and the assurance in his voice as he said them. Today is looking up. He poured himself a cup of coffee. He was, indeed, ready to go. All the facts had coalesced into one. It was time for Lucas Zane to cut his losses. Time to get out.

The only way out is the door you came in. Zane took his coffee and the phone into the bathroom to avoid waking Melissa, and dialed Jack's office number in New York. Jack answered with a tone of theatrical patience, demanded to know what he wanted.

"I want for you to give me a story."

"And I want you to give me a reason not to hang up right now."

"I'm not drunk."

"It's still early."

"That's still a reason."

"It's not a good one."

The conversation is not going as planned. The script is straightforward: Zane needs work. Jack can provide it. Zane calls Jack. They discuss the possibilities in friendly tones. As a matter of fact, there is some work available. Negotiations over his rate are perfunctory. He is, of course, willing to work for less these days. The exigencies of the situation. We have to start someplace. Above all, Zane does not wheedle.

"I need work. You need work done. And you need me."

Jack seemed to find this funny.

"The world does not need you. Nobody cares if the photos are any good, as long as they fill space on the page."

"I'm stung."

"Get over it. Let me put you in the picture."

Jack had already put him in the picture many times before, and Zane could recite the salient points by heart. It's ugly out there, good agencies are as rare as five-legged unicorns, and good agents like Jack are a dying breed. You should have fallen on your knees each morning to thank your deity of choice, or alternatively, Jack, that you weren't competing with the scrabbling mass of photographers for starvation wages on all-rights contracts drafted by the same lawyers who had advised Pontius Pilate in the matter of one Jesus of Nazareth. Instead, you bit the hand that fed you, and now Jack is fresh out of Milk Bones. So now you get to compete with hungry little upstarts who are only too happy to slide towards personal bankruptcy at seventy-five dollars a day in the vain hope of reaching the heights that the great Lucas Zane so recently abandoned. And I'm not about to take a risk on you given certain recent events that I'd rather not review. That about covered it.

Zane let it all play out.

"I mean it. I need a story."

"I'm a busy man. I think we're done here."

None of this is in the script. Has no one read his lines? Zane's lifeline was drawing in.

"You said you'd look at any story I came up with."

"Then come up with one."

"I'm starting to work on something."

"Good. What is it?"

We have failed to think this through. The perils of ad lib.

"The details aren't firm just yet. I'm going through the, ah, preliminary research. And I can't really get into the details just now."

"It's been nice talking to you."

"No, I really can't get into the details just now, you know, sensitive subject. Anyway, the thing is I need to cover costs. I need some work."

A long pause from New York, during which Zane could hear Jack's fingernails drumming on his desk. He took this as a positive sign. It was in any case more promising than a dial tone.

"Don't jerk me around. If you've got a story, do it. Alternatively, go to hell."

Zane heard the bedroom door open. She was up.

"I don't have the money to do this story."

"I'm from Missouri. You want back in the game, show me." Jack hung up.

"Fuck you if you can't get your lines straight," he said to the dial tone. I am tired of re-shooting this scene.

Zane went back out into the kitchen. Melissa had put her jeans on, for which he was thankful. Small mercies. She collapsed onto the couch and availed herself of Zane's blanket, covered herself from knees to shoulders. Her hair was a cascading disaster and she looked bleary and pale.

"I feel like crap."

"You look like crap."

He put the phone on the counter and dug a coffee cup out of the cupboard and poured her a cup. She requested cream and sugar. You might have guessed. One arm reached out from under the blanket to take the coffee. She sipped at it and then held up her right hand.

"I smashed your mirror, didn't I?"

"You cut your knuckles pretty good, too."

"I didn't mean to do that."

"Hit it by accident, did you?"

"No, I mean I didn't mean it."

"It was a shitty mirror, anyway. It made me look all blotchy and sick."

"I kind of remember other stuff. Please tell me it didn't happen."

"It did."

She groaned and rolled her head back. How much worse would she feel if she'd woken up next to you? Then again, perhaps she thinks she did. The worst symptom of hangover. However bad things look you're convinced that they're probably worse. Zane knew that territory well.

"You were pretty drunk. I had to put you to bed."

"Please say there isn't any more."

"There isn't any more. You said you wished you were my daughter. It was kind of cute."

"Oh, God. It's worse than I thought."

He finished his coffee and took the mug back to the kitchen and rinsed it and put it in the sink. He had nothing for breakfast beyond cereal but she said she couldn't face anything solid anyway. When she had finished her coffee, she levered herself up off the couch and announced that she was going to take a shower.

"Let's look at that hand, first."

He unwrapped the gauze and inspected the damage. He had been as thorough with the hand as he had cleaning up the glass. The cuts were still crusted with blood but they were clean. Nothing looked deep enough for stitches. She looked at her knuckles, winced and flexed her fingers, which opened the cut on her middle knuckle. This explained the blood soaked through the gauze.

"You're going to have knuckles like a bad drunk."

"Apparently, I am a bad drunk."

She didn't sing in the shower. Zane turned on the television. Nothing, save an endless round of talk shows and fake court cases. He switched it off again and stood at the kitchen window and watched life go by in the street. It was now coming on for afternoon.

You have to get out. You need a story. You just need one credible idea. You need to get Melissa out the door and then you can go and get the papers and find out what's going on in the real world. The names and details you can make up as long as the idea carries weight. Once you get something out of Jack you can tell him the whole thing fell apart. The subject backed out. All you need is to get moving, to convince Jack that you're back in the game.

All Zane needed was to get rid of Melissa.

* * *

Rows of lenses beneath the glass top of a display cabinet: a couple of well-used 50/1.8s for less than nothing, two slow mid-range zooms, an old 24 mm f/2 going cheap, a battered 300 mm f/4.5, an 85, a 20-35 zoom, some crappy third-party tele-converters. In short, nothing exciting. No good lens going cheap, no cheapie worth using as a beater, nothing worth playing with for its own sake. Nothing holds its value anymore. Returning from El Salvador, you sold those two battered F3s for three times what a mint F3 high-eyepoint will fetch now. Photography today is nothing but a game of technology. In the computer age, the philosopher's stone is merely a serviceable paperweight.

Poring over the used gear cabinet became unpleasantly like looking at Lucas Zane preserved in a museum. He had gone down to the ROM that summer, wanted to see the dinosaurs, felt he could deal with all those bones. But the place was closed for renovation. You want to see a dinosaur, look for your reflection in the glass.

Charlie, run-down, slightly stooped, thinning grey hair, asked if he wanted to take a closer look at anything. Charlie had worked there as long as Zane could remember. Longer than that, in fact. Charlie had worked there since the Nikon F, knew every good camera made since 1959. Tell him you needed to rig a remote trigger for an arcane motor drive that hadn't been made since 1983, and he'd drag a dusty box up from the basement and find the connector you needed. With a wink: you can have that free because I'm pissed off at the boss today. Charlie liked anyone who wanted things obscure and obsolete. He could have been an award-winning nature photographer but he drank too much. At least, that was the story as Zane heard it.

"Those prices are breaking my heart," said Zane.

"Used prices are way down. Great deals in there."

"That's what's breaking my heart."

Zane wandered away from the used cabinets to the back corner of the shop, where new equipment competed for space with the used. Tripods, light stands, studio flash heads, umbrellas, light boxes, reflectors, power supplies, all the assorted clamps and widgets of the mad engineers of studio lighting. Scars and scratches and wear marks and chipped paint. This stuff wears forever, changes hands. You always need a widget. The place was a photographic thrift shop.

On the back wall he found a shelf where assorted used developing tanks lay jumbled. Yard sale junk; no-one uses this stuff anymore. The shelf bore three lonely bottles of liquid black-and-white developer, Kodak HC-110. Zane picked one up and inspected it, taking note of the colour change at the top of the bottle, where the developer had reacted to the air. Easy to work with, has a long shelf life, but like any liquid developer it's heavy to carry. It was Zane's favourite, in the days when he still shot a lot of black-and-white. In El Salvador.

He set the bottle aside. The chemicals on the shelf were jumbled together in no particular order but he found bottles of rapid fixer and glacial acetic acid without difficulty. He still had his old tanks back at the apartment, in one of the boxes. He had all he needed.

He deposited the chemicals on the counter and Charlie looked at him dubiously. He rarely used Zane's name, probably couldn't remember it without reading it off his credit card. But he could tell you that the difference between an AI-S Nikkor and an AI Nikkor only matters if you own the Nikon FA. And who owns a Nikon FA, anyway?

"I always preferred D-76."

Which was exactly what Zane might have expected from Charlie.

"That's what Saint Ansel used?"

"It is indeed."

"Europe is in flames, and Ansel Adams is photographing rocks and trees. Cartier-Bresson said that."

"Did he?"

"But no doubt, someplace else was in flames when Cartier-Bresson was shooting guys jumping over puddles."

"No doubt."

Charlie put the chemicals in a plastic bag. Zane knew he was far more interested in the merits of HC-110 as compared to D-76, and could cheerfully have discussed contrast curves and push-processing characteristics all afternoon. What a dead Frenchman had once said about a dead American, he couldn't have cared less.

"Thing is, someplace or other is always in flames," said Zane. Now that he had the chemicals, he felt no real desire to take any pictures worth developing.

"And there are always rocks and trees."

"True, that."

Rocks and trees. Who cares? No doubt Charlie will shake his head sadly after you leave: what a pity that Zane guy hit the bottle. Used to be good, you know, a real pro. In any case, Cartier-Bresson had taken to painting by the time Capa got himself killed in Indochina. Zane was more or less sure of that. If your pictures aren't good enough, you aren't close enough. Then Capa stepped on a mine. Cartier-Bresson was better off painting.

* * *

Nothing lasts. The *Manual of Photography* burns through new editions faster than Hollywood burns through marriages. *Photographic Sensitometry* is out of print; contrast curves are now a problem for software engineers. A Tessar is all very nice in theory, but what you want now is a constant-aperture zoom, fourteen elements in eleven groups. Alchemy is black magic again, and even chemistry is too imprecise. Now, you can edit pixel by pixel, colour correction by the numbers. We have progress.

Zane was just old enough to have started his career in black and white. In San Salvador he ended his days standing by the window of his hotel room, watching the evening light turn soft and blue and fade as the sky turned purple, watching the city transform from a sprawling, ugly jumble of concrete and corrugated iron into a network of coloured lights splattered across the dark blanket of night: beauty distilled out of misery.

When the light faded, he turned out the lights in his room. He went into the bathroom and ran the shower to cut the dust, then stuffed towels under the door to complete the darkness and loaded the film he had shot that day into developing tanks. He used a beer bottle opener to break open the film cans. His companions in the darkness were a battery-powered radio tuned to an English-language station, its glowing lights covered with duct tape, a glass of rum and ice, and a towel to dry his hands.

Wet hands are murder for this job: wet film sticks in the grooves, refuses to behave. The job of threading the film onto the developing reels has to be perfect. If a loop of film jumps the groove and touches the next loop the result will be a half-dozen lost pictures. And each lost frame was of course a Pulitzer in the making. Still, Zane was not prepared to dispense with his Nicaraguan rum, which had a vague chemical aftertaste and sweated heavily in the tropical night.

With the tanks loaded and sealed he could turn on the lights again, pull the towels out from under the door and replenish his rum. The hotel bathroom became an alchemist's workshop.

In school he had learned consistent, controlled darkroom procedures: temperature control, distilled water, the stop clock with its luminous dial. Developing in a hotel bathroom in San Salvador was more art than science. Tap water at room temperature replaced distilled water. His developing time changed with the weather, an estimate pulled from a grubby graph he kept tucked in the pocket of his camera bag, although he had long since committed the time-temperature curve to memory.

On a cool night, the developer was in the tank for six minutes by his watch, transforming the events of the day into a permanent record through the action of light on photosensitive halide ions. Light into silver. When the time was up, he dumped the developer and hit the film with the stop bath, the pungent vinegar smell stabbing his nostrils. Then he exchanged the stop bath for the fixer, to dissolve the unexposed halides. Only silver then remained, suspended in a thin layer of gelatin. He estimated the fixing time by dropping a short piece of unexposed film in the fixer and keeping one eye on his watch as the film turned from opaque brown to clear.

Three baths of tap water, and he had pictures. The film came off the spools in shining black ribbons, which held to the light revealed images. Shadows glowed. Lights appeared as small black points. The wet film shone and twisted, dripping on the bathroom floor. Zane hung the negatives from the shower rod to dry. When he found good pictures, he would print them wet. The pictures made a pittance but they paid his hotel bills and kept him in the game until his lucky break arrived, in the form of a dead girl from North Dakota, whose name was Christine. Then the weeklies started calling, and he moved up to colour. The march of progress never ceases.

* * *

A loud and unceasing pounding on his door. It's eight-thirty: unholy early. Zane pulled on a pair of jeans, the first shirt he found.

The rent is paid. You didn't leave anything in the hall, did you? The pounding continued.

Melissa's balloon head again in his peephole. He opened the door. She looked healthier than last he had seen her, but this was saying little. Under her left arm was a brown paper bag. Groceries.

"And the dead arose, and appeared to many," she said.

"What?"

"Something my grandmother used to say. From the Bible, I think. Were you planning to sleep to noon?"

She brushed past him and put the paper bag on the kitchen counter. It was difficult to imagine Melissa having a grandmother. Still, certain things are immutable biological necessities. He had never asked about her family. He treated this as off limits, filed it under unwanted knowledge.

"What are you doing here?"

"Aren't you gracious. I came to make you breakfast."

"Breakfast?"

"It's the meal you eat in the morning."

"Why?"

"Because you have to eat."

"What are you, Meals on Wheels?"

"Someone has to feed the shut-ins." She opened the fridge, found the margarine, hunted through cupboards, turned on him and made a shooing motion. "Go take a shower. You smell."

Zane left her in the kitchen and quickly showered. Unable to ponder his reflection, he was forced to shave by feel. Since Zane shaved only sporadically, this took somewhat longer than usual. On the positive side, he was unable to fret over his blotchy appearance. Presumably, he was a new man. All setbacks have their countervailing compensations.

Cooking smells infiltrated the bathroom. As threatened, she was making breakfast. More to the point, she was cooking bacon. Probably, she was also cooking eggs. Diarrhea and dehydration, a day strapped to the toilet seat. These are the wages of sin, and of a bowel forcibly shortened by the transit of a machine gun bullet. She didn't know. Zane finished shaving and rinsed his face and then opened the door. We must now face the music.

He had guessed right: she was tipping scrambled eggs onto a plate. To his dismay, she added a sprig of fresh parsley, and held the plate out to him, beaming. She had made a lot of food.

"I'm just going to get changed."

"Hurry up, before it gets cold."

He fled to the bedroom with a feeling of doom deep in his gut. Fathers' Day: seven-year-old Lucas and five-year-old Connie cook breakfast, under minimal supervision. Zane's father eats the resulting burnt bacon and leathery eggs without complaint, even winks at Zane's mother and suggests the kids can teach her to cook. This girl, this fucked-up kid, she tries to be your friend. She gets stupid, busts your mirror, splits her knuckles, wants to make it up to you. She does what she can. You're about to get the hell out of this, get rid of her, make a clean break. Now you're going to turn down this kid's peace offering?

She made him sit on the couch, insisted on serving him at the coffee table: bacon, scrambled eggs, and toast, with orange juice and coffee. The coffee was weak, watery. He drank it without comment. It had been a long time since he had tasted bacon and eggs. He had missed them.

"You didn't have to do this."

"It's time you ate a real meal. It's not healthy, how you live."

He shovelled his food around on his plate. If only she hadn't served you, you could have gone light on the bacon and eggs, still made appreciative noises. Now you're obliged to clean your plate. Maybe you can decently abandon a little of the food, not that it'll make much difference to the outcome.

"You really didn't have to do this."

"I feel bad about your mirror."

"It was cracked anyway. Let's see the damage."

She had made her own crude efforts at wound care, a mess of Band-Aids. He peeled them off, carefully folded the sticky ends against each other, laid them on the coffee table. The cuts looked fine, but the skin was pale and waterlogged.

"Leave them open to the air," he said. "They'll heal faster."

"I feel bad about the rest of it, too."

"I've forgotten the rest of it."

The moment of ill grace approaches. The food will work fast. It's time to get rid of the kid.

"Look, I'm going to have to kick you out of here pretty soon. I have to go work on a story. A photo story."

"What's the story?"

"I don't know yet."

"You don't know?"

"I still have to come up with one."

"So you don't have a story."

"A minor detail that may yet derail my plans."

"Your problem is, you spend too much time in your own head."

She stood up, collected the plates, went into the kitchen. He heard the water running in the sink and followed. The pipes moaned as she started the hot water. She tested the temperature with her hand before putting the plug in the sink and adding soap.

"Keep those knuckles out of that dishwater." He took the dishtowel from the oven door and handed it to her. Time to say things that need to be said. "Anyway, if things work out with this story, I'm through with Barker."

"Lucky you. I don't know what I'm gonna do. I'm running out of acts."

Rich has plenty of new acts lined up for you. Nobody runs out of acts around here. None of us ever outruns himself.

Zane slipped the plates into the water and worked at them. He finished the dishes and scrubbed the frying pan and then let the water run out of the sink, ran the tap to chase the last of the suds down the drain. Then he watched her drying the plates in the morning window light.

"Thinking of taking my picture again, are ya?"

"Not really."

"Still looking for that story?"

"Not really."

"You're a' real dope, man. You ever think I could be your story?"

Porno girl struggles to make good. The stripper with a heart of gold. All the elements are there. This, you can sell to Jack: porn is the story of our times. You are, in fact, a real dope.

"That's perfect."

"So what do I get paid?"

"There's the rub. You don't."

"Doesn't sound like much of a deal to me."

"You get your story told. Not many people get their stories told."

You get turned into silver. And you get to save my ass. It would be, he thought, a more substantial contribution to his well-being than her bacon and eggs, which were already announcing their presence in the remains of his intestines.

"So you take pictures of me doing what?"

"Doing whatever it is you do. Drying my dishes, for example."

She looked at him for a moment with her head tilted to one side, and then wiped her hands on the dishtowel, put the towel down on the counter, and shrugged.

"Okay," she said.

CHAPTER SEVEN

Richard Barker, under the *nom de guerre* of Diamond Blue Enterprises, owned three establishments wherein patrons, having paid a nominal cover charge and a much less nominal charge for drinks, could proceed to view young women removing their clothes and dancing to music, and to enjoy certain other pleasures that at one time or another had been at or beyond the boundaries of the law. The least-known of these establishments lay in the hinterlands to the north of the city, a rundown building of pink-painted cinder block that drew bikers and farm boys to watch strippers long past their prime go through their well practised motions while absently wondering what, if anything, they might do in retirement. The second was close to the airport, and succoured weary travellers. The third was downtown, and it aimed to sucker everyone else.

The club's facade glittered in polished black faux granite with gold trim. White bulbs flashed in gold fixtures. No cheesy pink neon tubes here, no anatomically improbable silhouettes as seen on tractor-trailer mud flaps. The sign above the front door was lettered in gold, as at a law office: Gentlemen's VIP. At the door, a brass plaque. No Live Nude Girls, no triple-X, no Girls Girls Girls. Just as a gentleman does not talk about money, here one is expected to understate and to understand.

Zane had come for his pay. The bouncer looked him over, his face filled with doubt. Can this shambolic individual, with sunken eyes and unkempt hair, be a gentleman? What precisely is the standard? The bouncer possessed little actual experience of gentlemen, perhaps, on which to base his judgment. In the end he nodded and stepped aside to let Zane pass. A wordless exchange in which the message was clear: management reserves the right to kick the shit out of you at any time.

In a UN observation post in Croatia, Zane spent three hours with a massive British infantry private, who complained that he could not stay in a bar until closing time without getting into a fight. This problem, a genetic defect of sorts, had prevented his promotion through the ranks, as shortly following each promotion and its ensuing celebration, he found himself marched before his commanding officer and again demoted. His military career was a trail of broken bar stools, shattered glass, and battered challengers, and he lamented the cruelty of his fate.

"When you're the biggest bloke in the room, everyone wants to try you on. It's a pain in the arse is what it is."

"You can't escape who you are," said Zane.

"The fuckin' truth, that is."

All the soldier really wanted to do in life was to breed and raise his delicate and beautiful South American discus fish. But there was no money in that, so he was overseas in Croatia while his fish glowed aimlessly in their luminous aquarium, under the care of his girlfriend, Sophie. Discus, he explained, were expensive, delicate and difficult to care for. This guaranteed he would do right by Sophie.

"But I'm not complaining," he said. "It's a good life. The fish can wait."

O cruel fate, laments the bouncer, that has placed me at this door and charged me with the cracking of heads. No wonder he looks grumpy. Perhaps a sunny greeting, some cheerful comment will brighten his day, deflate his carefully cultivated aggression. Perhaps not. Perhaps another time. Today, Zane wants his paycheque. One must avoid mishaps. Also, getting one's nose flattened.

Zane remained mired in his job. Jack still had not read the script, and had dismissed his story pitch. The telephone call was cut short by the action of Melissa's cooking on his innards, and this had somewhat undermined his argument. Jack said he had a premise, not a story, told him not to call back until he had the story worked out.

This is the age of porn, Jack. This is the story of our time. Hardcore goes mainstream. A generation gets its sex ed from the Internet. Teenaged girls photograph themselves in the mirror and post the pictures online, call it empowerment, go wild with empowerment at Fort Lauderdale, demonstrate empowerment at Mardi Gras for cheap strings of beads, email their empowerment to boys they like. They're drunk with empowerment. Drunken starlets forget their panties, do Marilyn Monroe on the ventilation shaft, and it makes the papers. Every day, a new email promises to grow your dick one more inch. Now the thing is two and a half feet long, gets mistaken for a torpedo at airport security. A serious inconvenience to the air traveller, but it breaks the ice at parties, and in major shipping lanes. It seems to have forgotten its place.

Jack said, are you done? None of that shit is for real. Your average coed is still a virgin.

Zane didn't ask him how he knew. Doesn't matter, he said. We're still in the age of hardcore gone mainstream.

Hardcore goes mainstream is not a story. Stories have goals and complications. Stories have a plot. Cover your own expenses, then show me the pictures.

So a day in the life of Melissa is not a story. This escape is going to take longer than planned. We have goals, and complications: actually producing the story Jack demands means shooting Melissa at work, here, among the gentlemen. This is a delicate matter; it requires the cooperation of Richard Barker. The proposal itself will arouse suspicion, and you have nothing to add to Barker's bank account. Here at the entrance to Barker's lair, Zane still had no idea how to broach the subject.

Beyond the bouncer, appearances declined. If one expected to find gentlemen within Gentlemen's VIP, one would quickly be disabused of the notion. The entrance hallway turned sharply to the right, to block the view from the street. Artwork for the walls had evidently presented the decorators with something of a challenge. Gentlemen might be expected to favour oily, smoke-tarred landscapes of nineteenth-century vintage, scenes of antique nautical mayhem, and portraits of horses with improbably long noses. The decorators had settled on portraiture, but instead of horses had opted for pastels of women with similarly exaggerated anatomy. Several bore unidentifiable stains, and none hung straight. Today's gentleman, it seemed, had no appreciation for art.

Onstage, a skinny girl flexed herself awkwardly around the pole for the benefit of a sparse gathering of men who had either left work early or never made it there in the first place. She wore black heels and a matching G-string, had apparently forgotten how to smile, and stared vacantly into the middle distance, somewhere halfway up the wall. Her audience looked equally bored.

Bill leaned on the bar, his day job, idly watching her and chewing gum. His acting career didn't pay the bills; besides, he had recently been on hiatus. Jade had suggested some time off, some time to work out a problem with his fists. He nodded at Zane by way of acknowledgment and then pointed his chin at the girl.

"She ain't gonna last."

Zane didn't bother to consider Bill's opinion. He was about to ask after Barker when he remembered that he had a story to do. You want to investigate the culture, or something like that.

"You think so?"

"You think she's earning any tips like that? You gotta make an effort." He lifted his elbows off the bar and wiped it with a cloth, apparently more for something to do than out of any need to clean. "Chicks like that, think they're above it all, they drive me nuts. Look around you, understand your fuckin' situation. You ain't above shit."

"You gotta get over yourself." Zane adopted Bill's idiom. Look around, understand your situation. Do your story, get back in the game. Sayonara, Richard Barker.

"Fuckin' right. You think I want to tend bar for a living? You do what you gotta do."

Bill put the cloth away and returned to leaning on the bar. "Rich around?"

"Gone out," said Bill, and snapped his gum again. "Jade's upstairs, though."

"Know when he'll be back? I wanted to ask him something."

"Ask Jade."

"I need a decision."

"Rich might be the boss, but she's the boss of Rich. She runs the show, man. Believe it."

So much for your story. You're not about to broach this one with Jade. At least Barker thinks you're a genius. Jade thinks you're a dunce. The only saving grace was that she once called you harmless, but that appraisal could change. You're not doing some exposé, are you?

He found Jade in the office, a small room upstairs that contained two desks, one computer, a small refrigerator, a locker, and an enormous safe that occupied one corner of the room in squat solemnity.

Below this safe, in the kitchen, an anonymous cook toils, never suspecting that at any moment the ceiling will collapse under its weight. One day, the floor will collapse and this safe will fall to his doom. Like the witch in the *Wizard of Oz*, the cook is reduced to a pair of legs protruding from the wreckage, never again to siphon off his percentage of the dancers' tips. Stripes on his socks. Joyful munchkins dance and sing. The bouncer beats the shit out of them on principle: nobody dances here for free. Melissa clicks her heels: there's no place like home. Zane, her all-purpose companion, frets and wrings his hands. If I only had a story, if I only had a clue, if I only had a straw to cling to. Or some kind of faith, at least. Maybe the wizard can help.

Jade sat at the desk, fingernails clacking on the computer keyboard, overdressed as usual in soap-opera chic. Her hair moved in precise lock step with the turn of her head as she greeted Zane. She was the only thing in Gentlemen's VIP that matched its exterior pretensions.

"Did Rich leave my cheque?"

"You and your social graces."

She slipped a finger into the waist pocket of her jacket and retrieved a key, sat down at the other desk and fit the key to the desk drawer. From the drawer she retrieved a white envelope. When Zane reached for it, she snatched it back with a flick of her wrist, and smiled.

"You're not one for small talk, are you?"

She tapped the corner of the envelope against the desk, wearing a small smile. He felt like a wounded mouse. She kept this up for some time, fixing Zane with an unwavering gaze.

"I think we might get some rain."

Jade stopped tapping the envelope and laid it on the desk in front of her, carefully aligning it so that it was square with the edge, face up so that Zane could read his name in plain, hasty capitals, inverted. Satisfied that the envelope was just so, she raised her eyes.

"How are you and Melissa getting along?"

"Didn't we already do this?"

"I like to keep up-to-date."

"You want a play-by-play?"

Jade laughed and then realigned the envelope, as if it had slipped out of plumb during her moment of informality. She got up and opened the refrigerator, pulled out a can of diet ginger ale, popped a straw into it with a precise jab of her thumb and forefinger. Her lipstick left a smear on the straw.

"What I hear is you're taking pictures of her."

"And?"

"Pictures are for men who are afraid of women."

"I think you should stop making assumptions."

"I'm not here to judge. As Rich would say, whatever flips your cookie." Jade put the ginger ale can down carefully in the centre of the desk and picked up the envelope. She tapped it against her palm and looked steadily at Zane. "You're not on a leash here. But I want you to remember our previous conversation."

"I'll bear it firmly in mind."

"I trust you'll also bear in mind that publishing photos of Melissa anywhere without our permission will make Rich very angry."

"They're purely for our own enjoyment."

So much for that. The situation now mandates alternative methods. More precisely, you're just going to have to be sneaky.

Downstairs, Bill worked a mop on the floor by the bar. A smeared trail of spilt beer led to a pile of broken glass that glittered in the corner. The spill that Bill was working on looked dark, like blood, but it might have been the lighting. Zane felt the bullet whiff his hair again.

"Looks like you had a mishap," he said.

"Some asshole got out of line."

Zane stepped around the mess and made for the door.

* * *

Melissa lived in a basement apartment with pipes running across the ceiling and small windows that opened onto the parking lot of a medical walk-in clinic. The view from the windows, slightly above eye level, was of car tires and the worried feet and ankles of people who found themselves suffering from something they feared was more serious than the flu. After dark, it was necessary to draw the curtains to avoid being put on display, because as Melissa explained, being put on display on your own terms was one thing, but you had to draw the line somewhere. It was a matter of control.

Melissa shared this happy space with another woman, named Marilou, who also danced for Barker. On discovering this fact, Zane felt he had uncovered the truth of several others.

"I thought your roommate's name was Clarissa."

"I said she went by Clarissa, not that her *name* was Clarissa. You can't dance with a name like Marilou unless you're going for men with a thing for farm girls from Kansas. Or you want to do some kind of Gilligan's Island act. And in that case you need a Ginger."

"I think Gilligan's Island was Mary-Anne."

Melissa waved a hand in the air.

"Don't tell me about your fetishes. The point is, Marilou wants to appeal to a wider audience."

We are successful because we bring diverse product offerings to the marketplace. Everyone you meet, it seems, has a business strategy.

Marilou herself was splayed on the couch, reading. She looked not in the least like a farm girl from Kansas, although Zane had to admit that he was relying solely on stereotype, and his actual experience of Kansan farm girls was nil. In place of denim overalls or cut-off jeans, Marilou wore pyjama pants and a tank top that, in keeping with the current fashion, was many sizes too small. She had long, blonde hair that she wore in a simple, straight style, but dark roots and her dark eyebrows, one of which was pierced, betrayed her. A pierced and tattooed navel peeked out from under the tank top.

She paused a moment, as if to finish a sentence, and then looked up and turned the book face-down in her lap. Zane checked the cover out of curiosity; it was an old paperback copy of *The Edible Woman*.

"So you're the photographer."

"I am. And you're the roommate."

Marilou made no movement beyond the musculature of her jaw, working on a stick of chewing gum.

"How's the book?"

"It's pretty good."

"Don't get into that," said Melissa. She walked away.

"I never liked Margaret Atwood," said Zane.

Marilou fixed him with a look of withering contempt. Apparently his stock was falling. To probable pervert, we now add certified dolt.

"You wouldn't. You're a man."

"I take it you're some kind of feminist?"

"Like it's a dirty word."

"I get paid to be curious," he said.

She rolled her eyes, turned the book back over and went back to reading. She muttered something under her breath. Zane thought he heard *exploitive male*.

"How do you square that with your job?"

With exaggerated movements, Marilou again inverted the book in her lap and glared at Zane.

"How do you mean?"

"I mean being a feminist and being a stripper. Isn't that kind of oil and water?"

"What's wrong with being a stripper?"

"Nothing. I just – "

"So it's feminists you have a problem with?"

She pushed her jaw forward as she spoke and arched her eyebrows in a dare.

"Apparently it's just one feminist in particular."

"Well, I reject your fuckin' value judgments. It's my body. What I do with it is up to me."

"I warned you," shouted Melissa, from the next room.

"I'm in control. Stripping is an expression of my empowerment."

"I'm not sure I buy that one."

"I don't care if you buy it or not. Your masculine value judgments are just another way of denying our empowerment. Just another way to control us."

"I see."

"Yeah. I highly doubt that."

Marilou had refused to sign on for his story. Melissa had quoted Marilou as saying, anyone wants to take my picture better pay me. Zane now suspected that this was paraphrased from a longer speech containing the words *exploitation* and *male*.

"Well," he said. "It was nice meeting you." He summoned his most obnoxious smile; she rolled her eyes and turned back to her book. You can't win them all. Or, in fact, any.

Zane joined Melissa in the kitchen, a white-tiled room smaller than his bathroom, cramped by the stove, refrigerator and countertop. He had brought his old Leica rangefinder, dug out from the boxes in the corner, and two lenses, a twenty-eight and a twenty-one. Given the tight quarters, he'd only need the twenty-one. He threaded the ultrawide onto the lens mount.

"Shit, Zane, that thing looks about four hundred years old."

"More like twenty." He loaded a roll of film, snapped the base plate back into place and closed the film door. Not even film loading could be convenient on the Leica. "And I'm shooting this in black and white, too."

"Why not try cave painting?"

"There's technical reasons, to do with lighting."

"Your cave's too dark to paint in?"

"There's a thing called colour temperature. It's complicated."

For which we have white balance. But there was the smell of film and the feel of working with it, the alchemy of development, the control and the sense of serendipity when control lapsed. And something else, too, something that Zane couldn't quite pin down. It had that dramatic look.

"So what do I do?"

"Nothing. Do what you normally do."

"Like what?"

"Pretend I'm not even here."

"So . . . ."

"Just do stuff."

Zane favoured the direct approach: get the camera into the subject's face early and often, until eventually the wide-angle lens becomes an accepted feature of your victim's personal space, as mundane as a wristwatch or a light bulb. The first three rolls are a warm-up. Soon, having one's portrait shot from a distance of two feet becomes as normal as breathing, the lens just another feature of the room.

"Just do stuff," she said.

So Zane shot her looking doubtfully into the lens from eighteen inches away. The distance and the lens would make her look like the bubble head in his apartment's peephole, but she didn't need to know that. You keep on pushing until she writes you off as part of the background, like the sound of water gurgling down the pipes overhead.

She stuck her tongue out at him. Do what you normally do: she started picking dishes from the sink and piling them on the counter. When the sink was empty she squirted detergent in it with the water running, and started scrubbing at the sink. Then she plugged the drain and slid the dirty dishes into the growing mound of suds.

Zane shot eight nondescript frames of Melissa with her hands in the sink. The overhead light played in the suds that stuck to her arms. A strand of hair fell from behind her ear and tickled her face, and in brushing it aside she left a smear of suds on her cheek; he made sure to get that shot.

"It's okay," she said. "I'll dry."

"Just act like I'm not here."

"How convenient for you."

She tested her work by rubbing a finger against a plate until it squeaked, and then put the plate in the rack.

"Why d'you want pictures of me washing the dishes, anyway?"

"It is my duty to record this domestic scene for posterity. One day, historians may be curious as to how a porn star obtained clean dishes. Mine may be the only visual record."

"Porn star."

Melissa shook her head and continued scrubbing. Perhaps not the wisest choice of words.

"Shit, Zane, you were a famous photographer, right? You could be taking pictures of Nicole Kidman washing her dishes."

"Nobody will ever care how those people obtain clean dishes."

"Yeah, right."

The possible outcomes of letting Melissa believe that he found her more interesting than Nicole Kidman were not to be considered. He went back to the viewfinder and carefully photographed her washing a plate and then placing it in the rack.

"You a big fan of Nicole Kidman?"

114

"Just a movie fan."

She pulled the plug and let the water drain from the sink, then took a dishtowel from the stove and wiped the suds off her arms.

"When I was a kid I loved to go to the movies and imagine I was one of the people in the story."

Everybody does that, but we all like to think we're unique.

"You could do that," he said.

"What?"

"Movies. I mean, you can act."

"Shit, Zane, you know how many actors there are in this city? There's twenty actors for every fuckin' part."

"Have you done a lot of auditions?"

"I haven't done any fuckin' 'auditions.' The best I'd ever do is a bit part in some shitty dinner theatre production of *South Pacific*. Fuck that. I make good money from Rich."

"That doesn't bother you?"

"What?"

"Giving up."

"Just take your stupid pictures."

Melissa turned to the dish rack and started drying the dishes. Zane let her get back to it, then resumed taking pictures until he finished the roll.

"It doesn't bother you, settling for less."

She stopped and looked at him for a moment.

"Why d'you have to ask all these questions?"

"You're the story."

"And you think I'm settling for less."

"What do you think?"

"I think you're full of shit."

She turned back to the sink, moved on to the pots and pans. Zane shot a few more frames, but the irritation on her face wasn't the look he was after.

"There's no 'settling for less.' There's what you can do, and what you can't do."

"And this is what you can do."

"It's not complicated. I get up in the morning and I go to work. I come home and I watch TV and go to sleep. I do the dishes, I grocery shop."

Zane said nothing.

"It's just a fuckin' job, man."

"Same like anyone," he said.

"Same like anyone. All that other shit is just dreams. Kid stuff."

"But not for Nicole Kidman."

"Shit, get real. That's like a whole other fuckin' planet."

She folded the dishtowel, staring up at the wall. Zane suspected that she didn't see the cracked blue paint or the grease splatters.

"But she got there."

"She got a lucky break."

"We make our breaks." You have small parts and small actors.

"You just don't get it, do you?"

He waited.

"You dream this big dream and then take that part in *South Pacific*, that's settling for less. I'm not settling for shit. I'm just doing a job. I'm just normal, man."

Zane experimented with framing. She finished the pots and put them away.

"Sorry to disappoint you," she said.

"I'm not disappointed."

She hung the dishtowel from the oven door handle.

"Anyway, Zane: when I'm famous like Nicole Kidman, I'll let you come visit me in my mansion in Beverly Hills. Your job will be to remind me of my humble roots."

"Deal."

Everyone knows California is full of the undead. One more vampire will hardly be noticed.

* * *

Zane burned film. He photographed Melissa eating her breakfast, cooking her supper, watching television. He shot her at the bus stop and on the subway and in the supermarket. He shot her with carrots, with breakfast cereal, with milk and with chicken. He made sure to cover all four food groups: a balanced diet.

Bill came off hiatus, got back in the swing of things, renewed his commitment to his art. He had rediscovered his muse. His work now possessed an urgent subtlety, its violence more frightening in understatement. The critics praised his mastery of subtext. At least, that was Barker's view of the matter. He sold pixels like cocaine crystals, thousands of grains to feed that jones. Business was good.

Zane shot Melissa's sardonic smile, shot her laugh, shot her stare lost in the middle distance. On a bus, he shot her with earbuds in her ears, ignoring him. She was angry.

Over time, the lens wears you down.

* * *

Do you want another drink, the waitress wants to know. In splashes of coloured light spilling down from the stage she looks to be in her mid-twenties, fair, with blonde hair falling around her bare shoulders. A heavy eastern European accent renders her all but incomprehensible through the pounding music. The sum of her clothing is a black miniskirt, over which she wears a black waitress apron. Pretty, perhaps, under different circumstances, pretty in that fragile Russian way. She slouched hips-forward in front of Zane, evidently thinking this a provocative pose. To Zane, she just looked bored.

"I'm fine." His drink was two-thirds empty.

"You want me to sit with you?"

"No, thanks."

"A table dance?"

"You're wasting your time."

A scowl. Whatever circumstances she might have been pretty under, these were definitely not. The hip jutted farther.

"You can't sit all night with one drink. This is the rule."

Not necessarily Russian. She could have come from anywhere east of the Polish border, any land of Slavic cheekbones.

"Rum and coke, then."

She looked at him, an insect, and then walked down two tables and struck up conversation with two men sitting there, lit up with smiles. Both of them about thirty, wearing goatees. Hard hands give them away, hands that build things. Roofs, walls, floors, concrete, brick. Something you said about a documentary being something constructed. You say stupid things when you get too smart. It wraps around on you. Zane's hands were soft and smooth.

Slavic cheekbones smiled and tilted her head. These were the two most interesting and attractive men she had ever met. Gentlemen, in fact; apparently they'd paid five bucks each for a couple more beers. First, a table dance. Things were looking up for everyone.

She cupped her breasts, looked coyly at them through her eyelashes, drooled a long string of saliva down onto her left nipple. One hand smeared it over her chest. She turned and bent over, smacked her buttocks, a wobbling shock wave like so much rubbery jello. She looked back at them and repeated the performance. Cheekbones notwithstanding, the effect was more bovine than erotic.

Zane shot the entire performance. A tricky proposition, likely to provoke a mishap of the sort Jade so detested. But you learn all kinds of tricks. In Somalia, Zane had left his camera slung around his neck and leaned his hand on the shutter button while he argued with rifle-toting teenagers, the clatter and roar of truck engines covering the whine of his motor drive. Here he had the Leica in his jacket pocket and an undesirable corner table beyond the pool of light around the stage. He shot under the table with the camera on his leg, used zone focusing, luck, experience, T-MAX pushed to 3200 and a lens made for night shooting. The fact of the matter is, no-one's here to watch you, anyway.

Melissa weaved among the tables toward Zane, made a face, and flopped into the seat beside him.

"That's it. I'm on my fuckin' break."

"How many breaks do you get?"

"Not this one. But far as anyone can see, I'm sitting here with a paying customer, doing my job."

"You're a hard-working girl."

"You better believe it, buster. I just had this table dance, this jerk kept pawing me."

Too bad you missed that. That was a picture.

"That must have been very nice for you."

"Not now, Zane. Please."

"I thought they kicked you out for that kind of thing."

"Shit, Zane, you believe that? What they say is a long, long way from the real world."

He shot a vertical of her, the camera concealed behind the table, worried in the back of his mind about keystoning. You can correct it in the printing. It was a good shot.

"You okay?"

"Don't."

She looked away. He watched the stage show, the same show he had seen fifteen minutes before, an hour before, two hours before. Only the faces changed. It could be the same dancer, a thousand masks.

Coming back from Jerusalem he had a painful cab ride in from the airport with a driver who never stopped talking. He was about fifty and he kept repeating the same words: to me, it's just another shaved pussy, you know? A hollow laugh follows. This man had discovered the Internet. You come back from the Holy Land and your plane descends into this.

The cab driver's mantra rang in his head. You're a creature of memory, the sum of your experience, and all the useless brain can drag up is it's just another shaved pussy, you know. One more good reason to take notes.

The dancer was about ready to drop her top, according to formula. Where x is duration of music, $3x/16 = $ show yer tits. There were fines for deviating from the plan. Someone had worked it out, studied the male attention span. Marilou could no doubt clarify this research.

In the crowd a voice yelled get on with it. The dancer had her halter untied, her best I-know-you-want-it look on her face, when a hand came out of the shadows and grabbed her ankle. She dropped it all, came down hard. In the shadows, a tidal surge as the bouncers closed in. The dancer got back to her feet, wobbly on high heels, blood trickling down her leg from a cut on her knee. A smile like an escaped psychiatric inmate.

"I need to put my feet up," said Melissa.

She put her feet on Zane's lap. Her heels were an inch higher than the limit of reason and of good taste. They looked dangerous. This is not the kind of thing you want in your lap. Also, Zane was disinclined to foot rubs.

The song had changed. According to formula, $x/2 = $ floor show. The dancer rolled onto her back and spread her legs, rolled again to face the other way. The cut on her knee continued to bleed and each maneuver smeared blood down her shin and calf and over the stage. Every move she made smeared the mess around. Everywhere you go there is always blood; there seems to be some message in this, but it doesn't bear decoding. In any case, the show must go on.

The waitress returned with his drink and he handed it off to Melissa. She sipped it through a straw, an act that struck Zane as entirely too childish for the surroundings.

"I saw you the other day, when I was dancing," she said. "That was kinda weird. Normally, you know, I don't see anyone. I just tune it all out."

She kept trying to sink the ice cubes with her straw, but they refused to stay sunk. In high school he had once got badly drunk and had tried to slide down a banister. The feat was beyond him sober. This had cost him a boxer's fracture to two fingers on his right hand. Walking to the hospital, he worked the two fingers, discovered he was almost too drunk to feel pain. Such amusement. Thinking of Melissa onstage he had much the same feeling. This time it wasn't the rum.

You won't be seeing yourself in the mirror anytime soon. Roland the Headless Leica Shooter. Count Noctilux of Transylvania.

"Thanks for the break," said Melissa.

"You made short work of that drink."

"It doesn't help to be sober 'round here."

She swung her feet down to the floor, adjusted her skirt and stood. Zane knocked back the rest of his rum.

"What're you doing after work, there, sweetie?"

"I'm going to take a long, long shower, and then I'm going to crash on my friend's couch. What did you have in mind, creep?"

"You better get back to work," said Zane. "And try to stick around this corner, if you can. I'm gonna need lots more pictures."

CHAPTER EIGHT

When Zane was eight, a pair of robins built a nest in the tree outside his bedroom window, and by chance a gap in the foliage allowed him a clear view. Connie called it no fair: she didn't get birds outside her window. Even migratory songbirds, apparently, were in on the conspiracy.

Zane borrowed his father's binoculars and when the eggs hatched he adopted the entire family, offering four updates each hour on his hatchlings' progress. After school, he dug worms out of the garden and left them at the base of the tree, on a dinner plate. It seemed a reasonable way to help out. Inexplicably, on finding the use to which her china had been put, Mrs. Zane did not agree.

Two days later he found the tail feathers of a robin on the garden walk, a puff of down, a scattering of rusty breast feathers. From his window he could see no birds on the nest. He fretted, checked again, threatened death to all cats. His mother checked, told him not to worry. His father shrugged.

That night, a bird was on the nest. The following day he sighted a robin in the yard, hunting worms. It did not fly away as he approached it, and on drawing closer he saw the dangling leg, the absence of tail feathers. He worried that the mother bird could no longer fly, but at dusk she flew up onto the fence rail where he saw the other robin feeding her. He ran to the kitchen to tell his mother, knocked a glass off the counter in his enthusiasm.

The following day, the birds were gone and the hatchlings dead. His mother helped him to bury them in the garden.

Life goes on. The neighbours always own a cat; you do what you can. You turn black potting soil into the earth, plant your hostas ringed with marigolds and impatiens, water daily. The neighbours' cat shits in the garden, uproots the flowers, rolls in the hostas. He toys with you, waits until you've finished planting to do the deed. You have a hose with a spray nozzle, but the cat is quick. When you run for the tap he hops the fence. He has a sense of humour. He plays with his kills.

One morning you open the front door to find half a mouse, its entrails trailing over your front step, his calling card, his mocking advertisement: dormice, fifty percent off.

* * *

Before he connected with Richard Barker, before he dropped out of sight, before the string of blown assignments that followed his announcement that he was through with wars, before Liberia, Zane went through a brief but intensely sentimental phase. He was on hiatus, in physiotherapy, adapting to his new restricted diet. To keep a steady income, he did some photo editing for the agency, and he put out a book. He was not busy.

He opened a gallery show in New York. Giant prints of his best-known photos hung on mid-toned walls under neutral spot lighting. The opening was wine and cheese, all-purpose little black dresses. People drifted through the gallery and said intelligent things: look at the lighting, consider the remarkable sensitivity, isn't it extraordinary the composition. A critic in one of the papers wrote of people drinking wine and laughing between walls covered with blood and despair, people talking about art in the midst of mayhem. He called the audience pretentious and he called Zane a vampire. Zane read the review and threw it out with the rest of the paper and pretended that he didn't care. All he'd really done, he said, was collapse the critic's sense of distance.

That opening was also his book launch. He liked that expression, book launch, liked the connotation of ships sliding down slipways amidst explosions of champagne. But the *Titanic* had a launching of its own, and Zane's first printing went to remainders.

Don't let it bother you, said Jack. They all go to remainders, unless you're dressing babies up as eggplants.

Zane liked babies dressed as eggplants, in his sentimental phase. He liked the flowery sentiment of the cards he had received in hospital, of the poster of a kitten hanging from a branch in the physiotherapist's waiting room: hang in there! All of us fluffy kittens. We've sure got guts!

At home, he cried over television commercials for long-distance telephone service. The daughter off at college phones home on mother's day: Mom, I got accepted into med school! Mother calls father in from the garage, where he's been tinkering at restoring his MG-A, says, our little girl is going to be a doctor. Look at this photo; do you remember when she was just an eggplant? Our own little aubergine! Mother and daughter alike wipe away heartfelt tears of pride and joy. Father smiles indulgently, inflates with pride. Zane, on the couch, blubbers like a halfwit.

Eventually, he had to give up watching television. He couldn't keep up his supply of tissues. Also, Jack asked him to see a therapist. It was the eggplants, above all, that Jack found disturbing.

* * *

Zane stood at the kitchen sink and drained the developing tank, keeping his hand over the opening to keep the spools from falling out, cold water running out between his fingers. He let the first spool slide out into his hand and put the tank down on the counter, and then caught the end of the film with a fingernail and pulled it out of its cage. The shining black ribbon twisted and shone in the window light. Melissa pressed in at his elbow. He held it to the light, and she squinted at it.

"I can't see a thing."

"That's you doing the dishes."

"If you say so. All this messing around with lost arts."

"It's not a lost art."

Zane snapped weighted clips onto each end and took the film into the bathroom. He picked up a spray bottle from the counter beside the sink and held the film over the bathtub while he sprayed it down with diluted wetting agent. In school they learned to use squeegees but he found this led to scratches. You develop your favoured routines. He hung the film over the bathtub and went back out to the kitchen.

He lifted the second reel from the tank, rolled the film off the reel in a long, shining black strip, water dripping on the kitchen tiles. Three dozen moments preserved in metallic silver. Immortality by way of the philosopher's stone. Visual permanence, at least. If not immortality, the closest thing to it.

"Are they any good?"

"I don't know yet."

He handed her the strip of film with his left hand and stepped aside, picked up his camera from the counter. He shot her twice, peering at the film with the window light washing over her face. After the second frame she turned and raised an eyebrow at him.

"And how are pictures of me looking at your pictures going to be part of this story?"

"I don't know yet."

"Do you know anything?"

"How many of the usual photos did you ever want to look at?"

"That's different."

"There you go, then."

"There I go what?"

"I don't know yet."

She rolled her eyes at him and he took the film from her and hung it, and then unloaded the next spool.

Melissa reading the label of a jar of spaghetti sauce, in the supermarket three blocks from her apartment; a young man with thin stubble along the line of his jaw pretends not to appraise her out of the corner of his eye while his girlfriend buys rotini and an overweight woman in her late thirties recedes into the background. How a porn star obtained spaghetti sauce in the early years of our benighted century; or, I'm just another ordinary girl.

Sometimes, when Zane looked at old photographs, he found himself beset by a sadness he could not quite grasp, a certain melancholic restlessness of mood. A feeling of autumn. It was in the work of the usual suspects, in Walker Evans and Dorothea Lange. It was in anonymous blurred birthday snapshots and class photos, in wartime regimental photos whose panoramic sweep of khaki uniforms resolved on closer examination into doomed rows of youthful, nameless faces. Faces in silver prints smile forever after, none of them realizing that everything photographed, in a sense, is already dead. Photographs persist to haunt us, like ghosts.

Zane had this sense again as he lifted the negatives up to the light. And he regretted saying that he didn't know if they were any good. In a certain light even the most ordinary moment is ineffably beautiful. Zane just wanted to find that light.

"Did a goose just walk over your grave?"

"What?"

"It's what my grandmother used to say: did a goose just walk over your grave?"

Geese don't fuck with the undead. There's no grave to walk over.

"I was just thinking, you're immortal now."

"What's that? Me eating my immortal breakfast?"

"That's metallic silver you're looking at. These pictures are still going to be around long after you're dead. You're immortal."

"So when are you gonna make these into real pictures?"

Immortality didn't much impress her.

"Print them, you mean?"

"Whatever."

"Most of them, never."

"So what's the point?"

"You just take a lot of pictures and try to get some good ones."

"But you don't know if they're any good."

"When I get a good one, I'll know. I'll make you a print."

126

He pulled out the next reel, unspooled the film, and held it up to the window. Lights as black orbs emanate darkness, Melissa's face a pool of darkness ringed by bright hair, her eyes two bright points. Melissa at the sink in her dismal basement apartment, washing the dishes, watching television, eating breakfast cereal, clearing away Marilou's debris, waiting for the bus. He sprayed the film down and hung it.

Dressing room shots from the club: Melissa half-naked, alternatively laughing and looking tired. Mostly looking tired. Close-ups of drug paraphernalia, parts of costumes, pictures pinned inside locker doors. None of them pictures of men. Pictures of kids or friends or places where people would rather be. Some, he could never publish. Not the kids, certainly. None showed any faces save Melissa's.

Melissa turned and opened the fridge. She opened a beer for him and put it on the counter while he sprayed down the film and hung it to dry.

"What I need is a picture of you with your friends."

"Shit, Zane, you just don't get it, do you?"

"What?"

"You are my fuckin' friends."

He fished the last reel out of the tank and pulled off the film, looked at it closely. Unspectacular. He sprayed it down, hung it with the others. What he needed was a proper drying cabinet.

"Yeah," she said. "I didn't think you'd have anything to say to that."

He rinsed off the tank and reels and stood them on the counter to dry. He put the chemicals away in the cupboard and then wiped the counter down with a cloth. He had nothing. He needed to find that certain light.

* * *

You have to keep believing. In the face of all the evidence, you just have to go on trying to reinvent yourself.

The following week, Bill's renewed sense of commitment expired. He gave up on understatement, abandoned subtlety, slipped back into overacting. In short, he punched a woman in the face, three times. He gave no reason. It did not occur to Zane to ask for one. The woman in question was Melissa.

Zane didn't see it happen. The mirror was up. He heard a dull wet thud and a shriek. The mirror came back down and the frame was empty. He lowered the camera to see what was going on. Then things got confusing.

In Croatia Zane saw four people shot, four civilians, two women and two men. They scuttled around a corner and the troops opened up with AKs, chips of brick and mortar dust flying off the wall behind them. They all went down and the soldiers broke cover. One of the four, a woman in a bright green sweater, was still moving. Blood blackened her sweater just above the kidney and she reached out with one hand, fingers opening and closing, grasping for something that wasn't there. One of the soldiers walked up and kicked her, his rifle dangling carelessly from his right hand, kicked her in the ribs like a soccer ball and Zane heard the dull thud of leather into ribcage carry across the street as he took the picture.

Bill wore that uniform now. Zane pushed himself up and Bill hit her a third time and Zane took two quick steps and hit him with his camera and he went down. He hit the floor like a slab of beef. Zane kicked at his face, missed, kicked him twice in the ribs (there's your payback) and then Barker pushed him back, shouting at him. He wanted to kick Bill in the face, see blood and teeth fly, wanted to see the skull implode like a suburban jack-o-lantern after Hallowe'en, wanted to kick him until his breathing stopped. Barker shouted again and Zane pushed him, hard, and he fell. His jaw clenched so tight the muscles hurt.

Melissa sat backed against the wall, knees up, face full of blood. Blood ran from her nose and from a cut over her eye, the eye socket already swelling closed. Blood spattered her knees and chest as she breathed. Jade tried to talk to her and she screamed back to fuck off, go away, leave me alone. Barker was up off the floor now, yelling something and Zane turned and realized that Barker was yelling at him.

"Are you fucking crazy?"

"Fuck off," said Zane. His guts jumped, twisted, knotted. No butterflies here. Instead, three angry weasels fighting over a bloody lump of raw meat.

"You're telling me to fuck off?"

"Fuck off."

"I don't believe it."

"Believe it."

He picked up Melissa's robe. Barker yelling, Jade shouting let it go, let it go. Barker yelling now at Bill, Bill on all fours, shaking his head to clear it. Zane wanted to kick him again, to get his foot into his face, split his mouth and break his nose. He wanted combat boots, steel toes, hobnails. Teeth breaking like bone china under the poll of a single-bit axe.

He went to Melissa and helped her up and put the robe around her and shepherded her to the door. Blood ran down her face, stained her robe. Her hands were wet with it.

Why is my life so filled with blood?

"You get her cleaned up and get your ass back in here," said Barker.

Zane said nothing. He wanted to be gone before Bill's head cleared. He got Melissa into the bathroom and started the water in the sink and wet a fresh face cloth and used it to wipe the worst of the blood off her face. Then he handed her a towel.

"Get cleaned up. I'll get your clothes."

She had left her street clothes neatly folded on the chair in the changing room. Zane checked that his hands were not covered in blood and then picked them off the chair and went back to the bathroom door and knocked at it.

Melissa had cleaned off the blood but her nose and the cut over her eye were still bleeding, the eye now swollen almost shut, her upper lip puffy and split. With one hand she held a wad of toilet paper to her nose, while with the other she wiped at the cut over her eye.

"You'll want to put pressure on that."

She just looked at him.

"Wipe at it like that, it'll just keep on bleeding."

She stopped wiping at the cut and let it ooze.

"There's no fuckin' bandages. That fuckin' asshole."

"We need to get the hell out of here."

She put down the wad of toilet paper, now stained a dark, heavy red, and started pulling on her clothes.

"Is my nose broken?"

"Doesn't look to be. Get your shirt on. I don't want to stick around."

"And you think I do?"

In the studio Bill had put on his shorts and now sat on a chair, holding a hand towel to his head. A dark stain spread over the towel where it touched his scalp, and trickles of blood had run down from his hair, over his neck and into the teeth of the tattooed shark. Murder lay coiled in his eyes.

"You're gonna wish you hit me with something heavier," he said.

"Maybe I will."

"That's enough," said Jade. She had blood on her hands. The blood was drying, getting sticky. She held her hands away from her clothes, fingers apart. Jade was fresh out of latex gloves. What we had here was a mishap of the first order.

Barker looked up as Melissa walked in, took up his seat at the desk, opened the drawer and took out the bottle. He asked if she was okay.

"Do I look okay?"

"We'll take care of you. Have a seat."

Melissa didn't move. Zane picked up his camera bag and slung it over his shoulder, keeping his camera in his right hand and one eye on Bill and trying to stay between Melissa and Barker. His stomach had started again. The weasels had found a new scrap to fight over.

He tried to strike a conversational tone: "We're out of here."

"I want to talk to you."

"Call me tomorrow." Zane opened the door and held it for Melissa, without turning his back on Bill.

"Melissa, I want to talk to you, too." Iron in his voice.

"Then call her tomorrow."

"It's just a misunderstanding here," said Jade.

"I think we all understand perfectly."

"We should talk this out. Let's not blow this all out of proportion."

"I'll decide what's out of proportion."

Zane backed through the door and then put his hand in the small of Melissa's back and marched her down the hall. The streetlights had come on and glowed orange with light still in the sky. He made for the hospital without asking. The cut was going to need stitches. Eyebrows like a hockey player, a career minor-league scrapper. They drove for several blocks before Melissa spoke.

"I never took you for a tough guy."

She dabbed at her nose. It was still oozing. Blood had dripped onto her shirt. She essayed a smile but it came off hollow.

"I'm not."

"You sure took care of Bill."

"I hit him from behind. You know what that camera weighs?"

"Did you bust your camera?"

"I don't know."

She twisted, reached for the back seat where he had dropped the camera, and held it up for him to see. Blood and hair was stuck to the tripod plate and the polycarbonate body was cracked.

"Looks like it's fucked," he said. And Bill's skull is probably fractured. Zane felt badly about the camera.

"That sucks."

"It's insured."

She twisted again to put the camera back. Blood matted her eyebrow. He heard her trying to breathe around the wad of tissue she still held to her nose.

"You okay?"

"I'm okay." She inspected the tissue, drew a long breath and put it back to her nose. "Mind if I crash at your place?"

"Of course." He almost added something goofy, *mi casa es su casa*, decided not. He straightened in his seat, tried both hands on the wheel. Ten and two.

"I'm sorry. I'm making a mess of your car."

"It's already a mess."

After a few minutes, she inspected the tissue again. The bleeding had stopped. She looked for a garbage bag, found none, held the crumpled tissue in her hand.

"I want to go home."

"It's okay. I'll take the couch."

"No, I mean home home. Vancouver. I want to go home."

A half a block passed under the tires.

"Good idea, probably."

"Tonight. I want to go home tonight. I want to go back to my place and pack, and then I want you to take me to the train station, and I'm going home."

"You need a hospital."

"No, I want to go now. I want to get the fuck out of here."

The air vibrates with desperate harmonics. You better be careful. Let her get her stuff, and then take her down to the ER for stitches. By the time she gets out of there, all she'll want to do is sleep.

"Okay," he said.

* * *

Marilou sat on the couch with the lights off, the blue television light shifting and flexing around her. Men, she said; fuck. You get these creeps and stalkers. At night, you look up from the TV, there's this blue disembodied face leering at your window. Ever since that one time, they'd kept the curtains closed. The good thing in the basement was bars on the windows. You didn't want to be on the ground floor.

Melissa finished packing inside twenty minutes: a bathroom bag, some clothes stuffed into a gym bag, an old knapsack. Everything else stayed. Sell it to cover the rent, she said.

"What about your spider plant?" said Zane.

"I was the one watered that thing anyway," said Marilou. She hugged Melissa, said take care of yourself. Little late for that, Melissa said, and she hugged her again. She compressed her lips but couldn't hide the trembling of her chin.

Zane picked up her bags, shifted his weight from one foot to the other, put the bags down again. Women: all this emotion, everything a blubberfest. He'd long since forgotten his long distance ads, his affection for eggplants.

"You take care," said Melissa. "I'll call you when I can."

Zane took Melissa's bags, loaded them in the car. She got in, fastened her seat belt, stared fixedly through the windscreen. He put the key in the ignition, hesitated a moment, and then started the engine. The familiar rush of clattering valves.

"You sure about this?"

"I'm sure."

"That eye needs stitches."

"Just drive me where I want to go. Please."

He paused before pulling out onto the street, hand on the turn signal, then pulled out quickly. He neglected to check his blind spot.

"Where are you going?"

"My place."

"I told you, I want to go now. I don't want to wait for morning."

"I need to get my stuff."

"What stuff?"

"My stuff. You're not taking the train."

He drove with his left hand on top of the wheel, moved his right up from the gearshift to rest on his leg.

"Shit, Zane, don't be stupid."

"I'm not. I'll drive you."

"To Vancouver."

"To Vancouver. I'm fucked if I'm letting my story get on a train to Vancouver."

She looked away, through the windshield, and shook her head. After a moment she looked back at him.

"You sure about this?"

"Are you?"

"I'm going home. Where you think you're going?"

"Vancouver."

"You got a job. You answered an ad, remember?"

"You think I want to see Bill after he's got over his headache?"

She shook her head again, said okay then.

Zane packed one small bag and his essentials: the Leica, lenses, film, notebooks and developing paraphernalia. On impulse, he dug in his unopened boxes and packed his book. For Melissa. He was ready in fifteen minutes. Zane travelled light.

He made her sit and went into the bathroom and found some cotton swabs and the last of the disinfectant. Above her left eye the cut was deep and the swelling held it open. He found a cotton ball and dabbed disinfectant on it. She pushed his hand away and he told her to grow up.

"That's a bad cut. He must have got you with his ring." ·

"I'm not going to the hospital," she said.

Fair enough. What you need is a proper first aid kit, like you used to carry, tincture of benzoin and some wound closure strips. Even then it's like patching her up with tape. The valuables get smashed, the silver gets stolen, your books get torn up. You do what you can, but you know nothing's ever going to be the same. At the very least, you know this one's going to leave a scar.

Part Two

CHAPTER NINE

I see you're asleep.

In the soft grey light of the early morning, somewhere up past Sault Ste. Marie, coasting along the north shore of Lake Superior under an unbroken grey sky and a thin, incessant drizzle. On the right, forested hills, pine needles dripping onto wet ferns; on the left, the vast, pewter expanse of the big lake.

I remember reading somewhere that ferns are among the oldest plants on earth, and that pines came along long before broad-leafed trees. We could have slipped out of time to find ourselves here, could have slipped back to prehistory, violated fundamental laws of physics and somehow cut our moorings. The anchor dragging in the night, you wake up lost and out of sight of land. But this road cutting the landscape, these speed limit signs, fast-food wrappers and discarded pop cans: all this refuse places us in our own tarnished century. Lucky us.

I'm getting tired, kiddo. I feel worn thin, worn out, a watch spring winding down. The whole world is closing down, falling away from the sun, a planet tired of its orbit. The lights are going out all over Europe – who was it said that? They will not be lit again in our lifetime. They just keep on winking out. One minute you're alive and the next is nothing. Gone. And if we died now, nobody would notice, except the highway crew responsible for cleaning up the mess.

I just feel like my part is done, and in the end it all amounted to jack-shit. You strut and fret your hour upon the stage and it comes down to this. Maybe I've just been driving too long. Maybe I just need to find a place to stop.

See what happens when you go to sleep?

And look at you: one eye black and swollen shut, blood still around your nostrils and in your eyebrow. And I think this is the first time I've ever seen you quiet. But maybe I'm making that up. Maybe that just makes a better story.

You look so young. Strange to think that you can't remember a world without microwave ovens and personal computers and cellular telephones. You're too young to remember any of that. Too young to remember the Bomb. We don't even think about the Bomb anymore. Even the word now seems silly, a capital-B bomb that makes everyone capital-D dead. To you, I guess, the Cold War is just a history lesson. And I somehow doubt you're up on your history.

But I remember when the Wall came down. I was there when it happened. I was there when the Cold War ended. I remember the people hammering at it and pushing at it until it fell. I remember the soldiers looking on, unsure of what, if anything, they should do. I remember the dancing and the cheering, the delirium of victory. Because it was a victory, a great victory. And that particular victory will never be written up in thick serious books with campaign maps and biographies of its dead generals. But I was there, with my cameras. When you see some historical retrospective of it, when you see pictures from the end of the Dark Ages, some of those pictures are mine.

Someone said it was the end of history. Well, it wasn't.

I guess it wouldn't mean much to you, anyway. You can't understand what it meant to see that wall come down unless you lived through all that. Maybe you've seen a news report, when the anniversary rolled around, when people still cared. Maybe you learned about it in some high-school history course. But still, you wouldn't really understand it, you couldn't really feel all that it meant, unless you'd lived under the Bomb. Unless you lay awake late some night, thinking what you'd would do if the balloon went up, if the curtain went up. What you'd do if you heard the sirens sound, or if you'd even hear the sirens before the warheads hit. Whether you would see it coming. Whether you would do it the quick way, and simply walk out into the street to be incinerated, or if you'd die in your basement like a coward.

And when the wall came down, all that was over. Sanity and human decency had finally prevailed. We all got a death-row pardon. And the focal point of it all, the point at which the whole evil mess collapsed into rubble, was that spontaneous celebration in Berlin, when we took down the wall. Because that crazy fucker Reagan didn't take down that wall, whatever they might tell you now. That senile bastard had nothing to do with it. We took that wall down ourselves.

I guess I must be rambling. You go ahead and sleep; I might as well tell you a story. It's a fairy tale. Once upon a time.

All through eighty-nine the big story was Eastern Europe. I was in Hungary that fall, where the Communists simply gave up and there was nothing to photograph. From Budapest I travelled back to the NATO side, to West Germany. The East German government was losing its grip. Things were tense. People with power don't let go so easy. We used to talk about the curtain going up, and I was thinking that if the curtain went up now, well, that would be my last war. No need to open the shutter to catch that flash.

You have to understand, in 1989 the East Germans were still shooting people who tried to get over the wall. In February that year, they shot a man eleven times for trying to get to the west. His name was Chris Gueffroy, and he was twenty-one years old. He bled to death in the border strip, by the Berlin Wall. The men who shot him got commendations. So this thing was by no means a slam dunk. Anything could happen.

The East Germans said they were opening travel to the west for those with proper visas, but the need for proper visas had been lost in translation. Everyone headed for the west. Berlin went crazy, huge lines backed up at the checkpoints. And there I was, stuck in a hotel in Bonn. I tried to get a flight to Berlin but everything was booked solid. No trains, no flights, no buses. So I bought a map and took whatever transportation I could find. I made the last leg by hitchhiking. A bunch of Danish students picked me up and I wedged myself in the back seat of this tiny car between two blonde girls, who were both a little drunk. After a few miles of this arrangement their boyfriends, in the front seat, weren't quite so happy anymore.

I said, why are you going all the way to 4Berlin, from Copenhagen.

The girl on my right had a clean, boyish look, short blonde hair and little makeup.

This is history, she said. A revolution. How could anyone miss that?

There's an old cliché in the news business about having a ringside seat to history. So I knew all about history. I'd seen a lot of history. History was my particular specialty, and one thing I'd learned early on was that history is best avoided. If you're smart, you ignore it, stick your head up out of your gopher hole at age eighty and ask what you missed. Chances are you didn't miss much.

I said, you aren't worried what might happen.

What could happen? Why would I worry?

What if there are riots? What if there's shooting?

She snorted. The other girl laughed.

She said, why would there be shooting? All that is over. You are a very silly man.

* * *

Berlin was madness, chaos, anarchy. Germans rushed to the city to join the revolution, students from all over Europe poured in to join the fun, parents brought their young children to witness history. All these people slept in the streets or in the homes of complete strangers, because there were no hotel rooms to be had. Shops flouted the law by refusing to close. Pubs gave away free beer. And nobody knew exactly what was happening, or why, just that everything had changed, that nothing would ever be the same.

I lost track of the Danes soon after we arrived. I was there to take pictures, and they weren't there to wait around for me. The streets were utter confusion and thanks to my inability to speak German I soon had no idea what was going on. Rumours flew in a half-dozen languages: the East Germans had moved tanks in around the wall, the police were arresting people who had crossed without papers, unification talks had begun, and so on. Lessons of the wars: ninety percent of all rumours are false, and the rest are just plain wrong. I went with the flow.

I made for Checkpoint Charlie with my cameras because the checkpoint itself was a symbol of the Cold War. It made for a good visual. This was a place with guard towers and barbed wire and men with machine guns, a serious place. People had been killed there. Ronald Reagan stopped to have his picture taken there. But now the guard towers were all empty and the barbed wire was torn down and the guards were all smiling with their guns slung across their backs. You didn't even need documents to get through. The guards just left the gates up.

Checkpoint Charlie was a street party. Musicians walked down to the border crossing and played for the crowd, and people sang and danced in the street. The crossing itself was jammed with cars and foot traffic. It took hours to get through. People waiting in line shut down their engines and got out of their cars and talked to each other. Berliners made coffee and sandwiches and they brought them down to the checkpoint and gave them to the people waiting there.

I photographed an East German family crossing through Checkpoint Charlie in a Trabi, a cheap and noisy East German car with a dirty exhaust, like something out of an old movie. As the Trabi passed through the checkpoint the crowd started to cheer. Mother smiled and laughed and Father rolled down his window and shouted something and gave the thumbs-up to the people gathered there, and his kids' faces were pressed against the glass in wonder, as if they were entering Santa's workshop. I caught the kids just like that, a wide-angle shot with the crowd cheering and the soldiers in the background, bemused and sheepish, another photographer leaning in to make his shot, and the German flag reflected in the glass of the window. You've probably seen the photo. It ran everywhere. It was in *Life* magazine's photos of the century.

But maybe you've never seen it at all.

* * *

By the late afternoon, people had lit fires in the streets to stay warm. I shot some photos of the scene, thinking that to look at the photos you would not be able to tell if this was a brave new world, or the Weimar Republic. Some of the shops and restaurants were still open and people were sharing food in the street, but now places were starting to close as they ran out of food. There were so many people out in the streets that traffic just stopped. Drivers just abandoned their cars where they stood.

The Potsdammerplatz was jammed. It was impossible to work in that crowd: thousands of people chanting and singing and pressing in to chip at the wall with hammers and crowbars and even stones, police looking on in sympathetic impotence. It hardly seemed possible that anyone could start shooting, and the crowd in any case was heedless. They wouldn't dare.

The Germans already had a name for the people chipping at the wall with hammers: wallpeckers. I wanted to get in close to the wall and get a shot of the wallpeckers at work, something that would make the signature shot for the story. I got in there and shot several frames of a man whaling away at it with a carpenter's hammer. After he chipped a hunk off the wall he held the hammer out to me, so I took it and whacked at the concrete a few times. When I looked up, the man was gone. Whacking the wall with a hammer felt better than taking pictures of other people doing it, but I still had a story to do. I passed the hammer on to the first man I saw and then shot him knocking chips off the wall with it.

Later, a man with a more serious weapon, a sledgehammer, succeeded in knocking a big hole through the wall, and I shot several frames of people reaching through the hole to shake hands with the East German guards. Then a group of young men started pulling at the remains of the slab and succeeded in pulling the whole thing down. The crowd surged clear as it began to topple, like a stone falling in water, revealing two teen-aged East German soldiers in ill-fitting *feldgrau*. The crowd cheered madly and the soldiers just stood there and smiled sheepishly, with their rifles slung, clearly unsure of what they were supposed to do.

Towards evening, construction equipment moved in from the East German side and knocked down a big section of the wall. Every time a slab fell, the crowd erupted in cheers. People began setting off fireworks, with no fear of provoking shooting. The police simply watched. I shot some frames of police and soldiers from both sides trading caps and badges as souvenirs. None of them ever wanted to fight each other, anyway.

When the big slabs fell, people surged through the gap and hugged strangers and danced. Bottles of cheap wine passed from hand to hand and empty bottles rolled underfoot. There was broken glass all over the place. People climbed up on the hoods and roofs of parked cars to get a better view, danced on the cars.

Autobody shops getting rich. Some people climbed on top of the wall and stood there, which only days earlier would have got them shot.

I tried to photograph it all, but I couldn't keep steady and I couldn't get a clear shot. I was reduced to making the Hail Mary shot, where you put on a wide-angle lens and hold the camera up in the air and just keep shooting in the vague and desperate hope of getting something publishable. At one point, someone began to spray the crowd with champagne, which ruined my thirty-five to seventy zoom. There was champagne all over the glass and it was hell to clean it. Eventually, I just wrote that one off.

* * *

When the light started to go I moved back from the wall, where things were calmer, and I found a family from the East sitting on the curb eating oranges. They couldn't get oranges at home, so when they saw a bag in a shop, they bought it. The kids, a boy and a girl, about six and eight, sat on the curb and feasted on them, their hands and faces sticky with the juice. It must have played hell with their digestion, but that was a problem for tomorrow. I knelt in the street and made several frames of those kids, eating their oranges. I think those were the happiest pictures that I ever took.

When the sun went down I found a place to stay in a mechanic's garage, where the owner had set out some cots. I gave up my cot for a young woman who was heavily pregnant. Everyone had told her that she shouldn't go to Berlin in her condition, but she had ideas of her own. Those ideas caught up to her just before midnight, and one of her friends was sent out into the night to find a doctor. By one in the morning, with a medical student in attendance, she had given birth to a healthy baby boy right there in the garage, among the patient, half-assembled automobiles, the silent toolboxes, the drip pans sheened with oil. I took a photo of her with the baby before she was taken off to the hospital, and I promised to track her down and give her a copy. But I was never able to find her. It was as if I had dreamed it.

It was all over when you were just a little kid. The Cold War was over. History was over. War was over. Nobody understood how. It just happened, because enough people thought they could do it, and thought that if enough people did it, nobody could stop them. And right then, in Berlin with the daylight fading into deep blue, we all believed the nukes could be beaten into radioactive ploughshares and that we could stop poverty and we could save this rotten planet. The world really could be a better place. And people hugged each other in the street and cried with happiness, and I sat on the pavement taking pictures and wishing that I owned all the oranges in the world, if only so that I could give them all away.

That was how it all seemed, for a few days in November. But people forget that the year of Europe's great revolution was also the year that Slobodan Milosevic was elected in Yugoslavia. You can rack up all the debts you like, but sooner or later, you have to pay the bill.

And I guess the surest sign I'm getting old is expecting you to think that all this matters somehow. That's the self-importance you get into with nostalgia. You make the mistake of thinking that all your memories could actually amount to something more than a hill of shit.

Anyway, you're beginning to stir.

CHAPTER TEN

T he next gas station, oasis of the endless highway: two ancient pumps and a sign on a rust-scabbed pole, white paint flaking off the metal and red-brown stains weeping from the scabs. A small shop, set back from the road. A row of cars, half-cannibalized, rusting at the edge of the woods. The gas gauge reads below a quarter tank, hunger eats at your belly, Melissa complains that she needs to pee. It's about time.

We'll stop at the next gas station. An unwelcome image arises of Zane's own self as parent to a sticky-faced child with a road-swollen bladder. Stop that right now, young lady, or you can get out and walk. When Zane was eight, his father made that same old threat, carried through with it over his mother's angry protests, left him bawling at the side of the highway. Abandonment hit him like a deboning knife. The car was back in five minutes but it did nothing to heal Zane's hurt or to stop the attendant tears. Shut up, said his father. Did you really think I would just leave you there? Five full minutes of maternal rage had already flensed Zane senior to the nerve endings. The rest of the trip passed in silence.

Later, Zane understood that his father would have laid a charge of child endangerment against any other parent for abandoning an eight-year-old by the roadside, whatever the reason, and he threw the incident back at his father in a teenaged fight best forgotten but never quite forgiven. Twenty years later you discover a more truthful perspective but it's too late to take back what's gone before. When the glaciers melt and retreat they don't leave you much.

Zane signalled to turn into the gas station and Melissa commandeered the rear-view mirror, ran a careful hand over her face, felt the puffy eye and swollen lips, the blood matted in her eyebrow, the bridge of her nose now verified as approximately straight. Her first sight of the damage, as he'd refused to let her use the mirror while he was driving. An experimental fingertip explored bared teeth, searching for chips, then pressed against her upper incisors. This, presumably, was painful. There appeared to be some give. She rubbed her good eye and groaned.

"My whole face hurts."

Not much you can say to that. Zane pulled in beside the pumps and killed the engine.

A boy in his late teens issued from the shop, ducked his head and lifted the hood of his yellow rain slicker against the drizzle. He walked to the driver's side window. Long blond hair falling out from under his hood, pimples. Zane cranked down the window, thought of the chattering valves and asked him to check the oil while he was at it. He popped the hood release and cranked the window most of the way closed, to keep the rain out. As the kid lifted the hood, he tried not to stare at Melissa's face, and failed.

Zane paid in cash and then parked the car at the edge of the lot, beside a rusted-out pickup with flat, cracked tires, its windshield an opaque network of cracks, no glass in the driver's-side window. He stepped out into the rain and splashed through the puddles to the shop. Inside, he raided the shelves: two bags of chips, a bag of peanuts, four bottles of fruit juice, two cans of pop and a loaf of bread.

"Breakfast of champions," he said.

The attendant nodded and failed to smile.

Zane found a small, flat tin of Aspirins, then checked the rest of the first aid shelf and picked out some small bandages, a pair of tiny scissors, and a bottle of disinfectant. On impulse, he picked out a pair of cheap sunglasses and added them to the pile. The kid worked the cash register wordlessly. Zane paid and took the bag and the bathroom key, and the bell over the door tinkled at him as he walked out into the drizzle.

He dug the Aspirin and disinfectant out of the bag and handed them to Melissa with the bathroom key. She took her bag and ran for the bathroom. She'd neglected to pack a jacket. While he waited, Zane ate two slices of bread and drank half a bottle of juice, standing beside the car in the drizzle for the opportunity to stretch his legs. He checked his cellphone. It was coming on for eight, too early to get Jack, who worked on New York hours. You finally have a story, and it has to wait.

Melissa emerged wearing a clean shirt and made a face as she walked by, heading for the store. He waved at her to stop but she ignored him and went in. He checked his cellphone again: time's a-wasting. Presently, Melissa returned bearing two cups of coffee.

"At least I think of the essentials."

"Let's take a look at that cut."

He took her coffee from her and set it on the hood.

"I walked in there, first thing that kid did was ask if he should call the cops. I had to convince him you were my dad come to rescue me from a bad boyfriend."

"Did you actually put disinfectant on that?"

"He's a sweet kid. He woulda done anything for me."

"Fluttered your eyelashes at him, did you?"

"I can't flutter shit right now."

She flinched as he dabbed at the cut with the disinfectant. The cut was angry and deep and the swelling held it open.

"Hold still. You don't want this to get infected."

"So it seems you don't inspire much confidence."

There was no question that the cut needed stitches.

"Anyway, I convinced him," she said.

"Why do you do that?"

"Do what?"

This demanded delicacy. The effort defeated him. "Lie."

"You walk around with a face like this, people ask questions."

"What's wrong with the truth?"

"Who's gonna believe the truth?"

He dabbed with the disinfectant again and she winced.

"You want to explain all this to the cops? Shit, Zane, you got guilt written all over you."

He put the cap back on the disinfectant and she made to get back in the car, but he stopped her. He opened two of the small bandages and used the scissors to cut them down to form makeshift butterfly sutures, and then carefully pressed the cut closed, stuck the bandages in place and leaned back and raised her chin to look at his handiwork. Closed evenly, at least: good enough. If you get lucky it might not leave a scar. He found the sunglasses and put them on her face and appraised the result. Her hair was damp with the drizzle. The cut and his makeshift sutures still showed, and the sunglasses failed to hide the bruising.

"You really look like hell."

"You're so sweet."

"We should really get a doctor to look at that."

"Next town."

"And we should really think about calling the cops."

"The cops never do shit anyway."

She rummaged in her knapsack and took out a few things and threw them in the back seat of the car. Then she picked up the bandage wrappers and the empty plastic bag and Zane's juice bottle and she walked to the trash can and dropped the knapsack into it.

"Stuff best forgotten," she said.

Fair enough, he thought. You should have had your camera out, should have caught that on film. But to hell with it: I'm too tired for this shit. The picture probably would have been garbage anyway, wouldn't have made any sense without a caption to explain what she was doing. Winogrand said, there are no pictures when I'm changing film. Winogrand was right.

"You drive." He walked to the passenger side and got in and reclined the seat as far as it would go. Exhaustion spread through his bones as he settled into the seat, seeped from bone through sinew and muscle, settled into his ankles and knees. "Eat your breakfast. That's why I bought it."

"I'm gonna stop for a real breakfast in the next town."

Here's hoping a real breakfast doesn't mean bacon and eggs. She pulled onto the road, headed west, her driving jerky, out of practice.

"I was looking at the map." she said. "If we make Thunder Bay by early afternoon, do you think we can make someplace like Kenora by nightfall?"

Probably not. Maps make things look much more manageable than they really are. Zane wasn't even sure where they were. We are somewhere, we are anywhere, we are everywhere. You move around too much and the roots die. Every place starts to look the same.

"We'll just drive 'til we stop," he said. His eyes were already closed.

* * *

Melissa stopped for lunch in Marathon, where Zane overrode her objections and diverted her to the hospital after spotting the blue hospital sign on the road into town. It would take too long, she didn't like doctors, there would be questions; regardless, she needed stitches. You don't get that looked at, you'll end up looking like Tiger Williams. She said Tiger who.

The hospital was smaller than he expected. You picture a hospital, but you get a clinic. If not for the sign he would have driven past and kept right on looking. In the waiting room, an assortment of local colour waited on the doctor: an eight-year-old boy with a fish hook in his cheek, a pregnant woman with red hair, a young Indian man cradling an arm that appeared to be broken. The room swelled with that sense of polite and enervated expectation that is peculiar to hospital waiting rooms, to that interminable limbo that follows an accident, when those not critically injured await repair.

Into this scene Melissa entered as a small bomb loaded with impatience, reiterating her excuses.

"This is going to take too long."

"Just for once, do as I say."

Zane pointed at the chair facing the triage desk, cracked vinyl spilling foam rubber. The triage nurse looked up at Melissa and gave Zane a dirty look.

"Check yourself in. I'll go get us something to eat."

He left her at the triage desk and walked out into the street. So this challenge is now out of the way; looks like you just about got this thing nailed. This time, Zane felt he could get fully behind the sentiment. Hand me down my framing hammer and let's nail this thing. A strange feeling, his shoulders back and his head erect, almost a spring in his step. Something foreign, a feeling he hadn't experienced in years.

Zane felt optimistic.

* * *

Rain clouds have lifted into a high white overcast, a monotonous bright sheet under which puddles fade to damp patches on the pavement. A useless sky for photography. Over all this hangs the sweet, thick smell of the pulp mill west of town. Nevertheless, you work with what you've got. Dance with them what brung you. Zane left his car in the hospital lot and walked down Peninsula Road, overdressed for the weather in his rain jacket. The day was warming and the air grew humid. He took off the jacket and folded it around the weight of the Leica in the right-hand pocket.

Food was a problem; Zane's injury had complicated what was normally the simplest of matters. He bypassed pizza and burgers and found a sub shop, an outlet of a national chain. Problem solved: the magic of franchising guarantees a series of safe victuallers along the route. It remains only to decipher the menu, a bewildering array of choices. Zane looked over the options and realized that he hadn't the slightest idea what Melissa wanted, or indeed what she liked. Everything's a guessing game. The girl behind the counter, a gawky kid of about sixteen with mousy hair and a retainer, Katrina on her name tag, asked if she could help him.

"Well, what's good?"

Apparently, this was an inappropriate question. Katrina, flustered, uttered a self-deprecating giggle, and seemed to shrink.

"It's all good."

Zane looked up at the lighted sign behind the counter on which his choices were arrayed. Under the pressure of the moment, all these options become an insurmountable challenge. What, for example, is southwest chicken? How does it differ from ordinary chicken, and what is it doing north of Lake Superior? He ordered a turkey sub for himself, assorted for Melissa. Something for everyone; you can't go wrong.

"Small?"

"Please. Actually, no. Make them large." Something for the road; you don't know when you'll stop again.

"On?"

Puzzlement.

Katrina pointed at a display showing a half-dozen choices of bread. He dithered.

"I like parmesan oregano," said Katrina, having discovered new reserves of confidence.

"Sounds good."

"Cheese?"

"Sure."

"What kind?"

She pointed into a tub containing three unnamed varieties of cheese. One had holes in it, which presumably made it Swiss. Of the remaining choices, one was orange and the other white.

"Cheddar?" A shot in the dark.

Katrina reached for the orange.

"Lettuce tomato onions?"

"On the assorted. Just lettuce on the turkey."

"Anything else?" Katrina waved her hand over an array of possible toppings.

"Don't think so. No, thanks."

"Mustard mayo sub sauce?"

He frowned. Katrina paused with her hand extended toward the bottles. The entire exercise had become entirely too complicated.

"Mayo on the assorted."

Zane straightened his spine, confident. *My quest is now complete. Hail, the conquering hero; he is just about normal. Just put them in a bag and have done with it.*

"Salt and pepper?"

"No thanks."

Katrina hesitated. "No salt or pepper?"

Zane shook his head. She wrapped up the sandwiches and he grabbed two bottles of pop from the cooler. As he paid her he flashed his best smile and thanked her, and then walked back out into the street, clutching his bag of sandwiches to his chest like a trophy. Victory was his.

* * *

In a parking lot, a small gaggle of teenaged boys with shaggy hair attempt pointless skateboard tricks, presumably for the benefit of a separate gaggle of girls, who pretend to ignore them completely. All this scene lacks is a curmudgeonly shop owner to chase them all off, and thus to demonstrate that all is right with the world. *Clear off, you little punks; kids today, I don't know, when I was your age we never etcetera. Get a goddamn haircut. And you, does your mother know you dress like that?* Such poetry in the mouth of an aging barber, words of comfort that guarantee nothing ever changes in this town. Zane longed to live where nothing ever happens.

Zane's good mood was not marred even when one of the boys lost control as he passed, stumbled, and bumped into him. The boy

151

blurted a hasty apology, to the laughter of his friends, and the girls looked over. Zane said, watch where you're going, you young whippersnapper, but the kid didn't get the joke. He waited until he was safely back on his skateboard and twenty feet distant, and then told Zane to go fuck himself. Zane's laughter seemed to confuse him: this was not in the script.

* * *

Halfway back to the hospital, Zane's cellphone rang, an event sufficiently rare that at first he couldn't locate the source of the ring tone. Just when you think you've burned all your bridges, someone calls to talk to you. They never do learn.

Of all the voices in the world, Richard Barker's was the one voice Zane was least disposed to hear. You would think you could escape it, but omnipresence is exactly that. It was tempting to simply hang up, to turn the phone off and see how many times Barker called before taking the hint. But Zane felt it was probably best to formalize the break, to get it over with, like ripping off a bandage. No sense in dragging out the pain any longer than absolutely necessary.

"You were supposed to call me today, and you didn't," said Barker.

"I forgot."

"You have something of mine. I want it back."

"I don't think anything here belongs to you."

The day now seemed colder, less filled with possibility; the smell from the pulp mill increased in weight.

"Don't play coy with me, Zane. It distresses me. You know what I'm talking about."

"Nothing here belongs to you." Zane took the phone from his ear and stabbed the red button and put it back in his pocket.

The phone rang again, an insistent electrical chirping.

"You're wasting your time, and mine."

"That was rude of you, hanging up like that."

"I can't really hear you. You're breaking up. I think I'm losing the signal.",

"Don't fuck with me. You're not funny. I never took you for a thief, but you and Melissa, maybe there was something there I didn't anticipate." Barker paused, moderated his tone. "What's done is done. I know things got crazy there. I only want you to return what's mine."

"Why don't you call the cops, then, Rich? Tell them you've been robbed. Give them my description."

"I had hoped that we could talk like adults."

"Nobody here but us kids," said Zane.

He stabbed the red button again, looked at the phone briefly, and then switched it off. No point in having the thing ring at random intervals. He put it back in his pocket and put his jacket back on. The light was going and a cold wind was coming off the lake. So much for optimism.

* * *

Melissa was not in the waiting room. Zane stopped just inside the door and pondered the possibilities: either she's in with the doctor now, or she's decamped. A symptom of declining optimism, thoughts such as these. The triage nurse passed the desk and smiled at him, a victim of Melissa's charm, told him to take a seat while she checked on his daughter.

Zane sat in one of the chairs and picked up a *National Geographic* and looked idly through it. Despite the departure of so many of the greats the *Geographic* always finds a new eye to surprise you. A desert caravan, in this case, reflected in the eye of a camel; a new eye for a new eye. You wonder how many times the doctor tried to convince Melissa to call the police, and how long it took her to convince him of whatever story she'd told. No matter how good the pictures are you still get distracted by questions like these.

"Mr. Collins?"

A hand on his shoulder. He looked up to see the triage nurse, realizing as he did that she had called for him several times. Melissa Collins. You live, you learn.

"Sorry. I'm really tired."

He put down the magazine and followed the nurse back through a set of swinging doors to a room where Melissa sat on a hospital bed, propped on a pillow. A fresh set of stitches held her cut closed, dark ends bristling from her eyebrow.

The doctor displayed a confident smile and barely glanced at the chart.

"You're Mr. Collins?"

Zane nodded, quicker on the uptake than the last time.

"Well, it's not as bad as it looks." Competent smile, professional bedside manner; he did this a hundred times a day. "No broken nose, no fractures to the orbital bones. That was a nifty first aid job on the cut, the improvised butterfly sutures. Where'd you learn to do that?"

"Beirut," said Zane, without thinking. The problem was finding bandages without too much stretch.

"Beirut?"

"I was a journalist."

"Well," said the doctor. This you don't hear a hundred times a day. "Anyway, there's going to be some scarring. And you need to think about getting the police involved."

"I don't want to bother with the cops," said Melissa.

"You won't be the last that guy goes after."

This is no doubt an excerpt from a speech made dozens of times each week, to little effect. Melissa simply rolled her one good eye.

"Her mind's made up. You can't tell your kids anything."

"No kidding," said the doctor. We're all good people here. Kids today, you know how they are. But you're far too young to know that, doc. And furthermore, what the hell do I know about kids? All of us, making ourselves up as we go along.

* * *

Melissa drove the next leg, by dint of losing the coin toss. Somehow, although the chances are fifty-fifty, it always seems to come up heads. Zane called it heads and won. You've got a lot to learn about coin tosses, he said.

As they pulled out of Marathon Zane thought to call Jack. Jack answered on the third ring and asked, acidically, why he was calling.

"The game's afoot."

"Speak English."

"I'm on the road."

"So your porno project is toast. I told you there was nothing there."

"Wrong. It's all coming together now."

"It has nowhere to go but up."

"I have all the drama you could ever require." And I intend to rub it in your face, you smug, self-satisfied rat-fucker. When I tell you there's a story, there's a story.

"Do tell."

"The subject got beat up."

"The subject," said Melissa. "Now I'm the subject?"

Zane waved a hand at her: shut up.

"Is that her?"

"That's her. So now she's heading off home to make a fresh start."

"Home?"

"Vancouver. And we're in the middle of nowhere now, I'm going to lose coverage."

"And my name's Melissa, not The Subject."

Zane waved his hand at her again, glared.

"Stripper with a heart of gold," said Jack.

"If you like. I'm thinking some kind of redemption."

"Same thing. Working girl makes good."

"The Little Engine That Could. Whatever. You wanted a hook, I got a hook. It's a story."

"So now I'm the little engine that could?"

A pause followed, during which the phone emitted a strange sound that Zane identified as Jack sucking his teeth.

"How long?" said Jack.

"How long does it take to drive to Vancouver?"

"How long is a piece of string? How the fuck would I know? How long 'til you have a story?"

"Days, anyway. We have to get there, I have to shoot the tearful homecoming, develop the film. I'm doing it on film, everything takes longer."

"Time, you've got."

"I'm doing it on Tri-X Pan."

Silence from Jack. You know he gets the point, even if you yourself can't quite explain it. Somehow, this time, how you make the pictures matters more than what they say.

"She's driving to Vancouver now?"

"Technically speaking, I'm driving her to Vancouver."

Another pause.

"Just how close are you to this story?"

"I'm maintaining a professional distance."

"Ain't that the fuckin' truth," said Melissa.

He waved his hand at her again and she rolled her good eye in return.

"You need to keep that dispassionate eye."

"Trust me."

"I'm not even going to touch that one."

"You need to wait until you see the film."

"We're talking a week?"

Something like that, he said. The car nosed up an incline and Melissa began to chant I think I can I think I can I think I can. Now is not the time to start inexplicably laughing, now when Jack seems finally convinced you're back in the game. Melissa now making train noises. It suddenly seemed imperative to hang up. Quit while you're ahead. There never was a sequel to The Little Engine That Could.

CHAPTER ELEVEN

A t the edge of the road the neon sign proclaiming a vacancy flickers. The wooden frame of the office window bears a fresh coat of forest-green paint, and carefully tended geraniums flower in the window box. Crickets chirp unseen in the darkness, surprisingly loud; after some twenty-four hours of tires on pavement and engine sounds, of incessant hum and that worrisome valve clatter, the silence that the chirping penetrates seems unnatural. You fold yourself into the car seat and then set in that position like a gel hardening. At the end of the day it's difficult to move, to adapt to the change when you stand upright.

Melissa stopped Zane in the parking lot, hand on his arm.

"Let me do the talking."

A flicker across the background, perhaps a scratch in the film. Melissa in soft focus. What you need here, friend, is a trench coat and a fedora to go with the motel's flickering neon sign. Never trust a dame. Especially not a hard-luck dame in cheap sunglasses who speaks in B-movie clichés. Not as long as your film is noir – and at present, everything is monochrome. It gives everything that dramatic look. Also there are technical reasons, to do with lighting. We're doing the whole shebang on Tri-X Pan.

"I'm Mr. Collins again?"

"You got it."

"You don't think you're going a little far with all this?"

"You don't get it, do you?"

"Apparently not."

She glanced quickly toward the motel office as if checking for eavesdroppers; then it occurred to him that she was doing exactly that.

"You think we blend in? Shit, Zane, we're the talk of the town everywhere we go."

"I don't see that it matters."

"Rich knows where we're going."

"So what."

"So we stand out like a sore thumb. How long you think he'll take to find us?"

"Rich has better things to do."

"You don't know Rich."

You don't know anything, least of all the source of this paranoia.

"Point is, if some guy comes up the road looking for us, and we been telling everyone I'm bailing on my jerk boyfriend, he's gonna spend more time talking to the cops than following us."

"Jesus, Melissa. Nobody's following us."

"Like I said, you don't know Rich."

This is your brain on cocaine: full of cholesterol, crispy round the edges, gooey in the middle and more than a little wrapped up in itself. Paranoid, anyway. Zane let it drop.

Inside the motel office, a middle-aged woman sat reading a celebrity magazine while the television muttered softly in the background. An old, worn carpet, but no dust on the windowsills. Behind the counter, a bulletin board carried scattered community announcements, jokes, and photos of smiling men holding big fish. A large, mounted fish graced the wall over the window. Zane thought it was a pike.

"I need a room for the night," said Melissa, without removing her sunglasses.

"Oh, goodness me."

Eyes opening in shock on seeing Melissa's face. The phrase took Zane by surprise. Does anyone in the world still speak this way? The woman looked at Zane as the sun regards an ant through a magnifier. It was the same look he'd received in the hospital waiting room. You can only wither so much.

The woman turned her attention back to Melissa.

"The two of you?"

You don't want to be accused of robbing the cradle, on top of the rest. You have to draw the line someplace.

"We'll take separate rooms."

"I need the company, Dad," said Melissa. "You got one with twin beds?"

The woman rolled doubtful eyes over Zane and then, having evidently decided his innocence and confirmed the overall uselessness of men at solving anything more emotionally complex than clogged plumbing, turned her motherly attention to Melissa.

"I left the bastard." Melissa took off her sunglasses. "I'm going home."

"Oh, dear. Good for you."

The woman reached out and patted Melissa's hand, and began nattering about something that had happened to someone she had known, a mother hen clucking after her chicks. Zane wasn't paying attention. His eyes were on the television, on the evening news: hellfire in Baghdad, a car flattened like a fire-blackened beer can. Bloodstains in the street.

"Dad!"

Melissa squeezed his arm, fingernails sharp in his triceps.

"You look like you just seen a ghost," said the woman.

"On the news," he said. The desk, the stuffed fish, the television: you are in Dryden. "The war."

Nobody had an answer to that. Zane pulled out a credit card and laid it on the counter. When in doubt, pay. Grease liberally; keep the wheels moving at all costs.

"Just for the one night. We've got a long way to go."

"Where you headed?"

"Calgary," said Melissa.

Zane closed his mouth in some confusion. Let this hard-luck dame do the talking. She's the only cast member who's actually read this particular screenplay.

The woman commenced to cluck again as she ran Zane's credit card through the machine and put the slip on the counter for him to sign. She had heard Calgary was lovely but she didn't think she'd like it so much in the winter. Not the cold, mind you, it was cold enough here, but you just couldn't count on the weather. You would never know what to wear. Her neighbour's son had gone off to work on some oil job and they said the weather was just terrible. One day it was snow and the next it was spring, then it was snow again.

Zane signed.

"Room fourteen. You call if you need anything."

Melissa offered a wan smile and a promise.

This general flood of goodwill had left him high and dry. After that performance over the news you start to feel like a murder suspect. Time to demonstrate that you can still function normally. To this end, he addressed himself to the fish mounted on the wall over the window.

"That's a heck of a fish."

The fish was almost five feet long. Even stuffed, it had evil in its eyes, and its mouth was filled with long, needle sharp teeth.

"I wouldn't want to get bit by that thing. It's a pike?"

"A muskie. Pretty much like a pike."

"A fish like that makes me think twice about going swimming."

"Little girl got bit by one, last year." A story retold, no doubt, to every visitor. "Lots of muskie around here, if you like fishing."

"A fish like that makes me afraid to go fishing."

He held the door open for Melissa and waved as he went out into the darkness and the sound of crickets. She waited until they were out of earshot of the office before she spoke.

"Aren't *you* getting into character."

"I was starting to feel left out, the way you were carrying on with Henny Penny."

"Don't be mean."

"Since when are we going to Calgary?"

She waved a hand in the air: cease this nitpicking.

"We're going through Calgary. Good enough."

160

Room Fourteen was the kind of spare and functional space that defines a trans-Canada road trip: panelling walls and a thread-bare green carpet at least fifteen years old. The room smelled of dry pine and mothballs. Melissa closed the curtains and staked her claim by throwing her bag on the bed farthest from the door, then turned on the television and started flipping through the channels. Zane took a photo of her, and she stuck her tongue out at him. That's what you get for rooming with me, he said.

Shower first, then food. In the bathroom he locked the door and started the hot water. A weak sprinkle issued from the shower head, but it was hot. His bones ached from the car. The heat of the water gave him a chill and he stepped under it to drive the cold from his body. The tub enamel felt rough and worn under his feet and some of the tiles were cracked. All the discomforts of home. He put his head under the flow and let the water sheet down over his face, opening his mouth to breathe and spitting out the water that flowed in as he inhaled.

It's too long to sit in the car. You're too old for this. It's impossible to get a good diet on the road, and it's a long way to Vancouver. To Zane, the whole enterprise now seemed too much effort for too little gain. And he needed to find a liquor store.

Zane towelled off quickly, left his hair in a shambles and pulled on his jeans. He returned from the bathroom and threw his dirty shirt and socks onto his bed and started digging in his bag for clean clothes.

"Holy shit, Zane."

He turned to her in puzzlement, holding a clean T-shirt.

"Nice scars."

He looked down at the puckered scar of the entrance wound, and the neat surgical scars that accompanied it. And of course, she had already seen the big one, the exit wound.

"How'd you get a scar like that?"

"I got shot."

Zane dug in the bag for a pair of fresh socks and then tried to brush his hair into some semblance of order with his fingers before putting his shoes on.

"No shit? You got shot?"

He nodded.

"How can you be so matter of fact?"

"It's a matter of fact."

In matter of fact, he had been unable to talk about it for months without displaying a nervous tic he had developed, a fluttering in his left eyelid. He now rubbed at his eye, in case.

"Is that why you quit?"

"No."

There is no why-you-quit. Reasons for quitting are a complex structure, too complex to investigate. Best now stick to the facts; the facts don't move around. Any answer you come up with is probably bullshit, anyway. You can never trust yourself to tell the truth about this matter, or indeed about any other. You want to get from one day to the next, you make a deal with yourself: you agree not to dig to the bottom of certain boxes. And you try to forget that the stories you tell yourself are probably full of lies.

His Leica lay on the night table. He picked it up and checked the frame counter, and then decided to change out the roll. He could feel her eyes on him, unnaturally close, as he slipped the fresh roll into the camera and replaced the base plate. The feeling of being watched disturbed him. He shot a quick and pointless frame of her sitting on the bed.

"Jesus." She reached up and touched the entry wound on his belly.

Her touch unravelled him. He pulled on the T-shirt and tugged it down to cover the damage and then sat down on his bed and closed his eyes and covered his face with his hand.

If it's not the rage or the flashbacks it's the tears. We're done blubbering over long-distance commercials now, tearing up over televised kittens playing with toilet paper. Get a grip on yourself.

Melissa reached out and put her hand on his shoulder, which only made it worse. He shook his head and waved her off, fought himself until control returned.

162

"This other guy got hit in the head, got killed. I knew I was going to die. I kept talking to this guy to keep him awake, because I thought it was my job to take care of him. I didn't know he was already dead."

The eyelid had started to flutter. He blinked hard but it wouldn't stop.

"You don't have to talk about it."

"You just kind of took me by surprise."

No one had ever touched the scar. He had forgotten what it felt like.

"When the bullet goes through it makes a big mess. I lost a good chunk of my intestines. I can't eat anything greasy, pizza, fries, nachos, hamburgers, bacon and eggs. It gives me lethal attacks of the runs."

"I made you bacon and eggs that time, and you ate it."

"I had to."

"No, you fuckin' didn't."

"It was like breakfast on father's day. You eat it."

"Bullshit."

"And I paid for it, too. I spent the rest of the day in the can, feeling like death."

She swung and hit him in the shoulder, hard.

"It was a great breakfast."

"You're a fuckin' idiot."

"It was worth it." He picked up his keys. "Let's go get something to eat."

She said I want a pizza, double cheese, pepperoni, bacon and mushrooms. And I'm gonna eat it right in front of you. Serves you right.

* * *

"If you ask anyone, like our dear sweet Marilou, they'll tell you that they don't mind doing it and it's good money." Dinner in a family restaurant in Dryden, well after the suppertime rush. Three quarters of the tables empty. Their own table felt faintly sticky. "And it's all complete bullshit."

"That's what you told me."

"What?"

"Good money, etcetera."

"Well, that was all bullshit."

She waved her past statements away and took off the top of her burger. Its contents, a mess of grease and cheese and fried mushrooms topped with bacon, received a close inspection. Fries on the side. She planned to enjoy this, she'd said, just for him.

"Who's gonna say, it's fuckin' horrible, I can't stand it, it pays good but I still feel like a whore? You already know everybody's lookin' at you like you fell out of the bottom of the world and you're trapped in the shitpit. And you want everyone to think that you're really just a normal girl with this offbeat job. So you say, maybe it's just that everyone else is so uptight."

Melissa, having finished showing off her hamburger, reassembled it and took a bite.

"They tell you you're gonna make a thousand bucks a night, so you think, wow. You aren't going to get that ringing up groceries. But then they start pulling all this shit on you."

"Such as?"

She waved her hand in the air as she chewed and swallowed.

"This is good."

"I'm sure it is."

"Boy, if I couldn't eat like this, I'd just about die."

"You may die as it is."

"Is that a threat?"

"Think of your cholesterol."

She took another bite and made appreciative noises.

"I'm not old enough for that."

"So they pull all this shit on you," he said.

She wiped her fingers on her napkin and took a drink.

"You're a contractor, so you pay for stage time. Then they overbook the stage. You might not even get on. You got to pay a cut of your tips to the bouncers and the DJ. At the end of the day you got half what you thought you were gonna make."

She started picking at her fries. Zane waited. It had always been his experience that most people distrusted silence and would rush to fill it.

"But the money's still good, I guess. It's the work that sucks."

Zane had ordered a turkey sandwich, no mayo, and a garden salad with dressing on the side. The dressing was off limits.

"You dance for all these creeps, fuckin' misfits who can't talk to women. Sometimes you get these creeps waiting for you outside, following you home. Guys expect you to suck them off for twenty bucks. And girls do it, too. They just charge a little more."

A woman passing their table glared at Melissa but she had returned to her burger. Zane smiled up at her: these kids today, what can you do? No manners and no respect. I can't take her anywhere, you know. He felt an urge to ask her what she thought of the weather, this being the universal safe topic, but the look in her eyes suggested ice storms descending from the howling northlands. He waited, instead, for silence to overcome Melissa once more.

"You can call it what you want, man, but you're really just a fuckin' hooker. You know how that feels?"

Not exactly. What I want to know is when you say that all the girls are hooking, do you include yourself. But there's no diplomatic approach to this question. Best to file that one away forever under things you really don't want to know. And in future, you might want to fill in these silences yourself.

"So you get baked before you go on. It makes it easier. There goes half your pay. Half the girls are on fuckin' crack. But you know the worst thing? You wanna know the worst thing?"

Silence stretches out across the empty restaurant.

"What's the worst thing?"

"The worst thing is the money. Because you want that money. You want it bad enough to keep on doing that stuff just so you can get scorched again and make it go away. And it's like that joke, you look in the mirror, you know what you are. You're only haggling about the price. So yeah, you tell people that it's not so bad and you make good money. What the fuck, I'm just an ordinary girl, right?"

"You seem pretty ordinary to me."

"Don't pull that bullshit on me."

Zane picked at his salad.

"Shit, Zane, you just want to be *normal*. But I look in the mirror, I know what I am."

Melissa stopped and looked around the diner, and Zane belatedly became aware that the buzz of conversation was lacking.

"Shit," said Melissa. "Let's get the fuck out of here."

Zane signalled the waitress and wolfed his sandwich. Melissa ate a few more fries but left half the burger to congeal on her plate. Outside, a cloud of moths battered themselves senseless against the light.

* * *

Zane threw his bag in the car and closed the trunk lid with a satisfying thump that echoed through the morning quiet. Pale grey light and the air filled with birdsong. He took the Leica from his jacket pocket and shot a couple of frames of the motel parking lot, a desolate open space with a neon sign flashing "Vacancy." He couldn't identify any subject, any reason to take the picture. It just seemed like taking a picture was the thing to do. When you get the right light you can make a picture of anything.

He liked the sign, so he walked out to the road and shot the same picture another way, with the sign in the foreground so that the dead neon tube that spelled "No" was visible. The frame contained simple facts: a motel, a parking lot, mostly empty, and the sign declaring a vacancy. He liked the picture, liked the idea of it, although he didn't know what, if anything, he meant by it. There was a strong possibility that it was simply nonsense. Possibly, this was the very reason he liked it. He dismissed these speculations; you overthink these things, next thing you know, you're writing artist statements, talking about what your pictures interrogate. Why do you like chocolate? Is chocolate a metaphor for a certain aesthetic? Consider rum, on the other hand: not a metaphor, but a certain anaesthetic. Aren't we witty this morning.

The morning chill worked its way under his jacket. Zane had always liked dawn, the feeling of being alive, all senses alert. In the early morning light, everything seems simple, slender, reduced. Everything seems true. By noon, you've built a day on top of it, a day like any other.

A large mayfly rested on the window screen of Room Fourteen. He wanted a picture of it but the Leica was the wrong tool for that job. He left the camera alone and leaned in for a closer look. The mayfly, sluggish in the chill of morning, did not move.

Summer camp: big mayflies rise in clouds off the lake at night and in the morning you find them on window screens and canoe paddles and life jackets, drowned in a puddle of water in the bottom of a canoe that someone had forgotten to invert, drowned on the flat mist-smeared surface of the lake in the morning quiet. Someone said that they only lived for a day. It seemed like a rip-off, to be a mayfly. Zane suggested to a girl called Karen, if a mayfly only lives a day, it can't exactly afford to guard its virginity; I'm just saying. Karen, to his surprise, agreed. A disappointing fumble in the bushes ensued, Karen stopping short of his highest hopes, and thankfully no contact with poison ivy.

Here on the screen is northern Ontario distilled: the smell of dry pine wood, sunscreen, and bug juice, the rough feel of a weathered canoe paddle, the thrill of a girl's smile in the light of a campfire. He straightened and turned back to the parking lot. Some things, like the feeling you get from a song, you never can bring back.

Rumble and cough in still air, the bubbling sound of a big diesel exhaust: a tractor-trailer shakes off the night and pulls out onto the road, its cab rocking with the torque of the gear changes, groaning and wheezing air from its brake lines like an old man getting up from an easy chair. He wanted to freeze it, wanted to take a picture that no camera could take: not only the sound of the truck but the rocking motion of the cab, the brisk feel of the morning air on his skin, the stillness of the dawn and the sounds of the birds. He wanted to get that light.

The door to Room Fourteen was cheap and thin, no more secure than a curtain. He went in to check on Melissa. She was out of the shower, dressed in a T-shirt and jeans, with her hair still wet. Zane went to the window and rolled back the curtains to let the morning light flow into the room and then shot Melissa pulling the bandages from the cut and inspecting her face in the mirror. The swelling had subsided a little and the white of her eye now showed, red with blood.

He continued photographing her as she finished packing, and then put the camera back in his pocket. He loaded her bag in his trunk and then on impulse rummaged in his own bag and found his book, a heavy hardcover, and handed it to her before starting the engine.

"That's the whole story," he said. "And be careful with it. That thing's out of print."

His engine sounded unhealthy. The valve clatter was beginning to worry him. Nobody wants to find himself in the middle of nowhere with a dud engine.

"Thank you."

"Just don't spill your coffee on it."

"I think I'm having bacon and eggs for breakfast," she said. "With extra grease."

The light was getting harder now, as the sun came up over the trees.

CHAPTER TWELVE

Scrawny pines and white paper birches and road cuts strewn with chunks of blasted granite stream past the windows, blue lake water flashing Morse code through the trees. Wind buffets Zane's left ear, blasts his hair, blows his left sleeve up his armpit. This is the only way to keep cool. The air conditioning is banjaxed; it is essential, therefore, to keep moving, to maintain the slipstream. Hanging one arm out the open window carries a risk of sunburn; it's a trade-off.

From the waist down, Zane was a grease spot. He had considered driving with his fly open, to open all remaining vents to the cooling rush of air, but this might have communicated to Melissa certain notions that were ultimately incorrect. He chose to sweat and to suffer instead.

On the left, trees drop away to reveal the blue sheet of a lake, cold water. Ghosts of summers past, diving off the dock, body knifing into water, clean and cold, a girl in a bikini watching: you make certain not to lose your shorts. Humid summer nights, clouds of blackflies around your head, deer flies, mosquito bites swelling hot, red and uncontrollably itchy. All of which, surprisingly, filled Zane with a restless, non-specific nostalgia.

"This country takes me back."

"What?" Melissa sat slumped in the passenger seat, her feet up on the dash.

"Sorry. I thought you were asleep."

"You only talk to me when I'm sleeping?"

"I was talking to myself."

"You mean like a crazy person?"

"To stay awake."

The slipstream whipped at her hair, lashed it across her face. She reached up to tuck it behind her ear, tilted her sunglasses towards the sky.

"This takes you back to what?"

"Summer camp."

"Summer camp. Yeah, right."

This disbelief, the scorn in her giggle, stung him.

"I was a camp counselor and everything."

"Leading singalongs of Kumbaya?"

"Get your damn feet off the dash."

Sunburn and wet shoes and the smell of dry pine wood and sunscreen. When the car pulls away for the first time, gravel popping under its tires, your mother waving from the passenger window, you have never felt so alone. The conviction arises that this was a serious mistake.

It began, as far as Zane could conceive, as another exercise in Character Building; thus far, none had succeeded, but the elder Zane was not easily defeated. Like most of his colleagues he seemed neither to like nor to understand teenaged boys, and sending Zane off for the summer seemed to him an appropriate way to ensure the boy learned leadership and integrity. Instead, Zane took advantage of his barely-supervised time with girls his own age to learn lessons of his own. Legions of parents go unaware that their camp fees pay primarily for sex education. Zane could report, for example, that despite certain cherished national myths, a canoe makes a decidedly poor venue for an amorous tryst. It is for sound and sensible reasons that the thing across the middle is called a thwart.

At seventeen everything is a crisis and every adolescent crush a lifetime love affair. Zane fell in love anew every six weeks, each time with the conviction that if we can no longer be together then it's all over, in the best Romeo and Juliet bare-bodkin-to-the-aorta tradition. Driving over the same Canadian shield again, he wondered what had become of Suzanne or Karen or Sarah or whatshername. Especially whatshername. He remembered the striking ice blue of her irises, the precise curvature of her nose, but certain other identifying details now escaped him.

In any case, it had been a long time since Lucas Zane had fallen in love with anyone. You start to think you've forgotten how.

"You got geese walking on your grave again."

He watched the country slide by. All these geese, breeding and multiplying. You go to the park and your feet are slip-sliding in great gobs of goose-shit. They're everywhere, trampling all the best gravesites. Something ought to be done.

"I was just thinking what happened to all those people."

"What people?"

"Kids I knew from camp."

"Kids you knew from camp." She shook her head.

"I guess they all grew up and got married and had kids."

By now, those kids would be discovering the limitations of the canoe for themselves. The wheel turns again. The scale of the journey grows overwhelming and you just want to lie down and feel the sun on your skin and watch the clouds roll by.

"It's not like you to get like that."

"Like what?"

"All sappy like that."

"I don't know. This country is all happy memories."

"You'd think different if you lived up here."

"I guess I probably would." But everyone needs some happy memory to cling to. We need the happy memories to make us sad.

* * *

I still remember my first time, she said. He was driving at the time. They were right out in the middle of nowhere and had been talking far too long. He said, let's not go there. Too much information. I'm not gonna tell you about my first time, either.

"Not that. I mean stripping."

171

He wanted to reach for his notebook, but there was the small matter of keeping the car on the road.

"I guess you could say I answered an ad."

"It happens to the best of us."

"What would you know about that?"

Nobody will ever say she isn't quick.

"So I answered this ad where it said I could make two thousand bucks a night. And I was making like eight bucks an hour and I just split on this boyfriend who was an asshole and I didn't have any money, so I said, what the hell, right?"

You could swear you heard this one before.

"So I called the number and talked to this woman, and she asked a bunch of questions and said come on down Thursday night and try out. And I was in."

"Questions?"

"Just questions like why I wanted to do it and stuff."

"So you didn't always work for Barker."

She looked at him and shook her head.

"You think Barker's the be-all and end-all? I been doing this for a long time."

"How long?"

"I was seventeen."

Zane checked the gas gauge, mentally calculated the distance remaining to Winnipeg.

"They gave me a fake ID."

Zane pushed himself up in his seat and shifted his weight. His wallet was digging into his buttocks.

"That surprises you?"

He shifted his weight again.

"Anyway, I went in and they told me what I had to do and then I went out and did it."

"Easy as that."

"Easy as that. Shit, Zane, I knew how to dance."

So that's that. They tell you what to do and you go out and do it and there it is, easy as that.

172

"That really bothers you," she said.

"I'm just tired."

He could feel her eyes on him.

"Okay, it wasn't easy as that. I got baked first but it was still really fuckin' weird."

He didn't know whether to feel relieved.

"Shit, Zane, you're seven fuckin' teen, and you're up there in the lights and the lights are hot, and there's all these fuckin' guys out there and they're just watching you, just watching. And you're on this schedule and you know that by the end of the second verse you've got to be out of your bra. And it didn't excite me or anything. I just needed the money."

"It must have been hard."

Canned sympathy. You uncork it on demand.

"Fuckin' right it was hard."

He wanted to say something more but he couldn't find the words.

"Girls like coke for a reason," she said.

"And you?"

She wasn't watching him anymore.

"Everybody does it, man."

Fair enough. Enough of this sentimental shit. She's just another messed up kid and it's not like she owes you anything.

"Anyway, it gets easier. But the first time is pretty weird."

He didn't have the words to answer and then he decided not to look for them. You let it ride and then she stops and you can go back to driving on to Winnipeg.

"You know the weirdest thing? The weirdest thing is I was up there and I was taking off my bra, and then it was like it wasn't me, it was someone else. And I was watching her do it. It wasn't me. She was doing it, you could see her doing it, and I wasn't there."

You let it ride and then she stops and you can go driving on to Winnipeg. Zane drove on.

* * *

Eventually, every mile of this endless road looks the same: a river of blacktop, with its yellow line, divides scraggly pine forest. Periodic "moose crossing" signs serve only to reinforce the monotony. Mile after mile, the same thing, and the mind wanders. The mind wanders down alleys best avoided. It gets lost in bad neighbourhoods and asks directions of men with crude tattoos and hard, penetrating eyes. It has no fucking street smarts at all, the mind, no common sense. Like a dog that chases a stick into a sewage lagoon, it brings back the kind of things you can't bring yourself to touch, even to throw them back.

I was staying in Graz, Austria, ten days before Christmas, when Lapierre was killed. This was, I think, in '96. You lose track. I even lose track of cities, of places. They all seem the same. One hotel is just like another. Places become generic. But Graz, I remember.

Snow covered the rooftops of the old city, and lights glowed along the crooked streets, and Graz looked like a freshly iced cake, a gingerbread town built to excite tourists from Tackyville, Ohio, looking for the real Austria. It didn't seem real.

You have to understand, I don't like to be cynical. It's a cheap way to think about the world. But I was just back from the ruins of Groszny, taking a few days off between assignments. So that coloured my opinion of Graz, made the whole place seem as if it couldn't possibly belong to the real world. And I had got to the point where I'd started to feel out of place everywhere.

I went for a run that morning, and then I took my camera out for a walk around the city, just to shoot some happy snaps. I had no place to go and no one to see and I wanted to put this surreal Christmas in Graz on film, if only to stave off the loneliness that lurks quietly in hotel rooms. And I wanted to buy a postcard to send back to my niece.

You can only pretend for so long. Eventually, the light started to die and the deep streets darkened between the snowy rooftops. It was all of a sameness, anyway: snow, lights, and people walking through the slush with their heads bent down. Instead of rosy-cheeked Austrians, cheerfully inhabiting their gingerbread city for the sake of tourists from Tackyville, I had grumpy shoppers trying to get Christmas over and done with for another year. At street level it was all much the same as you might find anyplace else.

When I got back to my room, the message light on the phone was blinking. I left my camera out to let the condensation evaporate from the lens, and let the message wait while I kicked my boots off and ordered dinner from room service. Watching a foreign city sunk into the Christmas dispirit had left me in no mood to take messages relating to war or to hotel administration, and the message light was undoubtedly blinking for one or the other.

I did the postcard first. It was a winter scene looking over the old city, and I wrote that I was staying in a magical Christmas city but that it was filled with American tourists who were buying all the houses and taking them apart and shipping them home to give to their friends for Christmas, so it didn't look like the postcard anymore. When you looked out the window of the hotel you just saw all these Graz families sitting around the kitchen table or the television with no houses, but they were all happy because of all the money they got from the tourists, and everyone was getting a pony for Christmas. I thought that was pretty funny. Amanda was something like eight, then, and I wasn't fooling her anymore.

The message was from Jack. I had started working with Jack a couple of years before. He had also represented Lapierre for many years, which was how I met him. In a voice less brash than usual, he said he had bad news for me. Would I please call as soon as I got his message. Regardless of the time.

A message like that can mean nothing good. I dialed New York, where it was still mid-afternoon, with a stone in my gut.

He said, Terry is dead.

I was surprised to discover that I didn't feel a thing. You're supposed to feel anger or denial when you lose someone, but I had none of that. It was like, I suppose, learning that a relative had died after a long struggle with cancer, a battle that had gone on well beyond the point at which even the most deluded optimist believed that anything could be done. It was like when my mother died. Shock comes only from the unexpected.

When, I said.

Yesterday, near Vlasenica. It was a car wreck.

The war in Bosnia was over, but it had still killed my friend. So that was that. There really wasn't anything to say.

I don't have the details, he said. His car went off the road and down an embankment, and he was dead at the scene, I think. It took some time to get him out of the wreck. They were worried about mines.

I said, are you okay?

Jack had known Lapierre even longer than I had. And Terry was close to retiring. I figured that Jack would take the news hard.

Well, you come to expect.

When I get back to New York, I said, let's get together for a drink over it.

I'd like that.

We'll drink Talisker, I said. I knew Jack liked Scotch.

Silence crashed through the line and I tried to think what else to say.

Then Jack cleared his throat. Just one thing, he said. Terry was doing a story for *Time*, on a suspected mass grave, near Srebrenica. And they need someone to step in and finish it.

The last place I ever wanted to see again was Bosnia. I was through with Bosnia. But a story is a story.

So I took the details from Jack, and made a couple of phone calls to set things up so that I could get rolling in the morning. Then I called room service again, and ordered up a bottle of rum. I didn't want to hold a private wake in the hotel bar. Graz was the staging point for journalists covering the war in Yugo, and there was a good risk of running into someone I knew. Then you have a public wake on your hands, and I wasn't in the mood to go public.

And *Time* also wanted a short, personal obit. Terry had worked for them for years and they wanted to mark his passing.

They wanted me to write it. As a colleague, as a friend. It was to be a leading photojournalist's view of the great Thierry Lapierre. And I didn't know what to write.

Chemical assistance was in order. Terry would not have approved. He did not drink. He had, in fact, not one recognizable vice. He even eschewed wine, which seemed odd in a Frenchman.

You should not drink, he would say. It may help with sleeping but it opens the door to too many problems. When you drink you lose your grip on yourself and become careless. And to Lapierre, becoming careless was the worst mistake you could ever make. Lapierre was never careless. He was always in control.

I am alive, Lapierre said, because I leave nothing to chance. Luck favours the prepared.

I remember him sitting on his hotel room bed with his camera bag open, having carefully emptied it of its contents. He was cleaning his gear. It was his standard ritual.

First the bodies, two big Nikons, almost new but already battered, which he carefully wiped down with a cloth and then placed side by side on the table. Then each lens in turn, in order of focal length: wipe down the lens, remove the UV filter, check the front element, clean and replace the UV filter, and finally fiddle with the aperture lever, to make sure that the blades snapped back without sticking. Each lens took its place beside the camera bag, until they formed a neat row. Then he cleaned and tested his flash, which he never used but nevertheless insisted on carrying, counted and tested his supply of spare batteries, and sorted his film. That was back when we still shot film.

On one of the bodies, he mounted a wide-angle, and on the other a mid-range zoom. Then everything went back in the bag, in order, each item in its specific place. Lapierre could reach in his bag without looking and immediately come up with the lens he wanted.

He kept meticulous records, using only mechanical pencils because they continued to work in the cold or if they got wet and because their fine points suited his tiny, precise handwriting. He marked his expended film with the date and a roll number, using a felt-tip pen, so that he could relate it back to his notes. The final step of his cleaning routine was to check all his expended film against his notes, apparently out of concern that a roll had wandered off unsupervised.

Everything I know, I learned from Lapierre. Starting out, I copied him, down to this precise cleaning routine.

People will tell you that it is only the light that matters, Lapierre said, but this is all bullshit of street photographers who think they are making art. What matters is the subject you shoot, and how you see it. You can't wait for a certain light. All light is good light if you find a way to use it. You think a war will only happen when the light is good?

Wars never happen when the light is good. On the other hand they are full of subjects.

Lapierre shot for the symbol and composed with strong graphic design, and at first I copied him. His trick was to find symbols in the frame, so that Sandinista machine-gunners were transformed into the stylized, heroic workers of Soviet socialist realism, or a farmer carrying a scythe became the Grim Reaper himself. His trick was to find the symbol and then arrange the frame so that the symbol dominated the picture and defined the photograph. This was the source of his renown.

Eventually, I started shooting in my own way. Some critic in a New York paper called this the flowering of my nascent sensitivity, or some shit like that. I just thought I was finding a way to make good pictures. That's really all you think about, regardless of what the critics might say.

But I didn't even do that on my own. Lapierre picked up on what I was doing differently and pushed me down that path, before I even realized I was doing it. We were in a hotel room someplace, looking at contact prints, and he picked out one frame and pointed it out to me. It was a shot of a soldier attempting to flirt with a teenaged girl. I guess it must have been Nicaragua, or maybe Honduras.

You should work more this way, he said. You see how the soldier is standing, and you see her eyes and the way she hunches her shoulders? You can see everything that is happening here, without needing a caption. You should stop trying to make grand, graphic pictures and just make pictures like this.

Grand, graphic pictures work for you, I said.

I work like me. This picture, this is like you. He pushed the contact print closer to me and tapped his finger on the frame in question. When you try to make symbols, Lucas, you forget they are people. Then people are just shapes. You have no humanity.

Terry was big on humanity, but at first glance, you wouldn't have mistaken him for a human. He was too tidy, too compulsive, too cool and controlled. Even under fire, his hair remained neatly parted. And even after touring some refugee camp, filled with people in the final stages of malnutrition, ribcages protruding from emaciated frames, figures like the damned in some medieval painting of hell, Terry would return unruffled, clean his cameras and sort his film, and then go to bed. Lapierre was like a Swiss watch.

I think that, before the end, the humanity did go out of Terry's pictures, the people turned into shapes and ideas. If you go on long enough it's inevitable, in the same way that one hotel room after another makes all cities seem the same. You get your bed and the TV and the table and the neutral painting by some local artist, and outside of that is a whole city and a country and a people, a whole wealth of detail that you never see. It all just turns invisible like you're stuck inside yourself.

It was easy to think that Terry was stuck inside himself. He never showed much emotion, even in the early years. He said, it doesn't help anyone for you to cry or get angry or yell or get drunk. It only helps to do your job.

It certainly didn't help anyone that I was getting quietly drunk in a hotel room in Graz, looking out at a city disguised as a Christmas confection, but there was no one left for me to help in any case. Putting the bottle down wasn't going to restore Lapierre to

179

life. It wasn't going to do anything except to save me from a hangover, and I didn't much care about that.

And I couldn't see that doing my job really helped anyone, anyway. If my car went off the road as Terry's had, *Time* would just go ahead and find someone else. The world isn't going to suffer if I stop doing stories.

I mixed another drink and stood at the window and looked out on Graz. This is an old city. Living in Canada you have no idea of the ancient, no idea of history. The old walls of Graz once repelled Turkish invasions. There's a church there that was built in 1277. In its bones, this city still remembers the Black Death, the bodies of the damned in those medieval paintings.

Lapierre used to say that he was responsible to history. His photographs were court exhibits with which he intended to condemn humanity in posterity. They were witnesses for whatever reckoning might come, to trials presided over by future historians who would condemn the wicked long after it had all ceased to matter. The present, to Lapierre, was already lost.

But history itself is just bullshit, a sophisticated process through which the past effaces itself. Pictures don't preserve anything, much less the truth. What you put on film is 1/250th of a second. There are 15,000 equivalent moments each minute, 900,000 each hour – how can one such moment tell the immutable truth? What's past is as changeable as a badly told lie. History morphs and twists under interrogation. You can't even trust your own memory. I could have sworn I put the map in the glovebox, you say, but there it is. Or rather, there it isn't. Lost.

All those people carried away by the Black Death are dead and forgotten, as if they had never lived. And each of us suffers the same fate within two short generations. What can you tell me of your great grandfather's life, or even your grandfather's? Death is the great disappearing act. All of history is amnesia.

But Terry believed. He made every shot as a record, a data point, a middle finger raised at death. He had a joke about taking his own photograph to prove that he existed. And maybe, on some subconscious level, he was right. Maybe the point of all this is not to record the external world at all. Maybe it's about ourselves.

They say the Inuit put up inukshuks not only to aid in navigating the trackless tundra but to create a record of themselves, to prove they were there. Maybe we're all just putting up inukshuks. Maybe all the supposed subjects of all my photographs, and all of Lapierre's, were merely objects occupying space in the frame. Maybe the real subject is our own minds.

Anyway, Lapierre was right: normal people don't fuck around like this. They make babies and raise children, so somebody remembers them for a generation or two. They don't travel the world sucking the life out of people, trying to achieve immortality.

I was making inroads on the rum but wasn't getting anywhere useful with the obituary. None of *Time*'s loyal readers in barber shops in Michigan or dentists' offices in California gave a shit about the nature of photography or the root of the creative impulse, or about Lapierre's compulsive lens-cleaning habits.

All I needed was something short and simple about someone whose pictures they had been seeing for years, without realizing all that time that those pictures all came from the same man, or that the pictures made a mark on photography itself. Bob in a barbershop in Kalamazoo knew nothing of Thierry Lapierre from Sainte Nazaire. Not until Lapierre went off the road somewhere in the dismembered Yugoslavia and became the history he'd worked twenty-five years to record. And then barbershop Bob simply shrugged, and reflected that it was too bad, but it was a dangerous way to earn your living. Adrenaline junkies. And Bob got his short back and sides and carried on with his Kalamazoo life.

In the end, I wrote some drunken bullshit about Lapierre's faith in some future reckoning, which eventually I reworked into the foreword to his posthumous book. You read that shit. And Jack searched the files and found a photo of Lapierre and me, the same photo as in the book, of us standing in front of a church in El Salvador, and *Time* ran that photo with the obit, with a black border on the page. Someone snapped that with my Leica, my happy snap camera, about one week before Lapierre saved my life in that grenade attack. If I'd only known that they were going to run that picture, I might have written something about that, instead of some rambling bullshit about history.

It's always best to stick to the facts.

* * *

They stopped to change drivers a half-hour out of Winnipeg. Zane pushed himself up out of the driver's seat and stretched, trying to pull the ache out of his calves. Melissa took the keys and got in, but he remained at the side of the road. When you know it's up to you to take the first step, you develop a strategic inertia.

"I have to make a phone call." The cellphone weighed heavy in his pocket.

"Don't let me stop you."

Zane took his phone out and looked at it with loathing.

"Come on," she said. "Get in."

"It's kind of a personal call."

A truck passed and the blast of its passage blew through him. He felt suddenly fragile.

"I have to call my sister."

"You have a sister?"

"She lives in Calgary. I thought we could stay there, passing through."

The consequences of passing through Calgary without visiting Connie, should she discover the snub, did not bear considering.

"I'd like to meet her."

Oh, no, you wouldn't.

"We don't really get along."

"Why doesn't that surprise me?"

Or you can walk to Vancouver, kiddo.

He put the phone back in his pocket and crossed to the passenger side and got in. Melissa started the engine, checked her mirrors, and pulled out onto the highway.

"Why don't you two get along?"

A thousand possible answers, all of them facile. There never is a why.

"I don't know. The same old brother-sister thing."

When his mother was diagnosed with Alzheimer's, Zane was working in the West Bank. After he wrapped up the story he flew home to visit. As soon as he got in the door, his mother's dog rushed around his legs, barking, a flow of white fur around his ankles like a breaking wave. Buddy was a poodle cross, a small white scrap of fluff, and he loved Zane. This did not rank high on Connie's list of grievances, but it was there.

"She's asleep," said Connie.

Zane dropped his bags and stooped to scratch Buddy behind the ears, and Buddy whined at him.

"I think he needs to go out."

Connie opened the front-hall closet and handed Zane the leash, and then walked back into the kitchen.

Zane descended the front steps like an astronaut emerging from his capsule to explore an alien world: big, quiet houses with sprawling, precisely mown lawns over which sprinklers slowly rotated. Big cars gleaming in the driveways. In the West Bank he had sat in the evenings with a cool drink while rifle fire popped in the background, Israeli soldiers firing rubber bullets at rock-wielding teenagers. A week previously, he had photographed the aftermath of a bus bombing, volunteers collecting body parts and blood for burial in the Orthodox Jewish tradition. Now, he walked a poodle over the alien surface of Suburbia.

Zane hated them all: the Palestinian kids, the Israeli soldiers, the Orthodox Jews with their Zionist certainty, the suicidal fanatics with bombs strapped around their bodies. Ye shall reap what ye sow: fuck you all for the wages of sin. The pieces that the volunteers collected commingled the bomber and his victims and in that knowledge Zane found an angry satisfaction.

His head felt like a helium balloon tethered to his body by the finest of threads. In West Bank time, it was well into the small hours.

Buddy failed to do any of the business he had seemed so desperate to do, as if he had forgotten the purpose of his walk. When Zane got back and let him off the leash he trotted off without a backward glance.

More than anything, Zane needed sleep. He collapsed into his father's old recliner, which still occupied the place of honour in the living room. His mother had decorated the house in pastel colours and had hung flowery curtains and bad still lifes of fruit, painted in acrylic by artists with little colour sense. All of the furniture was overstuffed. The recliner threatened to swallow him, like a predatory flower. He fumbled with the lever to pull it back to the upright position. He laid his head back with the chair upright and closed his eyes.

Connie came into the room and made a snorting noise.

"It's two in the morning in the West Bank," he said.

"It's suppertime in Oshawa, and I'm making pork chops."

You just have to roll with it. Buddy was back at his feet. He whined, and Zane reached down to scratch his ears, which sent him into excited orbits, running to the door and then back to Zane.

This dog was clearly constipated.

"Has he been getting his walks?"

"I'm taking care of him."

Buddy positioned himself in front of Zane and emitted a single insistent bark. Zane made a point of not looking at him.

"Mom used to take him out," said Connie. "And then she'd forget, and take him out again. So now he wants twenty walks a day, but I can't let her out with him because she forgets how to get home."

"Why didn't you tell me?"

"I wanted you to learn the hard way." Connie went out into the kitchen, and the room was cold behind her.

But when Zane was wounded in Afghanistan, Connie flew to Germany to visit him in hospital, and brought Jim, the plastic surgeon, with her. She insisted Jim speak to the doctors and review the charts, and this he did, explaining to his peers and to Zane behind closed doors that he was a plastic surgeon, not a trauma specialist, and was only humouring his wife. Connie brought flowers to Zane's bedside and brought him books and read to him. She tidied his room and terrified the nurses, and she never once spoke of the past.

Zane took the phone back out of his pocket and dialed. She picked up on the third ring.

"Connie," he said, "it's Lucas. I'm coming to visit."

"Uncle Luke?" said the voice on the phone. "It's Amanda. I'll get Mom."

* * *

Saskatchewan is flat and boundless and seems to have no edges, but it does, and somewhere near its eastern edge, they picked up a hitchhiker.

That is to say, Melissa picked up a hitchhiker, as Zane was asleep when the decision was made and had no say in the matter. He awoke to the sound of the tires on gravel as the car lurched onto the shoulder and when he got oriented he saw the hitchhiker trotting up in the wing mirror.

"Why'd you stop?"

"We're gonna give this guy a lift."

"Didn't anyone ever tell you not to pick up hitchhikers?"

"You can protect me," she said, and waved her hand at him.

At that particular moment, Zane saw no reason why he would do so. There can be no peace in the rabbit warren if the ferrets insist on inviting their friends in to join the party. But the *fait* was in any case *accompli*, as the hitchhiker was now at the passenger window, a young man perhaps in his mid-twenties, tall and thin, with a hint of stubble on his chin and long, unruly brown hair held in place by a baseball cap. His hair and clothes suggested gap teeth and a badly done tattoo, but he had soft brown eyes and the features of a model. He paused, his orthodontically perfect smile fading, apparently taken aback by Zane's failure to open his window.

Zane resisted the temptation to swear at him and instead rolled down his window and smiled, hoping that the result did not appear obviously forced. The hitchhiker's smile returned.

"I sure am glad you stopped," he said, in a voice so sickeningly and effusively sincere that Zane momentarily considered rolling his window up and reaching across to stamp on the accelerator. The man's voice had the burr of the Maritimes.

"Don't mind my dad." Melissa activated her brightest possible smile. "He's always grumpy."

Zane turned to practical matters, namely the question of where the hitchhiker was headed.

"West," he said, waving vaguely in that direction.

This answer is inane; this road leads in only two possible directions and one is already out of the question, unless this young man is seriously confused.

"Edmonton. Grand Prairie, Fort MacMurray. Lookin' for work in the oil patch."

"Well, get in," said Melissa, who had apparently forgotten that the car was Zane's.

Zane sat up straight. Show any sign of sleepiness and Melissa will no doubt evict you from the front seat of your own car in favour of her new travelling companion. Fickle woman that thou art.

Melissa swung the car back onto the road with a heavy touch on the gas pedal that made Zane wince, unsure as he was over the state of his engine. Her touch didn't lighten as she worked her way through the gears.

"You're probably wondering about my face."

"I figured it was none of my business."

"My boyfriend liked to hit me. My ex-boyfriend, I mean. I'm Melissa. My dad's name is Zane. You ever hear of Zane Grey? He wrote all these cheesy western stories. My grandfather loved westerns so he named my dad after Zane Grey. How lame is that?"

At least you get to keep your real name, as Melissa freely reinvents your family history. Zane struggled to find a stupid reason to name a child "Melissa" but came up short. Their new passenger barely had time to introduce himself (Mike, he said) before she carried on.

"Bill was sweet until we got engaged. Then he turned into a whole 'nother person. We were together for like, a year, and then." She completed the sentence with a wave of her hand.

How much of this revisionist life story is worked out in advance? How much is ad lib? How long can she carry it on before she trips over a conflicting fact? You don't want to involve yourself in this. The trick to successful lying is to stay as close to the truth as possible, but the truth has a habit of putting its hand up and clearing its throat at inopportune moments. You have the right to remain silent. It seems prudent to exercise it.

"It happens," said Mike. "I just got divorced myself."

"That's too bad."

"Too bad for the kid but it's for the best. We got married too young. She got pregnant. Then things change and you end up blaming each other for all the ways you fucked up your life, pardon my French."

"I can see that."

"I was pissed off for a while. But then one day you realize the only person who fucked up your life is you. You make your own luck, man. She don't owe me anything."

Mike picked up after the divorce and took a job in a pulp mill for a year before deciding to go west, young man, to the land of opportunity. His truck broke down somewhere near Winterpeg and he'd been hitching since. But the truck was old. It didn't owe him anything. He figured to replace it once he got an oil patch job, figured to make good money to send back to support his boy who had just turned seven. He had pictures. Zane tried to be appreciative. The pictures were fuzzy and overexposed.

"It's good to make a fresh start," said Melissa.

"I made my fresh start back in Fredericton. Fresh start's all in your head."

Melissa drove on for a while before responding.

"I guess I'm not there yet."

Saskatchewan stretched limitless to the horizon, as empty as the moon. A small cluster of lunar cattle moved across a field to the north. One small step for a cow, one giant misstep for cow-kind; there's this rumour that we're all to become hamburger.

Zane wanted to say that there are no fresh starts. You carry your scars with you everywhere you go, a suitcase of troubles. All you can really do is learn to ignore them, although sooner or later someone will always ask where in the world you got a scar like that.

"I guess you're right," he said. "A fresh start's all in your head."

All Zane really wanted was to get back to sleep.

CHAPTER THIRTEEN

Christine, he said. Get lost. You're supposed to be dead.

Of course I'm not dead.

You're dead. I saw you dead.

Wake up, man. You're scaring the shit out of me.

Now the scene snaps into focus: darkness, sweaty sheets, his legs tangled in the blankets. Another foreign room in which the only light is the soft red glow from the clock radio. A woman holding him, pressing his head to her shoulder, rocking and shushing him like a child. The warmth of her body, an alien feeling of comfort. And in the strange warmth of Melissa's embrace, Zane felt a rising feeling of helplessness and loss.

He pushed away from her and sat up.

"You okay?"

"Bad dream."

"Don't freak me out like that."

She stood and turned on the bedside lamp, went briefly into the bathroom and emerged carrying a glass of water.

"You want to talk about it?"

"You've seen the pictures."

"Suit yourself."

Zane drank the water. He could taste the chlorine. The blanket was cheap, made from some fuzzy plastic material. There was a hole in it, a cigarette burn. That blanket will probably burn faster than newspaper. Things like this should not be allowed.

Chechnya was worse, much worse, than Sarajevo. The Russian way of war hadn't changed since Stalingrad. In Groszny you lived in the cellar and came up to the surface only briefly to scrounge for food and firewood. If you were lucky, you made it back to the cellar. If not, the shells found you and you became a patch of snow filled with frozen blood. A shell leaves not very much.

The Russian troops were ill-trained boys in ill-fitting uniforms, whose feet slowly rotted in the triangular footcloths that they wore in place of socks. The Russian way was to shell and bomb until the earth itself groaned and the air stank and shrieked with shrapnel, and then to throw the bodies of their soldiers into the maelstrom like logs into a wood chipper, to become more stains in the snow.

A thousand pictures could not explain Groszny. And Zane had been at it too long. No picture could ever explain that.

"It's not healthy to bottle things up."

"You're a shrink now?"

"No, I'm your fuckin' friend."

He got up and went into the bathroom and put the glass on the counter and splashed water on his face. Then he dried his face with a towel and went back into the room and sat on the edge of his bed, facing her.

"It was a dream about Chechnya. I was trapped in the shelling. That's all."

The splash of yellow light from the bedside lamp washed over her knees and left her face in half-darkness. High-contrast, highly directional light. You get dramatic, moody pictures. Zane got up to find his camera.

"What do you think it means?"

"It doesn't mean anything. It means I was in Chechnya once."

You get shelled, you get scared, you have a nightmare. And then some overpaid jackass starts in about repressed memories of your unhappy childhood and your secret fear that your father will cut off your penis with a carving knife. And people get paid for this.

Zane picked up his camera and checked the film counter.

"Don't you ever talk about it?"

"No."

"You can't hide behind that camera forever."

He took a picture of her, sitting on the edge of her bed in an oversized T-shirt. A flash of irritation crossed her face. He took another shot.

"I have better things to do." She flicked off the light. He got up to put his camera away, utterly blind in the sudden darkness. Looking for his camera bag, he stubbed his toe and swore.

"Serves you right," she said, but she turned the light back on. He put the camera away and inspected his foot. It felt as if he should have been bleeding, but there was no visible damage. Shit, Zane, you're just a big baby.

He sat down on his bed again and looked at her for a long moment before he spoke.

"They used to say, in the U.S. Civil War, that when you'd been in combat you'd seen the elephant."

"Seen the what?"

"The elephant. I used to think it meant something deep and important, like the elephant was so big and incomprehensible and I had to find it and explain it. But then I found out what it really means."

She sat and watched him in the half-light, and again he wanted to take a picture, drawn by the starkness of the light.

"Which is what?"

"It's a story: the circus comes to town and this yokel drives down there in his wagon because he wants to see the elephant. His horses see the elephant and they panic and bust up his wagon and kick the shit out of him. So he limps home, all beat to shit, and his wife says, how was the circus? Well, he says, I sure saw the elephant!"

He got up and went back into the bathroom and got the water glass. He had a mickey of rum in his bag and he got it out and splashed some in the glass and then drank it and waited for the glow.

"So you're the yokel."

He refilled his glass and raised it to her in a mock toast.

"I'm the yokel of fucking yokels."

"That Christine, she really messed you up."

"What?"

"You were babbling about Christine."

"She messed me up, all right." He refilled his glass for a third time.

"Who's Christine?"

He looked carefully at Melissa. She was about the same age Christine had been, and probably as different as it was possible to be.

"You know, when I started out, I thought I could save the world."

"Superman's dead, man."

This threw him for a moment. He finished his rum and decided not to refill it. It was coming back as heartburn.

"You get past that," he said. "And then you just hate everyone. It makes it easier. If you hate everyone then you don't have to hate yourself. And then you get tired of hating everyone and then you know how God feels."

"How does God feel?"

"Sad and tired and helpless," he said. He put the glass down and turned out the light and tried to go to sleep.

* * *

Somewhere near the eastern edge of Alberta, Zane gained a new and visceral understanding that the continent is just plain wide. He arrived at this after about thirty minutes of silent travel, Melissa staring out the window at the unvarying landscape. If I'd known how big this country is, he said, I would have stayed home.

She didn't reply.

The car covered ten further minutes of the continent's width before a motorcycle passed, a Harley Davidson that came up behind and swung out to pass before Zane realized it was there.

Melissa whooped.

"You got *owned*, man."

For the Harley, the continent was somewhat narrower.

"Man, you gotta pick it up," she said.

Pick it up and leave a smear of engine oil and bits of metal down the road as the engine drops out.

"I should hitch a ride with that guy."

"I can let you out here if you like."

"You gotta love a Harley. Get up on that thing with the wind in your hair and just go."

The wind in your hair and the bugs in your teeth.

"You ever actually ride on one?"

"I used to have this boyfriend owned a Harley."

"I guess it goes with the territory."

"What territory?"

He watched the road for a moment thinking how to put this tactfully, and then looked over at her.

"No, shit, this was way back. Before I got into stripping."

Zane found himself shifting his weight again, pushing himself against the seat back.

"How far back was that?"

"I was fifteen."

"And your boyfriend had a Harley."

"He was thirty-five."

At fifteen, Zane was momentarily in love with one Caroline Pearson, who was not in love with him, momentarily or otherwise. Caroline Pearson was going steady with the captain of the football team; this playing field was by no means level, and Zane didn't stand a chance. And this was the most serious personal crisis he faced during that school year.

"I didn't have anyplace to go. He kind of took me in."

"A real prince, was he?"

Melissa rolled her window down two inches.

"No," she said. "He was not a real prince."

A dull ache had formed in the small of Zane's back and he twisted in his seat in an effort to dispel it.

"I fell for the bike. I just liked the thought of myself up on the back of that bike with the wind in my hair like some kind of wild thing. It seemed like a good deal to me."

"We're gonna have to stop soon for gas."

She looked over and caught his eye and he looked back at the road.

"Shit," she said. "I wasn't looking for a deal. I just wanted to be his wild thing."

"Well." You want to say something about teenagers, about dumb kids, but you both know that you don't know the first damn thing about it. Not in this case.

"He was a bad dude."

"Thirty five, going after teenaged girls."

"No, I mean a bad dude. He was dealing drugs, all kinds of stuff."

"This was Vancouver?"

She shook her head.

"Just some little shit-ass logging town."

"So he was the local dealer."

"More than that," she said. "He was gonna turn me out."

"So you left."

"Shit, no. He fuckin' owned me, man. I had no place to go. There's no place you can run in a little shit-ass town like that. And the cops know all about him but they turn a blind eye."

"But you got out."

"He got busted."

"But you said the cops turned a blind eye."

"'Til I started fucking this cop."

Caroline has virgin lips, scrawled on Caroline Pearson's locker door in thick black marker, and Zane at first didn't quite get it. Or he didn't want to get it. But you get older and the goddamn continent just keeps getting wider, and eventually, you get to know how God feels.

And then Melissa was laughing.

"Shit, Zane," she said. "You fuckin' *fell* for that?"

And she leaned back in her seat and put her foot up on the dash and rolled her head back and laughed again. He didn't think it was quite that funny.

* * *

Zane's car expired just outside Medicine Hat. At one moment he was zipping along at his customary pace, somewhere just below the speed at which a cop on patrol would feel obliged to take notice, and at the next moment he found the car coasting as the accelerator needle rotated inexorably back towards zero. The engine note became a letter of resignation: it continued to operate to fulfill its existing obligations, but had given its notice and henceforth would take on no new projects. And nothing that Zane did could compel it to reconsider its decision.

Zane expressed his feelings concerning this turn of events in a single word. He pulled to the right edge of the shoulder and stopped, then took the engine out of gear and floored the accelerator. The engine responded that it would be working to rule from this point forward, but thanked him for showing interest in its career and future plans.

"What's the matter with it?"

"If I knew that, nothing'd be the matter with it."

This was, of course, wishful thinking; Zane's knowledge of motor vehicle maintenance was limited to adding gas and inflating tires. He put the engine out of its misery and then got out, lifted the hood and gazed upon the mystery within, while trying to conceal his bafflement.

At a time like this you realize how far removed you are from those hardy souls of yesteryear who, faced with inoperable Model T Fords, stripped apart their engines and fashioned replacement gasket-seal-grommet-bushing-things out of old tin pots. Humanity in general has declined. We soon shall see computer scientists and nuclear physicists starving in droves, simply because they're unable to open cans of baked beans without the aid of electrical appliances. Future archeologists will discover their shrunken bodies and their final scribbled notes: delivery of sufficient kinetic energy to can may cause it to rupture, allowing access to contents – could build machine for this purpose if only could find wood and nails to use with this hammer!

Al Joad, you are not.

"Do you know anything about cars?"

"I was hoping it was something obvious."

"So you were faking it."

"Not faking it, *per se*."

"So it's up to me to save the day."

Zane appraised her while he considered the possible meanings of this remark. This could be the final blow to your manhood: Melissa has a secret past as a licensed mechanic.

"You know how to fix this?"

"I know how to hitchhike into town and find a towtruck."

Which she did, leaving Zane at the roadside with a deceased automobile and a panicky conviction that she would not return. He thrust this thought aside by reminding himself that her bags were still in the trunk of his car. His story wasn't going far without its luggage.

Melissa returned in the front seat of a towtruck driven by a man who wore a battered ball cap, a shirt that declared his name to be Scott, and clean work pants that suggested he spent more time towing cars than working on them. Scott seemed disappointed to see Zane, a human signpost indicating the end of his role as white knight of the towtruck. He asked what the problem was, the question a challenge as clear as an oil-stained work glove thrown on the gravel at Zane's feet.

"It just more or less conked out."

"As in the engine died?"

Scott snapped his chewing gum and affected an air of boundless capability.

"Not exactly died. It won't go any faster than a crawl."

"Make any noises when it conked out?"

"Not really, no. In fact, it stopped making noises."

You bullshit artist. You're no more going to fix this bastard here at the side of the road than I am. Nothing will reveal itself until this beast is hooked up to diagnostic equipment that neither of us understands. Why not cut to the part where you tow us into town, and you go back to fantasizing about the girl in the Snap-On Tools calendar?

Scott knew enough to quit when he was ahead, and declined to look under the hood. On the way into Medicine Hat Melissa took the middle seat and carried on an animated conversation with him, and his ears turned bright red when she suggested that the disastrous and unrecoverable failure of Zane's engine was for her a stroke of luck. Zane, for his part, considered the terrain of southern Alberta.

Zane felt an imperative to keep moving. The Toyota was long past its best-before date. He left the car with a wrecker and took a cab to the nearest car dealership, where he stalked the lot looking at used cars.

The ritual of tire-kicking summons salesmen like demons to an incantation; in this case, in the form of a man in sports jacket and tie who said his name was Rod. Rod shook hands with great force and bonhomie, and favoured words such as "gosh" and "golly" which in Zane's estimation hadn't been used since 1953, and even then, not by real people. Zane took this to indicate that the salesman's name was Roderick but he adopted his Rod persona to come across as the kind of hokey, just-folks small-town Little-League-coaching everyman who you'd gladly give your money to in good faith, only to discover after the fact that you'd been screwed over on every aspect of the deal not expressly covered in writing. This understanding, Zane felt, was the basis of a solid working relationship in the field of automotive sales.

"I'll give you seven thousand bucks for it, cash on the nail, and forget the extended warranties and other bullshit."

Rod blinked and looked quickly at Melissa, unsure how to deal with the bluntness of Zane's offer. He had made a point of ignoring the state of her face, as if it was none of his business and certainly not something he'd allow to deep-six the deal. Consequently, he didn't look at her long.

"What about the fabric treatment?"

"No fabric treatment."

"And how much will you be putting down?"

"Seven thousand bucks. Plus taxes and assorted bullshit. And we drive out of here today."

For reasons beyond Zane's ken, the deal seemed suddenly urgent: he needed the car, now. He needed to be on the road again that same afternoon. And this problem, at least, he knew how to lick. What earnest towtruck Scott didn't comprehend, with his faith in tools and know-how, was that all mechanical problems are ultimately solved by a liberal application of cash. And this point, Zane was not ashamed to drive home to his adopted daughter.

"Seven thousand cash?"

Rod's mind had evidently recovered from its surprise at Zane's unorthodox purchasing procedures, and had seized on the essentials of the deal, to wit, the commission. The reasons for Zane's urgency, like the state of Melissa's eye behind her sunglasses, he chose to ignore.

"I'll get you a cashier's cheque. And I want to be out of here this afternoon. So let's get cracking."

Rod got cracking.

* * *

It transpired that in Medicine Hat, no amount of cracking is sufficient to close a deal on a used car and complete the necessary paperwork within two hours. The deal was not done until nearly one the following afternoon. Zane, feeling unaccountably agitated by his loss of momentum, soothed his nerves by proceeding to the local shopping mall. He felt an overpowering urge to own a wristwatch.

He had lost the habit of wearing one. On the rare occasions when Zane wanted the time, he ordinarily checked his cellphone. But now, a watch seemed suddenly essential. He fussed at length over a large display of watches and finally selected a stainless steel dress watch with a black dial and silver numbers. The hands glowed in the dark and the face lit up at the press of a button, and the crystal was flat and reflected the sterile fluorescent light of the mall. He was not ashamed to admit that it appealed to him mostly because it was shiny.

The watch did not fit. To adjust the band, he needed a pair of pliers, so he bought an expensive multi-tool featuring pliers, two knife blades (one serrated), Phillips and slot-head screwdrivers, a can opener, and a small saw. So equipped, and with his new wristwatch shining importantly on his wrist, he bought himself a pair of polarized sunglasses with blue mirror lenses, a mechanical pencil, two notebooks, a paperback novel to read on the trip, a new toothbrush, a thermos, two stainless steel coffee mugs and a compass for the dashboard of his new car.

He told Melissa that he needed supplies. In truth, the mere act of shopping was calming his unexplained attacks of nerves. He had been driving so long that it felt strange to be in one place. Also, once you drop seven thousand on a car, the rest seems like spare change.

He bought a new road atlas of Canada, with which he could navigate from Vancouver to St. John's via Whitehorse, should the need arise. The road map in his glovebox was useless, partially because it covered only Ontario, but more importantly because it was no longer in his glovebox. It had gone missing long before the Toyota reached the wrecker's yard, and Melissa insisted that she had no knowledge of its whereabouts.

He remembered Amanda. In his role as absent uncle returning from afar, it seemed proper that he bear gifts. She would be sixteen. He had no idea.

"You leave that to me," said Melissa.

"I don't know what she listens to, what size she would wear, what she likes. I don't know anything."

"As long as she's not a goth or something."

Melissa treated him to a questioning look. He didn't know; as an uncle, Zane was proving deficient. He hedged his bets with I-don't-think-so, and regretted it, realizing too late that this was simply moronic.

Melissa, having dragged him through a series of boutiques, picked out a pair of earrings, small oblong silver pendants with a design picked out on the face in gold.

"She's only sixteen."

"You really are a complete idiot."

Melissa snapped the box closed and handed it to him, and he added it to his growing bundle of shopping bags. A sudden panic seized him. With the act of buying the gift, his impending visit to Connie became a reality.

"I need some decent clothes."

He made Melissa wait while he looked at shirts, contemplated a tie. Perhaps a sports jacket.

"If you wear a tie, what am I going to wear?"

"Just be yourself. She'll love you. Especially if you keep calling me an idiot."

I guess I can keep it casual then, she said. Zane settled on a shirt, no tie, no sports jacket. He bought Melissa a new shirt. They got changed in advance. The car was ready, and he was out of excuses.

CHAPTER FOURTEEN

Connie lived in a sprawling new house on the south edge of Calgary, backing onto the Bow River flood plain. Its architecture recalled an older style, a style that predated the uniform suburban boxes, bungalows and split-levels of Zane's childhood and now was back in vogue. Gabled windows overlooked a driveway of interlocking paving stone, with sand still fresh in its crevices, leading up to a three-car garage. Three small saplings loitered in the front yard. They had yet to grow into the roles which fate and landscape architecture had assigned.

"Some house," said Melissa.

"Jim's a plastic surgeon."

"Big money in boob jobs, I guess."

You can dress this kid up but you can't take her anywhere.

"He does reconstructive surgery. On burn victims. He teaches at the University hospital."

Zane tilted the rear-view mirror and fussed briefly at his hair, and then gave it up as pointless. Too little, too late; you're not about to fool anyone, new shirt or no. Melissa's face will get all the stares in any case. She had donned her sunglasses, which as a disguise proved no more effective than his abortive attempt to tame his hair.

"Showtime," he said.

"It can't be that bad."

"You wait."

He got out of the car and closed his door. The latch punctuated the afternoon with a satisfying, decisive clunk.

A magpie called, a sound like a creaking gate, which confused Zane until he located its source, perched on the peak of the garage roof. Beside the front door, Connie had installed an ornate wooden mailbox with a painted wooden face peeking out over the top. Kilroy was here but has now gone kitsch, spelling out a welcome in chunky wooden capitals. It was the kind of thing Zane's mother might have put up, to go with her overstuffed furniture, her flower prints.

Something in this icon of suburbia, or in his own reaction to it, bothered him. You don't want to be a cynic but at the same time you instinctively write it all off as tacky, condemn each token of conspicuous consumption even as Lapierre's voice intones that it is not wrong to want these things. You recognize the road not taken even as you bomb it. Not one of us is incapable of pettiness.

Zane stopped on the front step to gather himself before ringing the doorbell, but the front door confounded him by opening of its own accord.

Revealed in the doorway, a cheerful family portrait: Connie in sundress, Doctor Jim in khakis with dress shirt open at the neck, daughter Amanda smiling between them. All this scene lacks is a mid-toned backdrop lit by a couple of studio flash units bounced off umbrellas.

Connie's smile seemed unnaturally rigid. Zane felt scruffier than usual, and acutely conscious of the bruises peeping from behind Melissa's sunglasses. The moment stretched thin. Then Zane remembered himself and introduced Melissa.

"What happened to your face?" Amanda, guileless and sixteen, broached the unbroachable.

Melissa removed her sunglasses.

"I got beat up."

"How?"

"Old boyfriend. Long story."

The tension deflates with an almost palpable sense of release. The important thing, it seems, is that Melissa did not incur these injuries by walking into a door. This would be embarrassing for everyone.

Connie took Zane's hand and tilted her head to one side and smiled weakly.

"It's been a long time."

"It sure has."

Watching a faint tremble in Connie's chin, Zane felt a sense of panic. Are we all supposed to be this fragile? You get the awkward sense that you're supposed to be equally emotional, that you're supposed to do or say something. All of us kittens, hanging in there; we've sure got guts. Then it occurred to him: the conventional thing would be to give her a hug. He felt stiff and uncomfortable as her tears wet his cheek.

Inside, the house seemed almost empty, the effect of its open concept design and vaulted ceilings. An awkward silence echoed momentarily through the space.

"Amanda, I can't believe how you've grown."

Melissa kicked Zane in the ankle.

"Your uncle is an idiot."

As an ice breaker, this was certainly unique, not to mention effective; everyone save Zane agreed. Zane flexed his ankle, indignant less over the kick than over the lack of a serious injury about which to complain. Being lame was not in itself a problem; it was the sense of the word that was troublesome.

"Anyway, we got you a little something." He held out the box containing the earrings.

"They're gorgeous."

"Melissa picked them out."

Amanda started chattering at Melissa. Zane felt his stature deflate, but he had no one to blame but himself.

"Come on out back," said Jim. "You want a beer?"

Zane nodded. He was going to be needing a beer.

Jim pointed to Melissa and raised an eyebrow.

"Just a pop or juice or whatever is fine."

At the back of the house a sliding glass door opened onto a broad wooden deck. Below, the Bow River snaked across its flood plain. Jim's barbecue, an enormous, stainless steel monster, lit with a push-button. No fumbling with matches, no eyebrows in peril as propane and air approached the correct explosive ratio. Zane felt this detracted somewhat from the manliness of the exercise.

"It's burgers," said Jim, and motioned to a platter where the patties were stacked. "But I got chicken for you."

"Thanks."

"Short bowel is no fun."

Talking shop, the consequence of being an expert on the one piece of equipment that everyone owns. Every body a conversation piece. Those 1958 Zanes, you know: good model year, but you really got to watch the head gaskets. After a while they start leaking all over the damn place. Next thing you know the thing blows a seal, one hell of a mess. And eventually they just more or less conk out.

"I'm off red meat, anyway."

The sight of loose ground beef ordinarily made Zane feel distinctly ill. He looked away from the platter and took a long pull from his beer. It was so cold that his teeth hurt. He couldn't taste a thing.

Connie emerged from the house and drifted over to Zane and squeezed his arm and pointed him at a chair at the patio table. Zane took up his indicated position, in the shade of a green cloth umbrella. Connie sat opposite.

"It really is good to see you." Connie possessed a fey, ineffable fragility, a wispiness that Zane could not quite fathom. Her voice was soft and seemed insubstantial, as if she was not there.

"It's been too long," he said.

Connie looked off over the river and he felt the need to fill the conversational space.

"I really can't believe how much Amanda's grown."

"Kids grow up," said Jim. He was a merchant of the obvious.

"She's just about grown up."

"Let's not rush things," said Connie.

"She'll be off to university soon."

"She has two more years of high school."

"What's she going to do?"

"I don't think she knows. She's not as grown up as she looks."

Connie nodded towards the back lawn, where Amanda and Melissa wandered together. They were too distant to be overheard, but their laughter carried up to the deck. Zane felt certain that he was the butt of the joke.

"It's nice for your friend to have someone to talk to, a little closer her own age."

"We're not together."

"You're driving her around just because?"

"I'm doing a story on her, Connie."

Connie sipped at her drink and looked out again at Melissa and Amanda, whose heads were now close in sisterly conversation.

"Women amaze me," said Jim. He turned away from the barbecue and waved his spatula in the general direction of the lawn. Zane suspected that he secretly wanted to wave it at Connie. "Five minutes, and they're old friends."

"Melissa has that effect on people."

"You two seem pretty close," said Connie.

"We're not."

"Pretty familiar, anyway."

"I've kind of adopted her. She's a nice kid."

"So you won't be sharing the guest room, then."

"I'm fine on the couch."

"What happened to her face?"

Connie was perhaps less fragile than she appeared. Zane pushed away his irritation. It's none of her business but then again, it is the obvious question.

"Like she said: she got beat up."

"What I mean is, how, and by who?"

"She told you, her old boyfriend."

"I'd say a current boyfriend. Those bruises are pretty fresh."

"A former boyfriend."

Connie raised her eyebrows. Is it possible to become so defiled that your own sister will not recognize you?

"You know me better than that."

"You've been through a lot."

"I haven't been through that much."

Connie sipped at her drink.

"Anyway, it's her story to tell."

Connie put her drink down and stood up. "I'll go get the plates."

"You want to watch those orbital bones," said Jim.

"They're fine, apparently. Just the stitches."

Jim stood by the barbecue and looked out over the valley and hefted his spatula, as if testing its weight.

"You should visit more often," he said, as if addressing the river. "It's good for Connie, to see you."

"It's a long way to come."

"She wants to see more of you, you know."

Jim lifted the lid and flipped the burgers, and then asked Zane if he wanted another beer, as if nothing else had been said. Zane accepted, and Jim pulled one from the icebox.

"Those stitches look like a good job."

Zane let that one ride, thinking, doctors.

"She's going to have a scar, though."

"Eyebrows like a hockey player."

"What about you? How are you doing these days?"

"The diet gets me down."

"You aren't looking so good."

Zane put the beer down on the table. It now seemed important that he not drink it. Melissa and Amanda, down on the lawn, were sharing another joke.

"It's just I don't sleep so well, these days."

Jim looked out at the river and hefted the spatula again.

"I love living on the Bow," he said. "I go down in the evenings to fish. I got a drift boat in the garage. There's nothing like trout fishing, Luke. It helps me get my headspace, you know?"

Headspacing, as it had been explained to Zane, was a measurement important to the correct adjustment of a machine gun. This was no way to live.

"I always found fishing a bit goofy."

"A jerk on one end of the line, and a jerk on the other."

"Something like that."

"No, it's relaxing." Jim opened the lid and checked the burgers again. "I can do skin grafts all week and then Saturday I do a float trip down the Bow with my fishing partner and all that stuff just flies away."

A magpie lighted in a tree at the edge of the lawn.

"I got a case last month. Young guy, British soldier. You know, they train down at Suffield, just east of here." He took a pull of his beer and then set it down and closed the lid of the barbecue. "Anyway, he was in a tank, or whatever, and somehow they got hit by friendly fire. In training. Can you believe that?"

Zane said nothing. This was precisely the territory he preferred to avoid. It gets so the sight of ground beef makes you sick.

"Anyway, the burns were pretty bad."

"I can imagine."

"I'm sure you don't need to imagine."

"No."

Zane picked up his beer again and took a swig. Despite the sun, the breeze felt cold. Jim continued squinting at the river, as if he expected to spot rising trout.

"Anyway, if you want to talk to someone, I can refer you to some pretty good people. There's a guy at U of T."

"It's okay."

"It's too bad you aren't staying a couple days. We could go fishing. Goofy as it is. You wouldn't believe the browns we get."

Jim now devoted himself to removing the burgers from the grill, as if they had been discussing trout fishing all the while.

They ate on the deck. The sun had dipped below the edge of the patio umbrella. Melissa, sitting beside Zane, dropped her sunglasses over her eyes. The sun felt warm on his arms and a cool breeze out of the southwest washed over him. He sat back in his chair and stretched out his legs and smiled at his sister.

"This is nice."

"We won't be getting many more days like this one." Connie turned her head to look out over the river, where the sun played on the riffles. "Amanda starts back at school next week."

Amanda, wearing her new earrings, scowled at the prospect.

"Your whole life can't be a vacation," said Jim.

"It's working out just fine for Zane." Melissa skewered a cherry tomato with her fork and smirked at him. He felt a sudden desire to critique her table manners.

"I miss the postcards," said Amanda. And to Melissa: "Uncle Luke used to send me postcards from all over, when I was a little kid."

"I don't travel much anymore."

Not to mention which, all the fun had gone out of it. The joke had run its course. The last time he sent her a postcard was from New York, a Manhattan skyline with the World Trade Center. He had no idea, when he mailed it, what was about to happen. He was in town to meet Jack, the day before. After she saw the postcard, Connie called him a sick man, told him never to send another.

"Those cards were so random. When I was in, like, Grade Two, I brought postcards from Sarajevo for show and tell. My teacher totally freaked out."

"Some of those postcards freaked me out," said Connie.

When the siege was on, there was no mail out of Sarajevo. Zane collected the postcards and mailed them from Graz, filled them with chatty remarks on such topics as Bosnian coffee, the weather, and all the new friends he pretended to be making. He never mentioned the wars. He told himself that he was playing a game with his young niece, so that she could look up all the places he had been in an atlas and learn about the world. but he was playing a game with himself, pretending that he was a simple tourist. Making up a different and more peaceful life.

"I bet you have some crazy stories." Amanda pushed the salad around her plate and looked at him expectantly.

"Zane's a bore. He doesn't like to tell stories," said Melissa.

"Your uncle's probably tired out from all that driving," said Jim.

Connie said nothing. Zane concentrated on his salad.

"Those postcards were so random. Uncle Luke was always my coolest uncle."

Jim had only sisters.

"I was there when the Berlin Wall fell."

"When the what?"

"When the Berlin Wall fell."

"You were there?"

"I sure was."

"Wow. We talked about that in History."

Melissa started to giggle. You get kicked in the ankle and called an idiot but chances are that Amanda's history textbooks include your photos.

"It was very exciting."

Melissa laughed out loud.

"Okay, well, she wanted a story."

"'It was very exciting' ain't a story, Zane."

"So what about this story you're working on now?" Connie had finished her meal and now neatly laid her knife and fork at four-thirty, as if waiting for a waiter to come and clear away the paper plates.

"Just a documentary thing."

Amanda made a disappointed face: "Documentary is a movie only four people watch, and three of them are sleeping."

"Sounds about right," said Zane. He was simply thankful that she had changed the subject.

"But what's it about?" said Connie.

Zane found it necessary to turn over his plastic fork and closely inspect the tines.

"It's about how I'm going home to make a fresh start," said Melissa.

"Why?"

"Why what?"

"Why a fresh start."

Zane picked up his fork again. Each of the tines had a small reinforcing rib near its base, perpendicular to the load-bearing surface, and the tine itself was constructed as a U-shaped channel. He supposed this gave the fork greater strength than a plain plastic fork would possess, although food would get caught in the U-channel. But then, you weren't supposed to clean and reuse these things. This was not among the design requirements.

He set the fork back down. The sun was in his eyes and he thought briefly of being interrogated under a bright light. Melissa watched him expectantly through her sunglasses.

"She's leaving the former boyfriend, etcetera," he said.

"And making a fresh start."

"Actually, there's more to it than that," said Melissa.

Zane inspected his fork again. Let's see what she comes up with this time.

"I'm starting my whole life over again."

"Like what?"

"I was a stripper. I did porn movies."

In the silence that followed, it seemed that the sun shrank appreciably toward the horizon.

"I don't know if the Flames are going to do anything this year," said Jim. "You can't ride Iginla's coattails forever."

Zane had never, until now, wished that he paid more attention to hockey. Connie shot Jim a look of contempt and then addressed Zane as if Melissa no longer existed, all of her wispiness blown away.

"What the hell is wrong with you?"

"It's a good story," said Zane.

"A good story?"

"It's a great story."

"I can't believe you."

"I'll go wait in the car," said Melissa, an announcement to which no-one responded.

"It's not such a big deal," he said.

"It's a big deal to me."

Zane motioned at the screen door, through which Melissa had now disappeared.

"She's a good kid, Connie."

"This is my home."

"Did she soil your carpet?"

"I have a sixteen-year-old daughter!"

Connie's chair slid back and teetered as she stood. Her balled-up paper napkin hit the table and bounced into Zane's lap.

"I'm not a baby, mom," said Amanda.

"Please excuse us."

"You think I've never been on the Internet?"

"Amanda, would you please excuse the grown-ups?"

"And I'll be happy to excuse you, too." Amanda departed.

Zane picked up the crumpled napkin and put it on his plate.

"Let's not overreact," said Jim.

"Oh, I'm sure you liked Lucas's little friend just fine, didn't you?"

"Connie."

"Maybe you've seen her before?"

"This is between you and Luke." Jim followed Amanda.

Every man for himself. At this time, the Captain asks that you identify and proceed to your assigned lifeboat station, and please refrain from running like hell on the quarterdeck. It had come time to announce a dignified departure. But first, there would be a certain amount of verbal abuse.

"Do you ever stop to think of the harm you do?" Connie began clearing up the remains of supper. Fortunately, none of the dishes were breakable. "Do you ever stop to think of the mess you leave behind?"

As if to underscore her point, she knocked over the salad bowl, swore, and then started to cry. Zane leaned down and started picking up lettuce from the deck, couldn't think where to put it, stood there stupidly with his hands full of salad.

"You're overreacting."

"Oh, I'm overreacting."

She made an ineffective attempt to sweep the remains of the salad up off the table. Leaves of lettuce stuck to her fingers as she tried to drop them into the bowl, and she swatted at them in frustration.

"You bring this whore to dinner, and I'm overreacting?"

"She's not a whore."

"Oh, I'm sorry, this goddamn *porn star*."

"She's a good kid."

"She's a good kid?" Now the potato salad took flight. Mayonnaise on his face. "Amanda is sixteen years old!"

Two years out of the university dorm. Two years from frat house parties, from wet T-shirt night, from come on baby, be a good sport, the pictures will just be for us. I won't put them up on the Internet, honest. Which is where kids get their sex ed these days, in any case. The angel at the gates raises his flaming sword and says, hey babe, yer kinda cute. Before you split town, whyn't you and me get to know each other better? What, you're going to listen to your *mother*?

"She could learn a lot from Melissa," said Zane, and Connie hit him.

The blow took him by surprise and she was screaming at him and clawing at his face before he realized what was happening, and he pushed her back, hard. She went back over a deck chair and fell. Everything stopped except the tears.

Well, now you hit a girl. Zane felt blood running from his nose and he touched his hand to it. There was blood all over his fingers and he held them out for her to see. His hands were trembling and he didn't care.

Connie sat on the deck amidst the salad.

"Get out of my house!"

Zane went back through the sliding door and through the house, cupping his hand under his nose to save the carpets. In the kitchen, Jim hunched over a bowl of strawberries, and Zane waved to him with his free hand.

"I'm really sorry about this," said Zane.

"I guess you miss dessert."

Jim pointed his fork at the strawberries, and looked down on them as if they had been carelessly broken. He had defeat in his shoulders. Zane heard the sliding door open again. He made for the front door.

Amanda stood by the passenger window of his car, talking to Melissa.

"What happened to you?"

"Long story."

Connie shouted to Amanda to come in at once. Amanda scowled, and stayed put. Zane opened his door to get in.

"Anyway, remember that," said Melissa.

"I will. Bye, Uncle Luke."

You say goodbye to your niece with blood streaming from your nose where her mother punched you. It is theoretically possible to sink lower, but no one has yet explained how.

Connie shouted at Amanda again. At the front door she told her mother to lighten up. Zane started the engine. He was getting blood on his new cloth seats.

"What was all that about?"

"Girl stuff," said Melissa. "What happened to your nose?"

"Girl stuff."

He'd had all the girl stuff he could take. He put it in reverse and backed out of the driveway without looking, into the path of a black convertible that swerved, honked, and then came to rest alongside him. The driver shouted something. He was about forty-five, with thin sandy hair. Zane gave him the finger.

The other driver opened his car door and started to get out. Zane put it in gear and waited until he started coming around his car, and then punched it hard. His tires left rubber on the pavement. In his rear view, he saw the sandy-haired man giving him the finger, and he fought down the urge to put it in reverse and go back and beat him into the ground. It was necessary that somebody display some maturity.

"All things considered," he said, "I feel that was a successful visit."

CHAPTER FIFTEEN

I don't remember a lot of the details, but somehow, I ended up here. I'm forty-six years old, somewhere in the Rocky Mountains, driving down the Trans-Canada to Vancouver with a would-be actress-cum-small-time porn model sleeping in the passenger seat. This would have all the makings of a first-rate, high-grade mid-life crisis were it not for her black eye, split lip, and stitches, not to mention the apparently irrecoverable failure of my erectile apparatus. This, at least, has guaranteed that our relationship remained platonic, regardless of what my intentions might otherwise have been. And to be honest I'm not quite sure what my intentions are. The trouser snake awakens in hospital to find himself paralyzed; he seeks a new vocation, but his talents are limited, and his motivation poor. It's a cruel fate.

You're not going to remember much of this trip. You've slept through half of it. But I guess Saskatchewan and Manitoba and southern Alberta really aren't that memorable anyway. They're just flat and endless. So you can wake up in Vancouver like a victim of amnesia, a woman without a past, without an identity. And then you can make that fresh start everyone yearns for. You can look out at the dismal Vancouver grey and find it all fresh and bright and beautiful.

But that'll never work in the end. The past always bubbles back to the surface. A man without a past digs for one, an orphan seeks his parents. Driven by a tragic curiosity, the cat digs too deep in the litter box; the anti-personnel mine coughs up a furball. You'll always have that hockey scar. No matter how many gaps remain in the story, the final frame is somehow connected to the first.

You asked why I took this job, with Rich – I should say, that job – and I said it was because I answered an ad. You think I'm being facetious, that I'm simply being evasive, but that's a truthful answer. It's the only truthful answer I have. Do you ever really know why you do anything? Why did you answer Connie flat out like that, when you made up stories for everyone else? I don't know, and neither do you. We just do things. The rest is our excuses.

So: it is a fact that I answered an ad, and I prefer to deal in facts. Anything else gets us into dangerous territory. You can't believe half the shit you hear, and the shit you make up, you can trust less. You start in on that, you end up trading on trust, and that's a slippery currency. That particular account is well overdrawn.

I'm sure you'd like a nice, pat explanation for my life. Something to tie up all my loose ends: I left it all behind after witnessing unspeakable horrors, etcetera, that left me reduced to a whisky-soaked shell. You'd like to think you're in some tale of sin and redemption. I guess we all like to think we're walking through some grand, redemptive story. Well, we're all going to be disappointed. Disappointment is one of the two fates that we must all eventually meet.

I ran out of horror a long time ago. You start with conviction, and then you just end up sad. You know you aren't going to stop anything. You'll be off to cover another war tomorrow and the day after that and the day after that and the day after that until you retire, until you just give up and leave the job to the next quixote. You realize that all the things you thought and believed were all bullshit. You just get tired out, and you can't feel anything anymore but a kind of distant sadness.

God looks down on his children and shakes his head. Free will, he thinks – what was I smoking when I came up with that one? You drop one tab of acid, eight days later you got snakes in the Garden of Eden.

Anyway, I don't know why I'm here. All explanations are suspect, especially your own. I don't know why I do anything – I don't think anyone really does. Maybe, if I was to trust the self who keeps the razor blades out of reach, I could say that this is all part of some plan I don't fully understand. But that kind of talk starts to get religious, and you can't trust that.

Maybe I'm not keeping the razor blades out of reach at all. Maybe you're my razor blade. Maybe I'm just trying to slip one past my guardian angel. You get down to a certain point and you just want to wipe out hard. You just want to go down like a plane on fire.

Who knows? Not me. We're supposed to be sticking with the facts.

The fact is my agency fired me over an assignment that didn't work out. Or maybe it was a string of assignments that didn't work out. Maybe it was more than that. Things got a little fuzzy there, for a while.

It was Jack who called to cut me loose. I think he felt he owed me that, to do it himself. I'd been with him a long time.

I'd blown an assignment to follow the Democratic campaign, down in the States. Jack wanted the kind of masterwork Elliott Erwitt had made of the Republican convention, which was like Hunter Thompson had figured out how to develop film in an LSD bath. Erwitt cast the powermongers and kingmakers of the great republic of the free and the brave as fat, backslapping hicks out of a small-town chamber of commerce, a bunch of used car and kitchen appliance salesmen. It was all done with an ultrawide. It was brilliant.

I didn't give Jack brilliant. I couldn't find anything to shoot. To me, all those people were just jackasses shouting slogans and waving signs. There was no point in it. I'd told Jack I was done with wars, but maybe I was just done. What Jack got was a collection of boring snapshots.

This is not what makes our reputation, he said. This is not what made your reputation.

What made my reputation was the suffering of others. I suspect that in fact, what made my reputation was a great deal of luck, that becoming the great Lucas Zane was largely a matter of continually being in the right place at the right time. It's my good luck to be there when your luck turns terminally bad. But I was beginning to think that my luck had run out. And I found that I didn't much care.

So I told him, maybe I just got lucky all these years.

Bullshit, he said. The magazine is pissed. They don't pay a Lucas Zane rate to get the same crap they could get from some guy from the Upper Plodsville Herald.

I said nobody can be on his game all the time.

Bullshit, he said. What you gave us was a few weak snapshots.

I'm sorry, I said. His pause demanded a response, and there seemed little else to say.

You're sorry, all right, he said. What's really pissed everyone off, is you spent most of your time locked in your hotel room, coming out only to get drunker in the hotel bar.

It was true enough. I had certain ghosts to keep at bay. More importantly, I simply didn't give a shit. I was pretty much adrift. But I didn't feel any inclination to communicate that information to Jack.

I know what you're up to, he said.

This declaration took me by surprise. I hadn't thought I was up to anything in particular.

What am I up to?

Let's say this: memory is the one thing you can't preserve in alcohol.

I could picture him, rocking back in his chair, tremendously pleased with himself. Yes, Jack, you're such a fucking wit.

And the other thing it won't preserve is your career. In that respect, it's a solvent. Do you know where your career is?

In the toilet, I said.

You pretty much don't have any career left to flush. This isn't the first time. The word is getting out: Lucas Zane is a head case.

What do you say to something like that? In my business, you can become a drunk, but you can't become a head case.

Anyway, I'm not a head case. I just don't care anymore.

Problem is, though, you say you're not a head case, that's denial, and denial means you must be a head case. So, I was now a head case. I let him stew.

You are in a whole fucking barrel of pickles, he said, and so am I in respect to your future here. So I'm going to tell you how it's going to be.

How it was going to be was, in short, you're fired. I'm not about to keep risking the agency's reputation and my own putting you on assignments you're just going to screw up. I've gone on long enough watching you try to get back in the game, and enough's enough. I'm tired of getting burned. We'll continue managing your stock, fair enough, but for assignments, you're on your own. Nobody's going to touch you at this stage. Even Canadian Press won't have you shooting at their lousy seventy-five bucks a day.

Jack took many more words to say this than were strictly necessary. And throughout it all, all that was running through my head was Mick Jagger singing "Not Fade Away."

"I'm a-gonna tell you how it's gonna be," sang Mick, in time with Jack's recitation of my numerous shortcomings. Something here was fading away, all right, but I found that I didn't really care. All things must pass. Fair enough. Get on with it.

One last thing, he said. At that point he'd already said entirely too many last things, none of them complimentary.

Don't hock your cameras to buy booze, because if you ever do come up with a story, if you ever do get back on track, I will still be here.

That's fair, I said. I felt I owed him that much. And the thing is I actually felt relief. Like a weight had been lifted. It's a cliché but it's true.

You have an immortal fucking eye, Zane. You just need to find a reason to give a shit, he said.

After he hung up I put the phone down and walked over to the window and looked out at the city. I was living in a condo downtown, by the harbour, an expensive place with a view of the city, of the centre of all the bustle and rush that fires the hearts of those who are fully caught up in the blood sport of commerce. Everything that mattered was there, where everyone who mattered could see it. I looked out on that and it was as pointless as a hamster on its wheel.

I stood there for a while and probed, experimentally, at how it felt to be unemployed, like you might probe with your tongue at the socket of a pulled tooth, to determine if the painkillers were still doing their job.

Evening was coming on and the city was outlined in electric lights as the sky faded to a deep, dirty blue, with the last sunlight illuminating the glass of the tall buildings in gold. The evening crowd was moving in to hit the bars and theatres, tail lights streaming red down the Gardiner while the outbound stream of workaholics headed home, stockbrokers and lawyers and commodity traders, people who worked until dark each day to justify their salaries, seemingly for no reason other than to buy yachts which they could find time to use only once a year. Hamsters.

I didn't have a yacht. Didn't have much, in fact, other than an expensive downtown condo, a closet filled with cameras and lenses, an extensive collection of photography books, and the kind of expensive but minimalist furnishings that you set up to warn visitors that they're now in the presence of Good Taste, just as the condo proclaimed that I was a Major Photographer, a success in a field in which most people survive, perforce, on ramen noodles. I was never one to accumulate things, mostly because with the life I led I had no time for them. The place was basically empty. I had spent twenty-two years on the hamster wheel for this.

Now, I was no longer a major photographer, at least, not in the current sense. Now I was a legacy. And it didn't matter how hard I jammed my tongue into that bloody mess of gums. I didn't feel a thing. I was done and that was fine by me.

I went to the kitchen and found myself a glass and mixed a rum and coke and then returned to the window to watch darkness descend, to see the glow of twilight fade until electricity provided the only illumination. The city becomes a splatter of lights: the same old light show all over again.

For a moment, I considered loading some high-speed black-and-white in the old Leica and going down to Yonge Street for an evening stroll, shoot some happy snaps, push the shit out of the film, produce odd and surreal visions of the urban crush. I could rediscover my muse. But I had never liked street photography. It's mostly derivative or downright imitative. Street photography has nothing to say.

I thought for a bit about calling someone up for company, perhaps this blonde Elaine who had recently expressed a strong admiration for my photography, but whose art education had failed to teach her that this need not translate into an admiration for me. When we met, at the opening of a Burtynsky show, she radiated an availability that materialized into a slip of paper bearing her telephone number. A practical demonstration of wave-particle duality, I like to think.

I didn't call her. Truth was, she held no more interest than street photography on Yonge Street, which is to say that it had all been done before, by people with more talent and more interest than me.

The last thing I wanted was to listen to someone enthuse about the guts and commitment it must take. I left that pretense in El Salvador, about 1981. People have been killing each other since the earliest caveman returned early from a hairy mammoth hunt to discover his erstwhile friend Thag, who was supposed to be repainting the antelope on the dining cave wall, making the two-backed hairy mammoth with the lovely Ughla. And all that's changed since then is we've gotten a lot better at it, and a lot more organized. Practice makes perfect, and we've had lots of practice. One guy with a camera isn't going to change all that.

Anyway, as far as Elaine went, things hadn't been working properly, both in terms of capability and of desire, since I'd had my guts shot out. I had experimented long enough. No need to explore Elaine's capacity for disappointment. Instead, I intended to explore my own capacity for rum. It keeps the ghosts from dropping by.

It seemed about time I faded away. I wanted to commit the great Lucas Zane to the trash can of history, once and for all. I wanted to leave myself behind.

I needed a job, and my qualifications were limited. I could tell from the sound if an incoming shell was likely to pass harmlessly overhead, I could turn light to silver through alchemy, and I could keep my lunch down when all around were losing theirs. These skills seemed of little practical use on the mean streets of Toronto.

Then I found Rich's ad. I needed only two qualifications: a camera, and an absence of qualms. It seemed the solution to more than one problem.

* * *

"You're awake," he said.

"I am."

Zane concentrated on the highway, which was now definitely descending. Wherever he was, it was somewhere on the long downslope towards Vancouver and the lower mainland of British Columbia. He drove for some time in silence.

"How long have you been awake?"

"For some time now."

So you keep driving. She's heard the whole monologue, more or less. It doesn't matter. It makes sense to lay it all out, anyway. Zane was surprised to find that he felt relief.

"So I suppose you know all."

"I suppose I do."

"I should probably express annoyance that you've been listening to me chattering on for some time, without alerting me to that fact."

"You want to express annoyance, I'll express you some fuckin' annoyance, man."

Zane drove. Where the hell was this coming from?

"I ask you a question, you brush it off, then soon as I'm asleep you're all chatty Cathy. So just go right ahead, express all the fuckin' annoyance you want."

It had not occurred to Zane that this could form a *casus belli*.

"I was just talking to keep myself awake."

"Whatever. Fuck you, anyway."

This is what it feels like to be torpedoed: you're cruising along, salt air on your tongue, watching a seagull wheeling through an overcast sky, and the next thing you know you're wrapped in a sheet of flame, wheeling through the air like a broken doll.

"I'm sorry."

He directed his attention to the road. You would not want to lose control of things here. A rolling ball of mangled consequences, a tangle of metal somewhere in the Fraser Valley, just another newspaper headline. A Tragic Weekend on Area Highways, soon to be forgotten. On page fourteen, below the fold.

"Why are you so fucking afraid to just talk to me?"

Zane let that slide into a long silence. I'm a man; what the hell do you want? We don't open up, don't explore our feelings, don't revel in the masturbatory pleasure of *sharing*. The silence lengthened until he felt it was safe to respond.

"I am not afraid, *per se*."

"*Per se*? What the fuck does that mean, *per se*?"

"*Per se*? Well, it means that – "

"I know what fuckin' *per se* means, smart guy."

So the road will now require your undivided attention. It seems reasonable to put off further discussion until you get to the next stop. A matter of road safety on these lethal switchbacks. It was now getting into late afternoon. One more stop, and then Vancouver.

"Is there a reason we need to do this now?"

"No reason. Fuck, why would you want to talk to me, anyway?"

I am just one lonely man, as helpless as all the rest. Why must I exceed your expectations? Why do you all expect so much of me, when the radio has nothing to offer but this worthless new country music? I don't know what you want of me. There is no why. Stop haunting me with your accusations.

"You want my life story?"

"Shit, Zane, I just want you to fucking *talk* to me."

"Go rubberneck at some other car wreck."

"Yeah, sorry for yourself."

I'm sorry for everyone. I'm sorry for everything. It's a stupid thing to fight about anyway. It takes a woman to pick a fight about something stupid like that.

A car is a small space, and Zane had a small car. Despite the hum of the tires on the pavement and the steel guitar noise pouring out of the radio, the space was pregnant with quiet.

"You're just like your sister."

"Leave Connie out of this."

"You'd be just fine with me if I worked at the supermarket."

"I am just fine with you."

"'Til it counts."

Now she starts to cry, chin a-quiver, face collapsing. It's one thing to keep your cool with bullets flying overhead, but the sight of this woman crying engenders the sense of panic that arises from helplessness. Zane tried to rewind the tape, to make sense of the discussion, but the recording might as well have been in Urdu.

"We're all good until it counts. Then I'm just your fuckin' *story*."

"You're not just my story."

"Like I say what I am and your sister freaks on me."

"I thought you were going to make something up!"

"Why would you think that?"

"You always make stuff up."

"Why's it all up to me?"

Zane felt a rising, desperate frustration. He had no idea how to put this fire out.

224

"I'm not my sister."

"You sure didn't want her to know what I am."

"It wasn't up to me."

"What the fuck does that mean?"

"I mean it's not up to me."

"You wouldn't even fuck me."

She spat this through her tears with alarming vehemence.

How does talking to yourself lead to this? I don't know what basis we built this thing on but whatever it was, it was clearly wrong.

"Melissa," he said, "I liked being your dad."

"My dad? What the fuck do you know about my dad?"

"I don't – "

"You want to know about my dad? You want to know how I was daddy's special girl?"

Oh, Jesus.

"I'm sorry."

You get to saying that a lot these days, but what else is there to say? Melissa carried on, reciting a litany of wrongs. He pulled off the road, onto the shoulder of a curve, put on the parking brake, and killed the engine.

"Melissa," he said.

She punched him in the face.

Zane heard the car door open while his head was down. He felt a trickle but when he dabbed a finger at his nostril there was no blood. When he looked up, she was sitting on a granite block fifty feet down the road.

Fair enough. She probably owes the world a few punches. Four or five in particular, and you probably deserve at least one of them.

Zane dabbed at his nose again but still there was no blood. You would expect Melissa to pack more of a punch than little girl Connie, but there you go. Some of us get lucky and some don't. How this all went south so fast, nobody knows.

Melissa got up from the boulder, walked to the edge of the highway, and stuck her thumb out. The theatricality of this gesture, given the lack of traffic, did not occur to Zane. Foremost in his mind was the thought that the first trucker to round the curve would think he had hit the jackpot, and would bring to their arrangement all of the expectations that Melissa had so recently decried. Zane swore and twisted the key in the ignition and threw the car into gear. His tires threw gravel as he stopped in front of her.

"Get in."

"Afraid your precious story's going to hitchhike away?"

"Your bags are in my trunk."

Melissa shrugged and got in, evidently choosing to treat that observation as an immutable fact rather than a problem easily solved by operating the latch. Maybe, by whatever scoring system she uses, she wins the day. At some point you stop caring to win anyway. Just as you probably deserved the punch, you probably deserve to lose. Zane pulled onto the highway without checking his blind spot.

"I'm sorry."

"Sorry's just a way of making someone feel guilty over something you did. Sorry's a guilt-bomb."

I'm sorry you feel that way.

"I don't mean that."

"Well, I'm sorry about your face."

"You hit like a girl."

"And it wasn't the fucking Stones did 'Not Fade Away,' it was Buddy Holly did it first. You fucking boomers are all the same, you think it all begins and ends with you."

She started to cry again. Over a remark like that. He handed her the box of tissue, the same box he'd used after Connie punched him, bloody fingerprints still on its sides.

"I see you giving up on your sister, man, I don't even have a sister."

"Leave Connie out of it."

"You just give up on her."

"It's complicated."

"Bullshit. You just write people off. You just leave them behind."

"Easy to say when you don't have a sister."

"How the fuck do you know if I have a sister?"

"You just said you don't have a sister."

"If I had a sister I wouldn't give up on her."

"This is just going in circles," he said. She was scattering balled up tissues all over the floor of his car.

"Last night? You were all sitting there, and the postcards, that story about the postcards. I just wanted to be a part of that, you know?"

He looked out the windscreen at the long gravel shoulder and the pines and the sky arching over the river valley. All the trees had moss growing on them and the gravel at the edge of the road was damp. Up ahead, the road disappeared around a curve. He wanted to say the right thing. He wanted to know what that was.

"Amanda likes you, I think."

She sniffled and wiped her eyes.

"I just need you to be my friend, Zane."

At some point you know all you're ever going to know and it has to be enough. You make the best offer you can.

"Why do you think I never slept with you?"

"Because you can't get it up," she said.

* * *

Zane sat on the hood of his car and watched a mile-long freight crawl across the rock face on the far side of the valley. The train somehow clung to the side of the mountain, a long and tenuous thread, its track a groove etched in the granite face. From where Zane sat, it looked as if the train could at any moment lose its grip, slip, and tumble down the long slope into the river below.

His new road atlas placed him in the middle of the Rockies, at a node on the Trans-Canada that had turned out, on arrival, to consist of a gas station, a motel, a roadhouse, and about four other buildings, which presumably housed the proprietors of these businesses and their employees. If not for Melissa's meltdown he would have blown through the place. But it had been a long day. They both needed to get out of the car.

Zane's head felt as if it was not properly connected to his body. He told himself that he was exhausted, but another voice in the back of his mind whispered that he was beginning to lose control. He feared he was suffering a relapse.

It was essential to remain grounded. Zane carefully marked his position, triangulating from the car, the motel room, and the freight train. One of these points was not stationary, and a second was only temporarily so; this may have explained his dizziness.

You conduct these periodic inventories, if only to keep things straight. Your driver's licence, in the wallet that you carry in your back pocket and which is now making an indentation in your buttocks, bears a photograph that looks just like you, except that the man in the photograph has shaved. In your pockets are said wallet, a set of car keys, a cellular telephone, and about twenty-seven dollars in cash. In your car are a book of photographs (out of print), a new road atlas with a shiny cover, two thermal coffee mugs, several empty juice bottles and paper bags, a bag containing someone else's belongings (contents unknown), and a brassiere, which drapes itself impudently across the back seat. This last is faintly disturbing. As brassieres go, it is a rather striking specimen, not in size but in colour and quality. If only it could behave more discreetly.

Inside your motel room are a camera bag, a small bag containing your clothes, another bag containing someone else's belongings (contents again unknown), and a striking young woman with a black eye and a sardonic eyebrow held together with stitches, whose presence accounts, at least, for the brassiere.

Inside the freight train are several thousand tons of wheat, perhaps, although it could equally be loaded with coal, or iron ore, or any of the many other things that freight trains are known to carry. It could be carrying marbles, or jelly beans. One cannot know everything. This aspect of the situation remains a mystery.

How can anyone expect me to get properly grounded, faced with a moving freight train carrying god knows what?

The woman in your room is the subject of a story that you're alleged to be working on. That story is now approaching its end. How it will work out remains uncertain. Whether you are still working on it, equally so.

Precisely who is this woman in your room? More importantly, precisely who is she to you? She has recently sown a certain confusion on this very subject, on where this relationship is going, on whether, as daytime television has it, we are moving to the next level. On what she expects.

Fact: a young woman, whose extraordinary brassiere now graces the back seat of your car, is now napping in a motel room rented under your name. Let us consider the possible reasons. First is her role in this alleged photo story. Second, we must consider that perhaps the same guardian angel who keeps the apartment free of razor blades now wants to get you laid. There are, indeed, certain technical issues, but it is also possible that your guardian angel knows the true score on that one. We have not experimented with this problem in some time.

Zane was making heavy weather of the question. The fact that vampires do not have guardian angels was not lost on him.

It was time to return to the territory of facts. It was not too late to catch Jack. Zane pulled out his cellphone and checked to see if he had coverage. He was not surprised to discover that he did not. There was a pay phone by the motel office. Zane walked over to it and dialed Jack's number. He did not want to make the call where Melissa could hear him.

"I'm going to wrap up, probably, in a day." He laid out the situation: he had a story, but the ending was in question.

"So you're calling to tell me that you don't quite have a story."

"No, I do have a story. But there's a question as to how things will work out."

"Is this a problem with your female companion? You make your girlfriend your subject, that never works."

"It's just that I have the sense that things could go south on me. That's the peril of non-fiction."

"I'm more worried about the perils of Lucas Zane."

The satisfaction in Jack's voice was palpable. Aren't you a wit. Zane discarded the freight train as a point of triangulation in favour of the pay phone. Compiling an inventory of the pay phone's contents was a simple matter: it contained Jack, who was an asshole.

"Don't be an asshole, Jack. It's messy out here."

"Just show me the pictures."

"We used to be friends," said Zane, and he hung up.

* * *

The window of Zane's motel room looked out on a bleak and empty parking lot where two crows fought over the remains of a small animal that had neglected to look both ways before crossing the road. You tell the kids to be careful, but they never do listen. Then a logging truck settles matters, permanently. It's the circle of life; cue the music.

The sun slanted low, backlighting the window grime, splashing long, dark slabs of orange light and dark shadow across the scene. Good light for photography, and gorgeous light for colour. It was light to make an evening look warm regardless of the chill and the wind coming down the valley. It was wonderful light for roadkill.

"I want to go out," said Melissa.

"So go."

"No, I mean go out. Go someplace."

"There's no place to go." A certain small animal has already made that discovery. Nevertheless, you're welcome to explore.

Seven buildings along the highway, including the gas station. Seven buildings positioned here for no apparent reason except to take advantage of the demand for fuel. You can't even call this place a village.

Melissa made a face: I'm running out of patience for your excuses.

"At least we could get a beer and a nice, greasy burger at that place up the road."

Out on the roadway, a sign proclaimed in faded, hand-painted lettering that they sold the best burgers in town. Zane saw no reason to doubt this assertion. Neither had he any desire to investigate its veracity. His guts squirmed at the prospect.

"That sounds just lovely."

"Party pooper."

"That's an apt turn of phrase, even if it is somewhat too explicit."

"You're disgusting."

She turned away from the window and Zane shot a frame against the light as she walked across the worn and cigarette-cratered carpet. On the wall by the bathroom door was a mirror, and she paused at it and looked carefully at her face as if studying the portrait of a stranger. She gently prodded at the bruising around her eye, purple now giving way to blue, green and yellow. The swelling had subsided but the white of her eye remained a livid red. She pulled gently at her eyelid and winced.

"I look like shit."

Zane shot two more pictures, framing her to make her a small feature of the squalid room.

"Shit, Zane, do you ever put that thing away?"

"How I see the world, kiddo."

"Creep."

She returned her attention to the mirror, turned her head one way and then the other, raised her chin and lowered it, raised her eyebrow and then relaxed it, judging the effect. She essayed three experimental smiles followed by a skeptical glance.

"Zane, d'you think I'm pretty?"

"You mean before or after you called me a creep?"

"Seriously."

"Are you going to ask if those jeans make your ass look fat?"

She turned back to the mirror.

"The black eye doesn't help," he said.

Echoes of the afternoon creeping into the room. Now you hold the lid on and stay clear of all known minefields. Melissa had been emitting electrical waves since morning and Zane had no idea of the cause or the solution.

He checked the film counter and snapped the lens cap back on and slipped the camera into the pocket of his jacket, which he had earlier thrown over his bed. Putting the camera away seemed a prudent response to her crystalline mood.

"I want to go dancing," she said.

The prospect of finding a place to go dancing in this node on the Trans-Canada seemed something less than dubious. And Zane was, at the best of times, hardly a dancing fool. A dishevelled man twice her age sporting a shock of unkempt hair and a haunted look seemed an unlikely dancing partner for a girl like Melissa, black eye or no. Zane hadn't danced with a woman since 1991.

"Nobody ever took me dancing."

"I find that hard to believe."

"Lots of guys want to see me dance. Nobody ever wanted to take me dancing."

Fair enough. Nobody goes dancing anymore, anyway.

"I doubt if there's anyplace to go dancing around here."

"Well, what the fuck." She made the two steps to her bed and flopped onto it with a theatrical flourish.

"Are you okay?"

"It's my birthday," she said. "I'm twenty-two."

"And all of a sudden you feel old age a-stalking you?"

She fixed him with a look that made it clear: you are an idiot.

"Birthdays get me down. My dad would buy me something nice but then he'd try to make it extra-special."

"I'm sorry."

"Stop saying that all the time, Zane. It's not you."

Zane looked helplessly at the ceiling tiles, noting in the corner the telltale signs of a leak in the roof. Must be brutal up here in the winter. One good storm and you're snowbound, trapped with the best burgers in town until the ploughs finally get through. A snow shovel would be no more effective than a teaspoon. You could dig clean through to spring and hardly make a dent in all that snow.

"Well, let's go get that burger, at least."

"I need to take a shower first."

Melissa went into the bathroom, and Zane laid back and tried to make sense of his situation. The motives of your guardian angel remain out of reach, and in any case the angel has poor timing. Any misstep will earn you another punch in the nose. That'll make three. The holy trinity. Give us a sign; the least any useful guardian angel can do is to drop the odd hint now and again. I've had about enough of this enigmatic silence.

Zane got up and retrieved a notebook from his camera bag and tore out a page and wrote, "Gone out dancing. Back soon." To this he signed his name, realizing only after the fact that the gesture was unnecessary. Then he walked over to check out the best burgers in town.

Yellow incandescent bulbs cast a warm light over the roadhouse's round wooden tables. A counter at the back of the room doubled as a bar, and through the order window Zane could see the kitchen behind it. The place was empty save for two men at one end of the counter, whose boots and hands marked them as loggers. A slightly overweight girl of about eighteen manned the other end of the counter, along with an older woman, similarly overweight but lacking pimples. Mother and daughter, in all probability. Mother stood between daughter and the loggers.

"I heard a rumour you have the best burgers in town," said Zane.

"That's the rumour," said the older woman. "But you know rumours and little towns."

Her name tag said that she was Darlene. Her daughter was Cathy. Two ordinary, small town names. The kind of names you can trust.

"Please tell me you also have a jukebox."

"We can move the tables if you want to dance." Darlene pointed to the corner. She clearly found Zane amusing.

"Maybe later."

"You want dinner?"

"Maybe later on that, too. But let's see what you got."

He picked up the laminated card that displayed the limited menu. It looked like he was going to be having salad, although the ominous behaviour of the younger logger suggested that Zane might be staying in. The logger had close-cropped blond hair under a dirty ball cap, and he moved like a kid who had recently graduated from crushing bones on a high-school football field, and now felt an overwhelming nostalgia for crepitus. He stared at Zane over his coffee cup with all the sympathy of a bull for the matador's cape.

Everyone on edge today. Must be something in the air, heat lightning. I have had my nose punched twice already in the past twenty-four hours. Thank you for your interest, but further tests of my blood clotting factors are unnecessary at this time.

"I'm here with my daughter. It's her birthday, it's not working out too good. All of a sudden she says she wants to go dancing. I'm trying to surprise her."

"That's nice of you."

"Well, she's been through a tough time. She needs some nice."

"That's the girl with the eye."

Rumours and small towns. This accounts for the electrical charge.

"That's her. Anyway, I want to do something kind of special."

"You want a cake?" said Cathy.

Zane almost came unpinned.

"You're a saint, Cathy."

"Oh, please. It's a freezer cake. But I'll put some candles in it for you."

"Just do one. First year of the rest of her life."

"Good for her," said Darlene.

"We'll be about half an hour," said Zane, and checked his watch. He walked to the door on a wave of approval. *For now, at least, you're one of the good guys. That'll change quick enough if the cake prompts Melissa to punch you in the nose again. That blond kid in the ball cap will go right ahead and land a few punches of his own. At least it'll be quick. Be sure to bring a supply of tissues, for the blood and for the mourners. If any bother showing up.*

The sun now filtered through the pine trees and the room had fallen into gloom. Zane turned on the light. The water had stopped splashing and Melissa had drawn the curtains, so he reasoned that she had already read his note although she was now cloistered again behind the bathroom door. He crumpled the note and threw it in the trash can and then sat down on the bed and waited.

She emerged from the bathroom in wet hair and a towel.

"Where'd you go?"

"I went to make dinner reservations."

"Yeah, right."

She fished a hairbrush out of her bag and began brushing her hair in short, quick strokes, with her head tilted to one side.

"For your birthday, I'm taking you out to dinner, and then I'm taking you dancing. But first, you have to do something for me."

The hairbrush froze in mid-stroke, and Zane realized the misfortune of his words. For a long moment, Melissa said nothing.

"Sing for me," he said.

"What?"

She held the hairbrush as if unsure of what it was for.

"I want you to sing for me. Anything you want. I never hear you sing anymore."

She put the hairbrush down and tucked the towel between her legs and sat down on the bed.

"You really are crazy."

"Shut up and sing," he said, and she laughed, and looked at him until it was clear that he was serious. And then she sat on the bed and started to sing, and tried to sing through her laughter. And then she gave up and said fuck it, Zane, let's go eat.

CHAPTER SIXTEEN

M elissa meanders through a fine drizzle, tracing a path along the water's edge with complete disregard for the deteriorating state of her running shoes. The Pacific, a grey and featureless expanse broken only by the dark mass of Point Roberts, stretches to the horizon under a flat, overcast sky. There will be no sunset tonight.

In the end it all comes down to this, at the end of the long downhill along the Fraser Valley: sitting on the hood while your engine cools, metal pinging as it contracts, its fading warmth rising through the soggy seat of your jeans. Drizzle finding its way under your jacket collar. And there she is, down on the beach, at the end of a trail of sodden footprints, at the end of the road. Taking her time. Not that it matters. Might as well spin this thing out as long as we can.

Zane hunched into his jacket and pulled up the collar and waited. She was alone on the beach.

When they hit Vancouver, Zane turned south off the Trans-Canada and drove down on through Surrey to White Rock because he wanted to see the water, and this was the route he knew. We are all of us creatures of habit. At the end of the road he pulled up and parked by the beach and then shook her. She opened her eyes and sat up, and he pointed at the ocean.

"There it is," he said, as if it was a rare and exotic animal instead of the boring, empty sweep of the open sea.

"The ocean."

"The Pacific Ocean."

"I love the ocean."

It looked as bleak as the endless prairies, flat and empty. Nothing to see and nowhere to go. The great navigator spins the roulette wheel, the ball bouncing and skipping and rattling to land on north-west by west; he tacks down the chosen bearing and finds greater expanses of nothing. Eventually we all sail off the edge, discover a greater emptiness. Might as well load up the old canoe and paddle off into interstellar space.

Zane put his hands in his pockets to warm them and his right hand came up against the hard, cold mass of his Leica. He framed Melissa walking down the empty beach, found a way to make it work, and took the shot. You won't get too many more pictures now.

At the point where her tracks turned back towards the car, Melissa paused and stooped to pick something out of the sand. For a moment, she stood and looked down at whatever it was, turning it over in her hand, and then she leaned over and flung it, sidearm, over the surface of the water, where it skipped once, and then twice, and then again, each time a shorter distance, until it dropped from sight and sank. A flat stone.

She stood at the water's edge as the ripples made by the stone spread and flattened once more, and then she turned away from the ocean and walked back up the beach to the car. Her hair lay flat, tangled with the wet, and her face had a cold, pinched look.

"Have a seat." He patted the hood. She tried to wipe the raindrops off the metal with her hand and sat.

"Now my ass is all wet."

Stop being a baby. This moment won't come again.

A row of cormorants flew low over the water, evenly spaced black silhouettes with long necks and rapid wing beats. Apart from the cormorants, the scene offered nothing to look at. Zane slipped the camera back into his pocket and hunched his shoulders. He shivered.

You got geese all over your grave again.

All of the pressure of forward movement had dissipated and now Zane wanted only to remain still in the emptiness of the present. He felt they had reached the cusp of things, and now hung suspended.

"So this is it," said Melissa. "The end of the line."

"The end of the line."

The end of the line could not have been less impressive.

"Where do we go now?"

"You can keep going, but you'd run out of road pretty quick."

"I guess I'll have to put down roots." Melissa hunched forward and hugged her arms against her chest. "I could put down roots in a place like this. I bet it's nice when the sun shines."

You won't be putting down any roots among the million-dollar condos of White Rock.

"When does the sun ever shine in Vancouver?"

"I bet it does sometimes."

Realization, which had been creeping up on Zane, now sprang upon him. He felt an odd sense of admiration. The cuckoo is a brood parasite that dupes other birds into raising its young at the cost of their own, but still you have to admire its ingenuity.

"What part of Vancouver are you actually from?"

Melissa pulled at the knee of her jeans with bitten fingernails. He saw the rough, uneven edges now, as he had never noticed before, and wondered how he had missed them and when she had discarded the artificial nails. That would have made a good photo, if he had seen it. But he had missed everything.

"I never been to Vancouver in my life," she said.

Zane laughed.

"What's so funny?"

He laughed again, and they looked at each other in strange wonderment. All of the facts had disappeared like landmarks under heavy fog. Zane was adrift.

"Where are you from, really?"

"North Bay." She shifted her weight, straightened her back and looked up at the overcast. "But I always wanted to go to Vancouver."

"Anyplace is better than North Bay."

He had never been there. She seemed to find this quite funny. Probably the disorienting effect of finding yourself adrift in the fog. Might as well laugh; nothing makes sense anymore.

A gull wheels across the flat arc of the sky, a dark shape in silhouette, gliding in slow and aimless circles down to the beach, where it flares and touches down and then shrugs and settles into position on the sand. The gull stands motionless in the drizzle, as if fixed there.

Cold drizzle on your skin, the smell of the ocean, the smell of fish and of salt water and of kelp stranded on the beach, and in that moment you feel alive, alert in all your senses as if the feel of drizzle on your neck had woken you to the beauty of the seagull's descending arc, backlit by the soft light of the overcast sky, aloft in that certain light.

You are only alive in fits and starts.

"Yesterday, was it really your birthday?"

She looked at him and then laughed and shook her head and looked down at the sand.

"Shit, Zane, I never even seen the ocean before."

Anyone driving past would have wondered what it was, down on the beach, that they had stopped to look at, and how it could possibly be that funny.

Zane took the camera out of his pocket and slowly turned it over in his hands, wondering how many photographs he had missed. Photographs never lie, but liars can take photographs. Lewis Hine said that. Lewis Hine had not addressed the problem of photographing liars. Zane's story, which up to now had described a perfect arc, now lay in an uncertain and shapeless mass. Meanwhile, Jack lay coiled inside the telephone, waiting to strike. He would hate to say he told you so, but would nevertheless do so at some length. It was a trial Zane was uncertain he could endure.

"I guess I messed everything up," she said.

Along the pier, the masts of moored boats stood motionless. Zane watched the blinking of the breakwater light. He was trying to calculate his expenses. The numbers had grown unpleasantly large.

"It doesn't matter."

This is what you get for building things up. Better to stick with the facts. The breakwater light, for example, keeps right on blinking regardless.

"Just tell me some of it was true."

"Shit, Zane, I can't even remember which parts are true anymore."

She tucked her hair behind her ear. The edges of her black eye had faded to pale yellow, and he could now see that the cut would leave a scar despite his best efforts. The white of her eye showed a livid red.

"It was true about my dad."

Only the painful things are ever true. The things you want to believe in are always the things you can trust the least. What you least want to believe, that's probably the truth. The bruises on her face are true.

I don't want to know anything more that's true.

They sat and looked out over the ocean while the engine cooled and the drizzle dampened their clothes.

"I fucked up," she said. "I fucked up bad." She began picking again at the knee of her jeans.

"Doesn't matter."

It didn't occur to him at first that she was no longer talking about letting him down.

"I got no place to go here. What am I gonna do?"

"Do what everyone else does: get a job."

Zane decided, belatedly, that this was an ungentle suggestion, but then changed his mind and decided that it was sound fatherly advice, and that it was about time somebody gave it.

"Get a job. Yeah, there's lots of jobs for me."

"Ring in groceries. Wait tables. Take a bit part in that bad dinner theatre production of South Pacific. Stop feeling sorry for yourself."

He wasn't sure that Melissa was up to it. The drizzle was gaining strength, and the engine had gone cold. It was time to move on.

"I'm just about outa road," she said. "And the worst thing is, I'm still in the same damn place."

Zane said nothing. He was getting cold. Her features were pinched and a drip had formed at the end of her nose. She wiped it away with the back of her hand without taking her gaze off the sea. Zane slipped the Leica out of his pocket and shot her like that, moved in close and shot her in profile, looking into the frame in the flat and even light. She might have been crying, or it might have been the drizzle. There was no way to know.

"Shit, Zane, put that thing away."

He put the lens cap on and then rewound the film and put the camera in his pocket and closed the zipper.

"That's it."

"What's it?"

"The end of the story." He slid down off the car hood. His backside was cold and wet. "Let's get dinner. There's a zillion good restaurants in White Rock."

They walked up the street and then turned at the corner, and as they climbed the hill a question struck him.

"What's your name, anyway?"

She stopped and looked at him for a moment, and then she smiled and said, "Janet."

* * *

Zane took stock. Cash flow presented a problem. To wit, cash continued to flow, but in one direction only. He had no story with which to recoup his expenses, expenses that in any case exceeded anything he might hope to collect in fees. At some point, he had lost control of everything. The pilot daydreams while the aircraft plummets, the flight attendants cheerfully serving zero-gravity coffee to the terrified passengers; at two thousand feet he snaps out of it, but there is the problem of momentum. Also, strain on the airframe.

Zane drove from White Rock to the outer reaches of civilization, and took a motel room in Port Coquitlam. The motel faced onto a rail yard, where dozens of freight cars sat slowly rusting in the interminable rain. Beyond them, the river slithered past rusting tugs and ancient pilings where rafts of logs awaited the saw mill. It wasn't much of a view.

On checking in, Zane got to work. He had film to develop. At some point, he had lost control of this also. How have you been remiss? Let me count the ways: thirty-six rolls of thirty-six exposures, some twelve hundred undeveloped frames of god-knows-what. Little wonder that the story got away from you. A thousand mysteries trace your route between Melissa's apartment and Port Coquitlam.

You don't even know what the story is. I'm just an ordinary girl who doesn't exist. I'm just the little engine that could. The developing backlog demands immediate attention, if only so that you can present to Jack some formless jumble of images. Perhaps an artist statement to go along with it. The case for the defence requires some evidence of a sincere effort. At this point it's a matter of snowing the jury.

Zane commandeered the bathroom and worked at alchemy. Processing his thirty six rolls took him the better part of a day. He had only one tank with him and it held four rolls. The room had a retractable clothesline over the bathtub and as he finished each roll he sprayed it down and hung it. By three in the afternoon the tub was filled with dripping black strips of film. Zane's roommate was not reticent regarding her frustration with the state of their shared bathroom. His dabbling in the black arts, which had so fascinated Melissa, held no interest for Janet. It can be difficult, rooming with a stranger. Relations became fractious.

"When are you going to get all this shit out of the bathroom?"

All this shit: a life, preserved in silver. Immortality was not among Janet's concerns.

"When it's dry."

"That's not an answer."

"Close the door."

She slammed the bathroom door and Zane cringed at the thought of the dust she had stirred up, now settling and adhering to his still-wet negatives. Hours of retouching loomed.

She stood by the door with the air of a woman who intended to stalk off in anger, but found her ambitions thwarted by insufficient stalking space. It was a small room.

What do you want from me? The work has to get done. That's why we're here. All those road miles, reduced to nothing. All that distance covered now lies between you. One morning you wake up to discover that you've never met.

"I'll take it down in the morning."

"I want to take a shower now."

"Then rent your own damn room."

"Fuck you, Zane."

Daylight slashed through the doorway as she walked out, stalking space no longer a concern. Her best efforts to slam the door were frustrated by a mechanism that slowed its swing. The point was clear, regardless. It's the thought that counts. She had no money with which to rent her own room, and he knew it. I'll take that punch in the nose now, please.

Zane sat alone in the room and flipped through his notes. A thread of a story began to form but the slash of light through the doorway replayed and severed it. Somewhere here is a story, a tale told by an idiot; problem is, the idiot can't figure out what exactly this tale is. For far too long, this particular idiot has disciplined himself to stick to the facts.

Faced with a lack of facts, Zane found distractions. Foremost now was irritation that she had left without her key. It suddenly seemed essential that he go out, if only to walk and clear his head. He needed to get back in motion. But her key lay on the wardrobe, beside the television, and mocked him. He was stranded with the wet black ribbons of his negatives and four notebooks filled with bilge and nonsense.

Zane watched television. He paced. He attempted to take further notes, and then crumpled those notes into balls and threw them at the wastepaper basket from various positions around the room, with a general lack of success. He attempted to read the novel that he had bought in Medicine Hat; it was moronic. He perused his road atlas; the road atlas reminded him of Calgary; Calgary reminded him of Connie. He returned to watching television.

When she knocked, he considered letting her wait outside but decided instead to demonstrate his maturity. She walked past him into the room without speaking and picked up her key from the wardrobe and then went to the window and looked out. He watched her in the window light. It was good light for a picture, flat and directionless light filtered through the overcast, washing through the window as if from a gigantic softbox. But he had no idea what this picture was supposed to say. And he was done with pictures, anyway.

"You forgot your key."

"I'm only staying 'til I find another place."

"Fine," he said.

"Fine."

He remembered her question, however long ago: when did we get married? Still she didn't look at him. He felt useless standing by the door. He walked over to his bed and sat down and found the remote and flicked the TV on. She swore at him and walked out again. This time, she remembered her key.

* * *

Zane had one thousand, three hundred and eleven negatives, from forty-three complete and partial rolls of film. In addition, he had the contents of the flash card salvaged from the camera he had wrecked against the iceberg of Bill's skull. Most of those pictures, given their content, were unusable, but he had saved seven frames of Melissa in full colour, dressed as a cheerleader. The remainder of the Melissa file was in four reporter's notebooks filled with neat, pencilled notes. This was all he had.

Of greater concern to Zane was what he lacked. He now realized that he had spent much of the trip either driving or sleeping, and too much of the remaining time messing around instead of taking pictures. He had failed to get a shot of her sleeping in the car, for example. This opportunity had presented itself on numerous occasions, but the shot had not occurred to him. It now seemed to him an obvious and glaring omission, and that he was driving at the time, a flimsy excuse. Winogrand was wrong: a thousand pictures had passed him by while he was loading film. It was gross negligence.

Consequently, Zane chose to slacken his editing standards. In making the first cut, he selected two hundred and fifty-nine negatives for a closer look. Making the cut took an entire day, and scanning his selects took another. After reviewing them on-screen, he felt that the quality of his output had been fairly high, although he could not shake the nagging voice that whispered wishful thinking from behind his ear. Neither could wishful thinking mitigate the fact that he still could not distill the thread of a story from those two hundred and fifty-nine pictures, those two hundred and fifty-nine disparate facts. Janet remained a mystery.

Zane's cellphone lay on the night table. He looked at it with loathing, as one might regard a coiled and dangerous snake. No good ever came of the cellular telephone; all its inventor achieved was to unleash the evil of Bell's original, wire-bound instrument. Then followed misery, plagues of rats, disease, pain in childbirth, and text messages. And this misery can reach you anywhere. It demands a non-proliferation treaty.

The time approaches when you will have no choice but to pick up the phone, voluntarily, and release Jack from its innards. Jack, who is an asshole, and who will undoubtedly remember that you recently told him as much. And this time, you will have to admit that you followed this story to its end, that its neat, symmetrical arc has collapsed into a hopeless tangle of yarn, and that you can't find either end. This time, you will have to admit to Jack that you have no story, that there was in the end no story to tell. And then, following a predictable dose of verbal abuse, the final, flickering light will go out.

You brought this on yourself.

Now for the hard part: with the developing done and the negs cut into neat strips, with the negs stored in archival plastic sleeves and filed carefully in manila file folders, and with the file folders secured with blue elastic bands that he had bought from the office supplies superstore down the road, nothing remained to Zane except to find the truth.

* * *

After the rain, the rich, dark earth steamed as if all the ghosts of Liberia would now arise to accuse the living. The dead emerged from sheltering doorways and stalked the streets with amputated limbs. Some of the dead were filled with anger, and they shouted and waved the stumps of their wrists at him. And some of the dead were crazy, and they thrust their stumps at his face to frighten him and they laughed at him with mad glee. When they grinned, the earth itself split open.

Zane rode in the front passenger seat of a crudely camouflaged Nissan pickup truck driven by a boy no older than fourteen. The boy had the glassy eyes of one possessed, and he did not speak. A half-dozen more boys rode in the open truck bed. None of them had ever shaved, and none spoke as the truck rolled down the main street of Tubmanburg. Only one of them had ever spoken to Zane. He had proudly recounted the number of men he had killed, and how he had killed them. Zane was thankful for the language barrier.

In Liberia, you needed protection, and the boys were Zane's assigned bodyguard. He travelled in a state of perpetual terror, afraid as much of his bodyguards as of any threat they might dispel. Nothing is so dangerous as a twelve-year-old boy with a brain full of drugs and a deadly weapon, and a deadly curiosity to explore its power.

Zane had no idea why he was in Liberia. He wanted only to get out again. He had read backgrounders on the civil war, but they made no impression. One group of people sets out to kill another; he could find no reason in it. There was no history but killing, nothing here more organized than the mind of a schizophrenic.

Only one fact made any strong impression. In the streets men armed with rifles carried machetes to hack off the arms of women and children. Before making the cut, the soldiers asked their victims if they would prefer their shirtsleeves to cover their stumps. And they honoured their victims' preferences.

"Just get the story out."

At a field hospital run by Medecins sans Frontiers. The doctor practised emergency medicine in Cincinnati.

"I don't even know what the story is," said Zane.

The doctor's name was Carr. At home, he played golf and collected jazz records of the Swing era. He waved his hand over the patients in the tent hospital, who lay listlessly on cots while intravenous fluids dripped into their arms. Most of the patients were women.

"The story's right fuckin' there," he said.

Zane saw rows of patients lying impassive in the heat, rows of people, but no story.

"You have to get the story out."

"Where did these people come from?"

"It's not fuckin' complicated. Just tell the story."

Nobody cares anyway. Zane took some photos and he fled.

The men with guns told their child soldiers that they were under magical protection, that bullets would pass through them and do them no harm, and some of them believed it. Much of the time, Zane was too terrified even to get out of the truck. Zane went where the truck went, and counted the days. All Zane wanted was to get the fuck out of Liberia.

Just outside Tubmanburg, the truck turned off the road and jolted along a muddy track that led through a rubber plantation.

Zane asked why they were there, knowing that it was futile. The driver said nothing.

They stopped before a low, whitewashed bunkhouse. A half-dozen men and boys kneeled in a row, their hands tied behind their backs and their heads hanging, staring at the ground. None of them looked up at the sound of the engine. Guarding them were two young boys with rifles, and an older man who, by virtue of being in his early twenties, was an authority figure. He, too, carried an AK-47, and wore an automatic pistol tucked into his belt.

Zane knew him: Sheriff Williams, a title Zane had thought odd until he learned that Sheriff is a popular first name in Liberia. Sheriff appeared to be the archetype of west African manhood: a wide smile, straight teeth, flawless dark skin and a chest sculpted by a lifetime of hard physical labour. He smiled often and was a good-looking man and Zane liked him on sight, except for the fact that he was an egomaniac, a psychopath, and a drug addict. And certain flaws are hard to overlook.

So now you know why you're here. You're here because Sheriff told the boys to bring you. Zane got out of the truck and Sheriff's face split into a wide grin, the earth again cracking open.

Sheriff extended his hand, and out of politeness, Zane shook it. Better a friend than the alternative. Sheriff smiled and squeezed Zane's hand hard and then walked over to the line of kneeling men, pulled the pistol from his belt, and waved it at the man at the end of the line. The man looked up at Zane. He was about thirty. He had crooked teeth, and his eyes rolled in fear. A queasy apprehension crept over Zane.

"This man is an enemy of our people. He has killed our brothers and raped our women. And we are going to show the world how we deal with such criminals."

Delusions of grandeur. For whose benefit can this man possibly be making speeches?

"Get your camera."

Sheriff pointed his pistol at Zane's camera, waved it about carelessly. Zane could feel the empty eye of its muzzle roaming over his body, an invisible force. Watching him. Don't make any sudden moves, just stand there, frozen like a rabbit. You don't want to get stupid here. Just get me to the airport, just get me on the first plane out of fucking Liberia, just get me off the runway. The pistol's wandering muzzle is one thing, but the look in Sheriff's eyes is worse. Looking in Sheriff's eyes, Zane didn't see a human being.

Zane didn't look at the eyes of the kneeling man.

"I am going to kill him, whether you take a picture or not."

The pistol muzzle wandering again, the remains of his insides contracting in fear. Feeling sick. No medevac helicopter for you in Liberia. No Special Forces to pull you out.

Aperture priority, f/8 and be there. Light falls on the subject, bends through fourteen elements in eleven groups, threatens the retina and the visual cortex frozen like a rabbit.

As the mirror blacked out the viewfinder, Zane heard the report of Sheriff's pistol. For a moment, he was pleased at his good shutter timing.

That was the last war Zane ever shot.

* * *

She stood in the parking lot, leaning against his new car with her arms crossed and her bags lying at her feet like patient dogs, and Zane mentally cursed the Vancouver rain that stopped only now, now when he finally wanted her driven back inside. A faint mist rising from the river and the puddles in the rail yard. He felt that there should be more to say. She felt that there was nothing more to say, and had said so, and had since proceeded to say nothing more, at length. All her things were packed, and the cab was on its way.

"You can't afford a cab," he'd said. "Let me drive you."

"I prefer to make a clean break."

She had found a place, found a roommate, found a waitressing job to pay the rent. She said it was a fresh start. What she'd hoped for. She said he should be happy for her.

He wasn't. He said he'd promised her a print, but he'd never made one.

Story of my life, she said.

I'll make one and bring it to you.

She said she didn't want one, anyway.

Across the road in the rail yard, freight cars stood silent like rusting oxen relieved at last of their burdens. Beyond, the river ran brown in early autumn flood. Soon the snow would hit the mountains, and the water would begin to fall. The endless cycle is always comforting when nothing else is. The Earth tilts away from the sun, our days shorten, and all of us at one time or another return to the soil. Interstellar space yawns. Events of the interim hardly matter. Zane wondered if oxen go to some eternal reward.

"You don't have to go."

"Sooner or later, all the little birdies fly the nest."

Zane thought of cats and window panes and falcons, and all the other perils that threaten small birds. Early snowfalls. DDT on your winter feeding grounds. You do your best but one day the kids have to go out on their own. From here, it could be Surrey or it could be the Downtown East Side, more human refuse circling a public toilet. Thinking he was better off being shut of her for good only made it worse.

"You can stay until you find your feet, I mean."

"I found my feet. I have a place."

Clearly, she intended to leave no forwarding address. He pulled out his wallet and found a business card, with the numbers for his cell, his defunct answering service, and the agency. Soon, all three would be useless. It was futile. Still, one has to make a gesture. He held the card out to her.

"If you ever need anything. Anything at all."

"Clean break, remember?"

She made no move to uncross her arms. Zane stood in the parking lot with its fading puddles, his arm outstretched.

"Don't make me stand here like a fool, Melissa."

You can't just write people off.

"Melissa's history. There is no Melissa."

Just when you get to know someone, she turns out not to exist. This is taking some getting used to.

"Melissa was just a story to you, anyway."

"I'm making an effort here."

"Too little too late."

That she seemed intent on bitterness filled him with a futile sadness: regret for that which he could do nothing to reverse, sweetened with a bitter dollop of bewilderment. To deserve this, I did precisely what?

"What was I to Melissa, then? A car and a credit card?"

"That's so fucking typical. She was your fucking friend, Zane."

She reached out and took the card and then held it up in the air for him to see before dropping it. It fell to the pavement and came to rest in a puddle, water darkening the paper.

Gulls wheeled above the freight yard, above the wet freight cars jumbled with graffiti, above stone and steel and cold and wet. Zane dug his hands in his pockets and looked at the sky, ignored the card soaking in the puddle. He wanted to leave her there, to simply turn and walk back to his room and leave her alone in the parking lot. But it seemed essential that he see this thing through.

"You don't even know me," she said. And you never will. "You never made an effort." A gust blew her hair across her face and she reached up to tuck it behind her ear. "I'll go my way and you can do whatever. Find your next windmill and go take pictures of it beating the shit out of people."

Zane felt again the pangs of worthless regret, the futile wish that things could be made different by the intervention of some higher power.

"None of us can change anything," he said.

"You never made the effort."

"I'm here now."

"Whatever."

A white taxicab with blue doors nosed into the parking lot and prowled slowly among the parked cars. She waved to the driver.

When the cab drew up the driver popped the trunk and climbed out in his Sikh turban and pointed to her bags with his eyebrows raised in a question. He seemed reluctant to speak.

Zane opened the door for her and thought himself a gentleman for doing so. She climbed in and reached for the door and tried to pull it closed, but he held it open.

"Take care of yourself."

Only after he said this did he realize what an oafish utterance it was.

"Goodbye, Zane."

He let go of the door and she closed it and the cab rolled off along the row of parked cars. Zane watched as its brake lights glowed briefly, before it turned down the road and was lost in the traffic. He was still trying to make it out when the drizzle started again.

* * *

After her cab disappeared into traffic, Zane went back to his room and turned on the television and went into the bathroom. A mirror ran the full length of the counter. He didn't like what he saw.

Shit, Zane, look at you: just like a lost puppy. So many things that we never will undo. Sorry is a guilt bomb, and regret an endless mud wallow. All this and he could still hear her voice.

On the pillow of his bed he discovered a slip of paper torn from one of his notebooks. He picked it up and unfolded it.

> Dear Lucas,
> I never meant to let you down like that. I wish I knew what to say. All I ever do is make up stories. I don't think you can change who you are. And I'm really sorry about the camera. I need the money bad.
> Love,
> Janet

She had left him the one he smashed. This is what you get for disregarding Lapierre's first law, trust your instincts.

He stared at her note, unable to read the words: a generality, a piece of white notepaper with faint blue lines, words written in blue ballpoint pen. Her handwriting formed neat, girlish loops, as if she was stuck at age sixteen.

You sure saw the elephant, all right. You are the yokel of fucking yokels, Zane, the original bumpkin. Hick meets huckster; step right up. Just seven thousand bucks to see her egress.

He walked to the window and looked out over the freight yard. A steady drip fell outside the window and splashed on the aluminum sill, and he heard the small smacks of its impact and the hiss of wet tires on the road below. The smell of the rain through the open window and the cold air outside.

Sometimes, you get that certain light. A mayfly rests on a window screen in the chill air of dawn as a diesel rig coughs into life and strains for the empty highway. Or cloud tops catch the light of the setting sun as their bases fall into evening shadow. You stand in the back of an armoured personnel carrier, legs bruised and aching as an armoured column rolls east into the sunrise, and the light paints the dust enveloping you orange, silhouettes the squat and violent shape of the tank ahead in glowing dust, and you forget for once to take a picture, all your senses now alive, alive within a flame.

A gull soars over the flat, empty Pacific as a cold drizzle damps your cheeks and the girl sitting beside you on the car hood picks at her jeans with bitten fingernails and shares with you the final truth. This is how the story ends. And no one ever knows what happens outside the picture space, outside the frame.

Zane stood at the window in the failing light and looked out over the freight yard, over gulls wheeling above steel and crushed stone, over wooden railway ties slick with rain, the river beyond sliding and eddying down to meet the sea. A lone man in a rain slicker walked between the rails. He carried a plain aluminum lunch box and a thermos, and with every step his feet slipped in the wet gravel. The man walked with his head down, plodding, and Zane watched him until he disappeared behind the graffiti-scarred freight cars that still stood patiently rusting in the endless rain, long after discharging their loads of mysterious freight.

About the Author

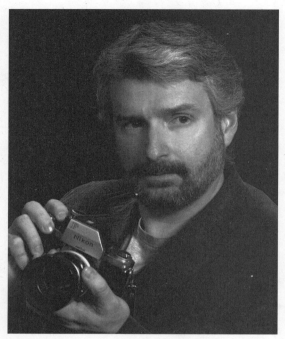

A.J. Somerset has been a soldier, a technical writer, a programmer, and a freelance photographer. His non-fiction has appeared in numerous outdoor magazines in Canada and the United States, and his articles have been translated into French and Japanese.